WHAT IS FOUND, WHAT IS LOST

WHAT IS FOUND, WHAT IS LOST

A Novel

Anne Leigh Parrish

SHE WRITES PRESS

Published 2014
Printed in the United States of America
ISBN: 978-1-938314-95-7
Library of Congress Control Number: [LOCCN]

For information, address:
She Writes Press
1563 Solano Ave #546
Berkeley, CA 94707

To John, Bob, and Lauren, as always. And to the memory of my parents, Stephen Maxfield Parrish (1921-2012) and Jean Jacob Parrish (1922-2002). Lastly to my grandmother and namesake, whom I never had the chance to know, Anna Dominian Jacob (1890-1956).

Part One

One

2012

In a quiet Sioux Falls neighborhood, a widow walked her Boston terrier along a shady street. The dog moved slowly and without much purpose, as if he, too, were grieving. The woman, Freddie, considered the loss of her husband, Ken, in practical terms, like the empty space in bed and the closets she cleaned out. She also reckoned a deeper loss—the light he could bring to a room, and the soft glow in her heart when she caught his eye.

Her dreams were full of him. In one, they were at a lunch counter. They shared a piece of cherry pie. The cherries were dark and drippy, and bothered Freddie because she knew that they represented his cancer. She put down her fork and said, *So, what's it like being dead?* And he answered, *You know, it's not bad.*

She was certain that she and Ken had never eaten at a lunch counter. The symbolism was clear. In the dream they were side by side, equals. In life, they hadn't been.

Freddie was sixty-two. She was tall, with a robust manner, clearly of Nordic descent. In her youth she had been slender and fair-haired. Now her body was thick, and her hair was what some would call "salt and pepper."

The dog, Pudgy, was eleven; he had been Ken's adored friend, a gift from Freddie to celebrate his initial recovery from the disease that ultimately killed him. Ken was sixty-six when he died a few months before. Theirs had been a long, hard marriage. Yet love persisted always.

She had no friends to speak of. She never had. She didn't find it odd.

3

The way she grew up made friendship impossible. She and her younger sister, Holly, were so isolated as children. Holly now lived in Minneapolis. Although they spoke on the telephone every other month, and saw each other once a year, Freddie knew only the outline of Holly's life, not the actual fabric of it. She was aware that Holly had something of a circle. Social events were sometimes alluded to. She supposed Holly needed them, while she didn't. Freddie possessed a richness of spirit—an inward bent—that allowed her to tolerate solitude.

The approaching summer would be another hot one. Holly would come for a couple of weeks. Before then, Freddie's daughter, Beth, would bring her little boy out from Las Vegas. That Beth resembled Ken so much might be difficult. This would be her first time home since he died.

Recently on her walks with Pudgy, Freddie had noticed a man driving a red pickup. The couple across from her had seen him, too. They assumed he was a landscaper, though his old truck bore no logo or advertising of any kind. The woman behind them thought he was drifter down on his luck, back home to help out in exchange for a place to stay. Freddie didn't see how the man could be connected with any one house, because his truck turned up on different streets.

The driver of the truck wasn't young. His beard was flecked with white, and his eyes were sharp and knowing. Other neighbors were leery of him and wondered if he'd break into their homes and steal. Freddie doubted that. He'd be the prime suspect if anything like that happened. When he was spotted, he was either driving the truck, or sitting in it, sipping coffee from a paper cup. No one spoke to him, and Freddie thought that was a shame.

✧

One morning, the man's truck was parked across the street. He was behind the wheel, head thrown back, probably asleep. Freddie dressed, poured a mug of coffee, and made her way across the road, Pudgy in tow. She tapped on the window, which was tricky with the mug in one hand and Pudgy's leash in the other. The man's mouth was open. Freddie could see silver fillings on his back teeth. On his neck below an overgrown beard was a small scar, perfectly straight, as if put there by a surgeon. She tapped the window harder. The man's head lifted and he stared at her with deep blue eyes. He rolled down his window. Neither spoke. Freddie went first.

"Thought you could use this," she said. He stared at the mug. *Kiss me, I'm Polish*, it said in blocky, childlike lettering.

"Got a shot of whiskey for it?" he asked.

"Don't think so. Not much of a whiskey drinker these days, truth to tell."

"I was only kidding. Never touch the stuff myself."

He took the mug. His fingernails were smooth, even, and perfectly clean.

"What are you doing here?" Freddie asked. The man blew into the coffee to cool it. Then he stared darkly into the mug.

"Looking for someone," he said.

"Who?"

"You ask a lot of questions."

"You spend a lot of time in my neighborhood."

"Guess you're right about that."

Inside, at her dining room table, he explained. His wife had left him three months before. He was from Omaha. The wife had family there in Sioux Falls. The brother lived two blocks over. The man—Nate—was sure she'd surface sooner or later.

"Why don't you just ask him if he's heard from her?" Freddie asked.

"I did. He said he hadn't. He said they didn't talk anymore, and hadn't for years. I told him that was bull, because I'm the one that pays the phone bill. She called his number plenty, and stayed on the line a while each time. He said I was a liar and that he'd punch out my lights if I didn't get off his porch."

"Sounds like a lovely fellow."

"That he is."

"You know, if she doesn't want to be found, she won't be. You're easy to avoid because you're so easy to spot," Freddie said.

"She's pretty easy to spot, too."

"How's that?"

"She's in a . . . what do you call it . . . you know, the black dress and head scarf."

"You mean what Muslim women wear?"

"Right. She converted," Nate said.

"What was she before?"

"Miserable."

Freddie laughed.

"Also Episcopalian, sort of," he said. "She never went to church. I didn't take too well to her newfangled view of things. Not Islam, in particular, you understand, just the way she went at it. All gung ho."

"What made her do it?"

"Looking for something, I guess."

They all were, Freddie thought. People who depended on religion to get them through life wanted an easy answer, the responsibility in someone else's hands. Freddie thought that was stupid. You had to think for yourself, no matter what. You had to realize the incredibly random nature of life. And you had to know that you could believe in God without following any particular religion. God was one thing, religion another. It was religion that messed everything up. She knew that first-hand. Her mother, Lorraine, had been a firebrand Bible-thumper. She gave birth to Freddie in a revival tent one spring night in 1950. Holly came along four years later.

Pudgy entered the kitchen and stared up at Nate with mucous-streaked eyes. Nate held out his hand, and Pudgy obligingly sniffed it. Then he turned away, and clicked across the floor to his tattered dog bed. He lay down, and kept his eyes on Nate.

"I've taken up enough of your time," Nate said.

"Not at all. It's been a pleasure."

Freddie saw Nate staring at Beth's high school picture on the side-board. Beth wasn't smiling. Her hair over one eye made her look both sultry and mean.

"My daughter," Freddie said.

"Nice. We don't have any ourselves. I wanted them; she didn't."

"They can turn you inside out. Especially that one."

Beth was an only child, Freddie told him, and maybe that was the problem. Only children had some advantages, of course, but some dis-advantages, too. All of their parents' expectations heaped on them, for instance. Growing up under a microscope. At least, that's how Freddie had explained Beth to herself for years now, though she didn't mention this specifically to Nate.

Beth's father only wanted the best for her. Isn't that what fathers did?

Want the best? Anyway, Beth didn't appreciate the constant pressure to measure up. She found it too demanding. So, in rebellion she left home and got a job as a pole dancer in Las Vegas. That's right—a real, live, exotic dancer, taking tips in her G-string. It just about broke Freddie's heart, but her husband, well, his heart was broken, too, of course, but he put all his grief straight into rage. Not the yelling and screaming sort of rage (that was earlier, when Beth still lived at home), but a deep, burning, silent rage. He wouldn't speak to his daughter, and she wouldn't speak to him. Then Beth got pregnant. The father refused responsibility. Freddie said they should press the point through legal means. Her husband wanted nothing to do with that. Beth had the child, a little boy, and went back to pole dancing. She brought him back to Sioux Falls a couple of times—by then Freddie had gotten her husband to relent and agree to let them in the house, though he made himself scarce—but she always went away again, back to her seedy life. Beth defended that life on the grounds that she was independent. What she meant was, independent of a man. She supported herself. Freddie didn't, and Beth accused her of being a bad role model while she was growing up. Then Freddie pointed out that Beth was, in fact, entirely dependent upon men, because who else went into those places and threw money on stage for her?

"Probably a lot more than you needed to know. Didn't used to be such a talker. Been on my own too long, I guess. My husband died about six months ago," Freddie said.

"I'm sorry to hear that."

Nate looked around her dining room some more. The walls were a cheerful yellow. The sideboard had two pairs of brass candlesticks and a heavy ceramic bowl that was probably Mexican, judging by its bright reds and yellows. Two small paintings of birds, one green, the other blue, hung at eye level on the wall opposite where he sat. The wood floors and rag rugs gave the whole place a homey feel. It was the kind of house he wished he and his wife had. They lived in a one-bedroom apartment in Omaha. The air conditioner didn't always work, and the people on either side were noisy. They talked about moving. They had a little saved. Then she took over a thousand dollars out of their joint checking account the day she left. He'd been scraping by since then. He only worked part-time, driving a delivery truck, and he quit that job two weeks ago to come and get her, so the apartment would be the next to go unless this lady here could give him a few bucks. She was talking again, and he hadn't been listening.

"So, you see, we have that in common," Freddie said.

"Ma'am?"

"My daughter. Your wife. Both of them lost."

"Uh-huh."

"Well, maybe not lost, really, but . . . *elsewhere.*"

Freddie's gray eyes were sharp and clear, and it occurred to Nate all of a sudden that she was the kind of person who probably spent her whole life acting dumber than she really was. Her manner was unpretentious, plain, and direct, but there was something in those eyes that brought him up short. As if she were seeing deep inside of him, and knew all the good and bad things he'd ever done. He told himself to take it easy, that she was just some woman who'd invited him in for coffee.

"So, you'll just have to find her," Freddie said.

"Come again?"

"Your wife. Go out and find her."

"I told you I've been looking."

"But have you been looking in the right places? You tried her brother. You've been cruising the neighborhood. What about the mosque?"

Nate hadn't considered that there might be a mosque in Sioux Falls, although there was at least one in Omaha. He felt like a fool under her gaze, though he was also sure that Freddie wasn't being unkind, only practical.

"You know whereabouts I could find it?" he asked.

"No. But you'll track it down. Now, how do you plan to handle the situation when you meet up with her again?"

"I'm going to tell her to get her bony ass back home."

Freddie smiled. She stood up. Nate stood, too.

"Where are you staying?" Freddie asked.

"My truck."

"Try the Motel Six on Jasper. The manager used to work with my husband."

"What was he?"

"Police officer."

Nate stood up a little taller.

"Then a private investigator, once he retired," Freddie said.

"Sounds like a handy guy to have around."

"Yes."

Freddie paused. A look of intense sadness swept over her.

"In fact, one of his passions was looking for missing people," she said.

"Really?"

"A mentally retarded man wandered away from the mall one morning, and was never heard from again. Ken—my husband—went over every square inch of prairie for miles and miles. There was no trace. Nothing."

That episode had been particularly painful for Ken, and made him drink even more for a little while. His fondness for whiskey almost got him kicked off the force several times. His inattention at work was one thing, but at home, it was worse. He once left his service revolver, loaded and unlocked, on the coffee table and staggered off to bed after being in a bar for hours when his shift ended. Freddie found Beth playing with it and almost lost her mind.

Freddie said nothing of that to Nate. She made her way to her front door. Nate followed. She stood a moment with him on the porch. It was time to pot her geraniums for the summer, she thought. Ken had always appreciated having color out front, though he found her taste in other things questionable.

"I didn't catch your name," Nate said.

"I'm sorry. Freddie. Short for Fredrika."

"German?"

"Swedish. My grandfather."

Nate nodded. He agreed to return the following day, knowing he wouldn't. If Freddie knew it, too, she didn't let on.

Nate drove through Freddie's neighborhood, feeling lost. He could find his wife easily enough. She wasn't living with the brother, he was sure of that. He'd hung around enough to have seen her, if she were. All he had to do was get a hold of their card activity, see where she was spending money on a recurring basis—a grocery store, maybe, or a pharmacy—and get over there and wait. Instead he'd stayed on those dull, quiet streets to think things out. He always ended in the same place. Who was she to walk out on their five years just like that? Didn't she understand what a commitment was? She hadn't been a good wife. She deplored housework. She seldom held a job. He was the one who brought in the money and kept things going. He'd fallen in love with her because she was beautiful and fiery, and he might love her still, though if the doubt of that was now in his mind, it might have been in his heart long before.

He was forty-two years old. His wife said he was a dreamer entertaining fantasies instead of facing the harsh truth life never failed to serve up. Her comments were ironic, given the relative privilege she came from. Her father owned a successful grocery store. Her mother was the town beauty. Her older brother adored her. Nate, on the other hand, had been raised by a single mother whose words were often critical. He met his wife in college. She was in her last year; he was a freshman. She got pregnant, he dropped out of school and got a job, she graduated, they married, she lost the baby. She didn't want to try again. Her degree in Anthropology wasn't good for much. She held a number of different positions in nail salons, dog kennels, a dry cleaner or two, and even at the public library, where she'd helped people look things up on the Internet. She was an intelligent woman, a fast learner. One day a Muslim woman came into the library. Her clothes fascinated his wife. *You'd never have to figure out what to wear in the morning. Think how freeing that would be*, she said. There was a new light in her eyes. He thought little of it. Then she showed up in a black dress, her head covered, and said she was studying with the imam at the mosque. Nate couldn't believe it. Not long after that she said, *I go into a wider country than you will ever know.*

Two

1977

In the early days of their marriage, disagreements were often about money. Freddie was used to earning her own, and Ken wanted her to stay home. His job was stressful. It soothed him to think of her there, making the place comfortable for them both. But she missed seeing the people who came through her line at the grocery store. Holly was gone, married and living in Minneapolis. Freddie hadn't thought she'd feel her absence so keenly. What Holly took away with her were truths no one else shared. Freddie held those truths fast. Ken resented her long moments of silence, so she forced herself to babble gently about things that irritated him even more.

"I don't give a crap about the garden. I'll mow the grass, I told you that, but please don't expect me to get out there and dig," he said.

When she talked about painting the dining room, he put down his newspaper and sighed.

"Anything you choose is fine. Just don't go overboard. I don't want to come home and find pink walls, or something," he said.

Yet other times he grew suspicious of her demeanor.

"There's something you're not telling me," he said.

"What makes you say that?"

"Well, is there?"

"What wouldn't I be telling you?"

"That's what I want to know."

She wanted to talk more about her mother. What she had shared so far was a blend of truth and fiction. The truth was Lorraine was a religious fanatic. Also true was that she lived out of state. But then Freddie had said she was too ill to travel, which explained why she wasn't at their wedding, and why she never visited. Ken had asked why they didn't get even a postcard or a simple phone call. Freddie said her mother was strange that way. Then as time passed and Lorraine's silence continued, Freddie relaxed. Her mother had given her a great gift by removing herself from her life.

Then one day she showed up. She reeked of whiskey. Her hair was wild. Much grayer than before, Freddie noted. Streaked all the way through. She had a gift in her hands, a box badly wrapped in silver paper. The paper was torn, and the carton beneath exposed. Freddie immediately saw that she was being given a toaster. She had a toaster. She in fact had two toasters, a broken one from before her marriage, which Ken promised to fix, and one she'd bought recently when she realized he wasn't going to. When he complained, she said she needed to finish putting her household together. Everything else was more or less in order. Absent a clothes dryer. Made up for with a line out back, where she was pinning Ken's T-shirts and undershorts when the doorbell rang.

Lorraine didn't ask to be invited in. She strolled past Freddie, put the gift on the dining room table, looked around, and helped herself to a chair. She was wearing a poncho with fringe that might once have been white and now was gray. Her thumbnails were long and well shaped. The rest were short and ragged.

"I came to see the blushing bride," Lorraine said.

"Take a good look, then, and be on your way."

"You are discourteous."

"You're drunk."

Lorraine waved her hand vaguely. "I admit to having had a few. My spirit has been in a state of disrepair." Lorraine glanced at Freddie, offering an invitation for her to follow up. Freddie didn't.

"I hope you didn't drive in that condition," Freddie said.

"Took the train."

"Where's your suitcase?"

"With Pastor Banner."

"And he gave you my address."

Freddie wished she hadn't told him where she lived. She ran into him at the market, he noticed her ring, polite questions followed. He would have written Lorraine with the news. He'd have thought it his Christian duty.

"I would have called first, but you're not in the phone book," Lorraine said.

Ken wanted it that way. *Don't want some shithead I arrested calling up in the middle of the night when he gets out of the joint.*

Ken's shift ended in just under an hour. What the hell was she going to tell him? She'd have to modify her story, and say that Lorraine's illness was never physical, as he could clearly see. It seemed so easy—she didn't know why she hadn't thought of it before.

My mother's always suffered from some sort of emotional imbalance.

You mean she's nuts.

Ken didn't mince words.

She was out on a walk and ditched her companion. It's happened before.

But then Ken might offer to make the call himself, given his official capacity, as it were, and Freddie would be caught in another lie about where Lorraine supposedly lived, and what sort place it was.

"Why don't you beat it?" Freddie asked.

Lorraine shook her head. She seemed genuinely sad. If she broke down crying, there was no telling how long she'd go at it. Once she got started, she could weep for hours.

"You can't be surprised that I'm not glad to see you," Freddie said. "You must understand that you're a part of my life I don't have room for anymore. Not that I ever did, really."

"How cruel you are."

"Don't talk to me about cruelty. You never gave a damn that I was your daughter, so why show up now? What is it you really want? Money? I haven't got any."

Freddie's anger felt good. She wished it hadn't taken so many years to rise within her.

"I came to give you my blessing," Lorraine said.

"Uh-huh."

"I want to meet the man you married, and bless him, too."

"That might be hard. He's Jewish."

Ken wasn't Jewish, but if Lorraine brought it up, it would just add another layer to her nuttiness.

"There is hope for him. Our Lord Christ was a Jew," Lorraine said.

Freddie went into the kitchen. She washed her hands. The chicken she meant to serve sat on the counter in a metal pan. It looked feeble and exposed. Freddie put pats of butter on the bumpy skin, and turned on the oven. She had potatoes to peel and a salad to toss. She set to work. Maybe Lorraine would realize how much she was in the way, and take herself off.

Lorraine crossed her arms on the table, laid her head on her arms, and snored. She stayed that way the whole time Freddie was in the kitchen. If she weren't making so much noise, Freddie could pretend that she wasn't there and never had been. Thinking this brought back all the times Freddie had pretended when she was growing up. After gaining a bit of confidence, she became something of a storyteller. Her mother was a scientist who traveled the world. Her mother was a famous concert pianist. Because she never pushed the point, she was seldom teased for her obviously extravagant tales. In time she stopped talking about Lorraine. Reinventing her mother wasn't as interesting as reinventing herself, which marrying Ken allowed her to do. She was a housewife, albeit an unwilling one, but she had an identity. People recognized it when they saw her at the store, or the gas station, or just working in her garden out front. Before Ken, she was a struggling single woman with an empty past, where some misfortune had befallen her that was perhaps a bit sinister. Before that she was an abandoned child with a sister to raise. Being a housewife earned her more acceptance than the other two roles, but what she was accepted into wasn't entirely clear.

Now Lorraine's presence would bring the storyteller back to life.

Except that Ken didn't show up. That meant he'd stopped off somewhere. He made no secret of enjoying a couple of beers after work. Sometimes the couple turned into a few. Once, he had to be driven home. His patrol car stayed parked behind the bar all night. The owner wasn't happy about that. He said it scared some of his business away. The car suggested some wrongdoing, even something dangerous. Ken quipped that some customers would be drawn to an atmosphere like that. The owner said he wasn't interested in attracting that sort of clientele.

Freddie picked at the dinner she made. The light faded, and a chill came into the house. She hadn't closed the back door after Lorraine rang the bell in front. That's how surprised she'd been. She wasn't surprised anymore, though, just rueful. Her mother was sleeping off another one, and would no doubt wake up in a robust, energetic state. She thought about calling Holly. Had Lorraine visited her, too? But Lorraine didn't know where Holly was. Holly had instructed Freddie to tell no one that she moving to Minneapolis. By no one she meant Pastor Banner, the man who had tried to watch over them when they were children while Lorraine was off preaching the gospel. He'd asked after her, too, the day he ran into Freddie. Freddie lied and said they weren't in touch anymore.

Holly would just tell Freddie to shove Lorraine out the door. Bold words from someone who'd never had to do so herself.

Freddie saved what she hadn't eaten, covered everything with plastic wrap, and cleaned up the kitchen. Lorraine mumbled, lifted her head for a moment, then pressed her other cheek to her folded arms. The snoring resumed. Freddie didn't look at the time. She put her apron away and watered the three ferns that hung from the ceiling in the corner of the living room. She set up the ironing board and pressed several of Ken's blue shirts. She hung the shirts in their bedroom closet. She left the bedside light on—she never liked returning to a dark room. She tried to ignore Lorraine's presence. She stopped wondering what she'd tell Ken when he finally came home. She no longer cared.

Yet at the sound of his car and the sweep of his headlights across the living room, she froze. Lorraine's snoring lessened, as if in sleep she, too, were registering Ken's arrival. Freddie went to the back door to greet him. She took a dishtowel from the oven handle where she always kept it. She needed something in her hands.

"Sorry about that. Frank needed a buddy tonight, and my number came up," Ken said.

Frank was a sergeant in the police force. His wife had left him the month before without saying why. A group of officers took turns taking him out so he wouldn't have to go home right away after work.

"Ken, listen, I have to tell—"

Ken looked past her into the dining room.

"Who the hell is that?" he asked. He'd been in the process of removing his holster.

"Well, you see, she just showed up."

"Who is she?"

"I have no idea. She rang the bell, and there she was. She said she was looking for some people who used to live here. I didn't want to invite her in, but she looked pretty bad. She'd been drinking, and obviously down on her luck."

"You let a strange drunk into the house?"

"No harm came of it. I mean, look at her. She's been that way for a couple of hours now."

"Honestly, Freddie, sometimes I think you don't know left from right." He was being polite, because of Lorraine's presence, even though Lorraine was still asleep. *Don't know your ass from your elbow* was what he usually said.

"She hasn't been any trouble, really," Freddie said.

Ken poured himself a drink from the bottle of scotch he kept in one of the cabinets.

"And just what did you intend to do with her?" he asked.

"I was going to ask you that."

Ken sighed. He looked down at her. His face softened.

"Okay. Let me have this first, then we'll get her up and on her way."

He had his drink. Then he called a taxi. He prodded Lorraine gently, then more firmly.

Lorraine lifted her head. A line of drool escaped the corner of her mouth. She wiped it away with the back of her hand. She coughed. When she saw Ken, she stiffened. Ken was still in his uniform.

"I think I'll be running along now," she said.

"Taxi's on its way," Freddie said.

Lorraine looked at Freddie, then at Ken. She stared at his badge, which said Officer Chase.

"Fitting name," she said.

"Come again?" he asked.

"'Render unto Caesar what is Caesar's, and unto God what is God's.'"

"Anything you say, sister." Ken got Lorraine on her feet. She tried to smooth out the wrinkles in her poncho. Ken steered her to the front door. The taxi wasn't there yet. Freddie wished it would hurry.

"Where you headed?" Ken asked Lorraine.

"The kingdom of Heaven."

"Someplace a driver can find."

"I have a bag at a friend's house. Then the train station."

Freddie came forward and shoved the fifty-two dollars she kept in a ceramic cookie jar into Lorraine's hands. She had been saving it for a new coat that Ken said was too expensive. Ken stared at the money crossly. Freddie prayed he wouldn't berate her for her generosity later.

"Take this, and remember please that those people don't live here anymore. You mustn't come to bother us again, do you understand?" Freddie said.

Lorraine looked at the money. She took it. From somewhere beneath the grimy poncho she produced a small red-vinyl coin purse. She had trouble closing the purse after she added the bills. Freddie saw that there had already been a fair amount of cash in there. Swinn's money, no doubt. It was always Swinn's money.

The taxi came slowly up the street. Ken put Lorraine in. Lorraine told the driver where to go. Ken and Freddie watched as the taxi drove away.

Several days passed before Freddie found the courage to tell Ken who Lorraine was.

"That crackpot? Seriously?" Ken asked. It was a weekend, just after lunch. She chose her time strategically. Breakfast was no good, because Ken was always in a bad mood right after he got up. Evenings were problematic. Sometimes he started early, and wasn't very receptive after the first few. The middle of the day at home tended to be the least contentious moment.

"Why did she come in the first place?" Ken asked.

"She heard I got married."

"Why didn't you introduce me?"

"She'd have preached at you."

"I could have handled it."

Ken was on the porch, painting a small wooden table. The old shirt he wore made him look rugged and capable, two qualities that had strongly attracted Freddie to him in the first place.

He drank from his bottle of beer, and wiped his mouth on his arm.

"I can see being ashamed of her. But not saying who I was made it look like you were also ashamed of me," he said.

"Why would I be ashamed of you?"

"Because I'm just a cop."

Holly's husband was a CPA, a partner in an accounting firm. Freddie only brought that up once, when she and Ken were thinking of going out to Minneapolis to visit. Ken was curious about Holly's new husband. They got married so fast there hadn't been time to include family. *Your sister won't like that you married down* was what he said. Freddie didn't think he meant it. She thought he was joking with an edge, the way he often did.

"I'm proud of you for being a cop," Freddie said. Ken rinsed his paintbrush in the sink. His back was to her. She couldn't read his mood.

"Look, if I said you were my husband, that this was your house, she'd still be here. She would have worked her way in. The way it was, she probably figured I called the police, and that you were the one they sent over. You were the face of authority. She was always afraid of that," she said.

"And if I belonged to you, I would have had no authority?"

"Yes."

Even so, Ken felt his position in the household should be known, even to a loser like Lorraine.

"I didn't have to tell you the truth. I could have stuck with my story. Don't come down on me for being honest," Freddie said.

"I wonder how honest you really are."

Freddie let it go. She didn't have the strength to defend herself further. She wanted to forget Lorraine's visit. She wanted to forget Lorraine. She never would, though, at least not in this lifetime.

Three

1980

Ken had promised to be on his best behavior. Holly and her husband, Jack, were coming over for drinks. They were visiting from Minnesota, where they'd lived for three years. Freddie had offered to put them up, but Holly wouldn't hear of it. Neither would Ken, though Freddie kept that to herself. Ken found Jack a little full of himself, too much of a social climber. Freddie agreed. One of the things that attracted Jack to Holly was the elegance she'd cultivated for years. She dressed well. She read difficult books. She took adult education courses in things like Reading the Ancient Greeks and the Art of the High Renaissance. Freddie knew that Ken thought her snooty. He didn't understand her need to compensate for the past.

Freddie cleaned the house. Ken complained that he couldn't hear the ball game over the sound of the vacuum cleaner. He told her she looked dumb with curlers in her hair. She told him he looked like a brute, sitting around in T-shirt with a can of beer in his hand. He laughed. Lorraine's visit was three years before. Freddie hadn't quite stopped fearing another.

Holly didn't know that Freddie was pregnant.

Ken was getting used to the idea. The guys at the precinct had slapped him on the back. The dispatcher who was in love with him went to the bathroom and cried at the news. She confessed to him that she prayed every night that Ken would leave Freddie. Ken was flattered, but didn't return her affection. Freddie knew about her and pretended not to. She was good at looking right at a truth, and ignoring it.

Holly was thinner than before. She remarked at once on Freddie's plumpness. Freddie had no choice but to say why.

"I thought you swore you'd never have any kids," Holly said. Her color was high, as if the news had upset her, which Freddie assumed it did, because it made them both think of Lorraine.

"Well, nature had other ideas," Freddie said.

"Divine intervention," Jack said. Whereas Holly was thin, Jack was on the heavy side. When he sat down, the buttons on his shirt strained and made small gaps between them.

"Not likely," Freddie said, and Holly laughed.

Freddie was suddenly embarrassed. She didn't like being the center of attention. She brought out a tray of cheese and crackers. Ken mixed a pitcher of martinis, and poured four drinks. The one he gave Freddie was smaller than the others.

"You need to watch it now," he told her.

The conversation took the usual turn. Did she want a boy or a girl? Would they make a nursery out of the spare room? Did she have a good obstetrician? Had they talked about names?

"Lorrie, if it's a girl," Ken said.

"That's not funny," Freddie said.

"God, you haven't heard from her again, have you?" Holly asked. Freddie shook her head. The elegant wave she'd tried to produce with the curlers had fallen flat, and her hair, recently shortened, wiggled unpleasantly.

Jack said he wasn't one to ever speak against a family member, but from everything he'd heard, Holly's mother was something else. Ken snorted. The story of her visit, which Freddie had shared with Holly in a series of phone calls, was repeated for Jack's benefit.

"You can't blame her for not coming clean right away. I mean, sheesh! Who wants to own up to a nightmare like that?" Jack asked. He leaned forward and helped himself to the nut bowl on the coffee table, further straining the fabric of his shirt.

"A nightmare I thought I'd never have again," Freddie said.

"At least she came alone," Holly said.

"And thank God for that. I don't think I could have handled Swinn, too."

"Swinn?" Jack asked.

"I'll refill this plate," Freddie said and went into the kitchen. Jack prompted Holly to continue. She hesitated. It was a tale that needed careful telling.

Swinn was their mother's spiritual advisor, for want of a better term, Holly said. He ran the Baptist camp in Ohio, where she and Freddie spent time as children. He was a very committed person. Freddie was eavesdropping, and when Holly described Swinn that way, she poured herself another martini from the sweating pitcher on the counter. Years later, she would wonder whether getting drunk that day had had any lasting effects on Beth. Sometimes she even thought Beth's need for stimulation had stemmed from the gin that had flowed through her blood on that very odd and disturbing afternoon.

Holly had moved on to something else—buying a new car—when Freddie finally reappeared. All three looked at her. Ken took the tray out of her hands. She wasn't carrying it very well. Several crackers had fallen to the floor.

"Looks like the martinis kept you company out there," he said.

"Aren't you supposed to be careful with alcohol?" Holly asked.

"Nonsense. My mother drank a glass of beer every day when she was pregnant with me. Doctor's orders," Jack said.

Freddie sat down. Holly handed her a couple of crackers and told her to eat them.

The men went into the kitchen so Ken could mix up more martinis, and Jack could steal a smoke out back. Ken said he didn't have to—he could enjoy his cigarette in the kitchen like a normal person. Jack said he wanted to spare Holly, who had just quit and was trying not to relapse.

"So, a baby," Holly said.

"Yup."

Freddie chewed her crackers. She wondered where the cheese was, then realized she hadn't added any to the tray while in the kitchen.

"I went by the old house," Holly said.

"Why?"

"Just curious."

"Uh-huh."

"I drove past Banner's place, too. He was pushing a lawnmower around. And he's no spring chicken. Gotta be in his eighties now, at least."

"Did you talk to him?"

"No."

"Did he see you?"

"Doubt it."

Holly nibbled on a cracker and brushed the crumbs daintily from her lap.

"But what if he did? He'd recognize you for sure," Freddie said.

"So what?"

"He'd write her, like he did before."

Then Lorraine would show up again, demanding information. And if she came now, in the next few months, she'd see that Freddie was pregnant.

"What's the matter?" Holly asked.

"She'll find out about the baby and make my life hell."

"No, she won't. Remember, you're stronger than she is. You kicked her out once. It wouldn't be so hard to do it again."

The sound of laughter came from the kitchen. Freddie couldn't tell how long they'd been out there. It was fall. A fresh breeze wafted in, along with the smell of cigarette smoke. Farther off was a smell of burning leaves. Halloween was only a few weeks away. Ken was saying something she couldn't make out. He was jolly for a change. Maybe he was talking about work. From a distance, out of the patrol car and away from the speeders, drunks, bashers, and abusers he dealt with every day, the events that made up his working life took on a comic tone.

Ken and Jack returned with a fresh pitcher of martinis and clean glasses.

"I hope you know I was just kidding about the baby's name," Ken told Freddie.

"It's fine."

Jack took his place next to Holly. Freddie stared into space. Then she poured herself another drink. Ken took the glass out of her hand and put in on the floor by his chair.

"Let's do something to lighten the mood," Holly said.

"My mood's fine," Jack said.

Holly gestured at Freddie.

"Come on, hon. Out with it," Ken said.

Freddie shook her head.

"Yeah, out with it," Jack said.

"Leave her alone," Holly said.

"Tell them," Freddie said to Holly.

"What?" Holly asked.

"Tell them what she's like."

"Who?" Ken asked.

"My mother."

"I met her, remember? Had so much booze in her, she could've floated away."

"What it was like *living* with her," Freddie said.

"They don't care about that," Holly said.

"From what I hear, she had the maternal instincts of an alligator," Ken said.

"Let's just say she had other priorities," Holly said.

"Tell them," Freddie said.

Holly sipped her drink. She smoothed down the front of her dress. Her hands were strong, like Freddie's, but her nails were manicured, well cared for.

Lorraine was a woman full of fire, she told him. Deeply passionate, with no concern for personal appearance. She dressed badly, never minded looking ragged.

"I took her for a homeless person," Ken said.

Freddie nodded.

"Which is why I probably work so hard to look good," Holly said. The men laughed.

Holly continued. Lorraine may have been cold as a mother, but people sought her guidance all the time, because she was so single-minded. God was the answer to everything. Prayer was always the solution. Holly could remember lots of despair in that camp that Lorraine lifted with her energy.

She had peculiar notions about death. Holly always found that strange.

"I don't understand," Freddie said.

Lorraine followed the Christian doctrine of eternal life after death, Holly explained, but she also believed that death was only experienced by other people, never by oneself.

"It was her one attempt at science. She said that one could never be aware of the moment of one's own death. You were just there one minute, then not there the next, so you never knew you were dead, or had died. Only the world knew. Death was held outside yourself," Holly said.

"That's not science," Freddie said.

"Okay, well, maybe I misspoke. I should have said her one attempt at some other sort of rationality that didn't stem from religion."

Freddie didn't remember her mother ever talking in those terms, but then she had been different with Holly, and might very well have shared that with only her.

"She talked to the dead," Freddie said, and pulled quickly at her clumpy hair.

"What do you mean?" Holly asked.

"There was someone she was always talking to late at night."

"She was praying."

"No. She was talking to someone named Miss Dormand."

"Who was that?"

"I don't know."

"What did she say?"

"Things like, 'Tell me what to do, Miss Dormand. You're there now, on the other side.'"

"She used those words, 'the other side?'" Jack asked.

"Yes."

Jack scratched his meaty head. His forehead glistened with sweat.

"I had an aunt who liked to contact the spirits. You know, séances and all that," he said.

Holly signaled Jack to drop the subject. Freddie felt pretty glum again, and it must have showed. Jack talked instead about the house they'd just bought in Minneapolis. All the pipes had to be replaced. The plumber made more in a year than Jack did, he was sure, and Ken agreed that it was likely. Gradually Freddie's silence thawed, and she said it must be awful to live without running water. But that only made her remember Swinn's camp, and her mood suffered once more. Though Lorraine was still alive, her power to haunt was as strong as any ghost's.

Four

2012

For a long while after Ken died the phone would ring and Freddie would think, *Oh, he's late again.* That had passed. So, too, had the people who came by with good wishes. No more people, no more wishes. Sympathy was at first a flood, then a stream, then a wobbly wet line across the desert of her heart.

The service had been simple, held in the funeral parlor. They hadn't been church people. She asked that no scripture be read. Yet now, and at other random moments, scripture returned.

For if we live, we live to the Lord, if we die, we die to the Lord. So, then, whether we live or whether we die, we are the Lord's.

Lorraine, ministering to a new widow. The wind lifting one side of the tent's canvas flap. Joseph Swinn patting his face with a red handkerchief.

Freddie didn't question why memories came when they did. Time was a loop, from now to then and back again.

Freddie went to the mall. Her pace was slow. She'd learned to hold herself back, to accommodate Ken. She'd made him walk there with her in cold weather to keep his spirits up. He'd been a pill about it, but she prevailed. *Exercise is just as important for the soul,* she said. Usually he told her to shut up.

It was just past noon, and the mall was crowded. Freddie would have come later, but Beth was on her way, and the guest bathroom needed a new shower curtain. The one Freddie chose was bright and cheerful, with yellow suns and wide rainbows. Beth would probably hate it.

Outside a store that offered the cheapest cell phones in the whole state a woman in a long black dress caught Freddie's gaze as she swept by. Her head was covered by a black scarf. She was tall and confident, just as Freddie imagined Nate's wife would be. From her shoulder swung a red purse.

Freddie followed her past a kiosk selling watches, a children's shop, and to a kitchen store where the woman paused in front of the plate glass and studied a display of enamel pots in green, blue, and red. She went inside. Freddie did, too.

The woman wanted to see a blue enamel seven-quart Dutch oven. It looked heavy and expensive. The sales clerk described its advantages— easy to clean, distributes the heat evenly. The woman lifted the oven off the counter. Her hands were young and smooth, but her face, which Freddie now saw up close, was tired and lined around the eyes. She had a mole on the left side of her chin. Freddie wondered if it bothered her, or if she were so used to it she never noticed.

"Do you do much cooking?" the clerk asked. The clerk had a nasal, singsongy voice that all young women seemed to have these days.

"I'm trying to learn," the woman said.

You didn't make his meals? What's wrong with you? Freddie thought. She was sure now that this was, indeed, Nate's wife.

Freddie stared at her dress. Nate's wife looked down the length of it, too, maybe wondering if it were stained or soiled. The fabric was clean.

"May I ask you something?" Freddie asked.

"Sure."

"Is that awkward to wear?"

"Not at all."

The clerk was watching them both.

"I'm sorry, I didn't mean to be nosy," Freddie said. She was uncomfortable all of a sudden. She saw herself the way Nate's wife must—a frumpy senior citizen with twenty extra pounds and a bad haircut.

The clerk left them to help another customer who'd come in, a man carrying a small, curly-haired dog. The dog barked when the clerk approached, and the man put him down. Freddie and Nate's wife watched the dog sidle up to a basket on the floor containing a bunch of red and blue placemats. The dog lifted its leg, and peed on the basket.

Nate's wife's eyes were full of glee. She clearly appreciated the dog's nerve and bad behavior. She turned her attention back to the Dutch oven. She sighed.

"Not sure if it's worth the money," she said.

"They say copper pans are best. I wouldn't know. I could never afford them. Doesn't really matter, though. I don't cook much anymore," Freddie said. Nate's wife looked politely curious.

"I lost my husband last year," Freddie said.

"Misplaced him?"

Freddie's cheeks warmed.

"I'm sorry. Sometimes my sick sense of humor gets the better of me."

Inside Nate's wife's purse a cell phone rang a cheerful tune, something from a sixties sitcom, Freddie thought. Nate's wife removed the phone and answered it.

"No, I'm still there. I'm almost done," she said. "Yes, all right. Soon." She hung up.

Freddie smiled politely when Nate's wife found her still standing there next to her.

"Kids," Nate's wife said. "Can't fend for themselves for one minute."

But Nate said they didn't have children. *It's not her*, Freddie realized.

"I know what you mean. Well, you have a good day," Freddie said, and left the store past the clerk, who'd just discovered the puddle of dog pee by the front door.

⚭

The rhythmic creak of the old swing set out back reached Freddie through her rolled-down window as she pulled into the driveway. Beth and Lawrence were already here, two hours early.

Freddie walked around to the backyard. Lawrence's blond curls caught the sun as he rose and fell. Beth stood aside, smoking a cigarette. She wore tight jeans pushed into cowboy boots, and a silver shirt with a red vest. Freddie thought what she always thought when she first saw her after time had passed—that she looked like a hooker.

Is that wrong of me, Ken?

Not at all. He always believed in calling a spade a spade, even if you kept the words to yourself.

"Hello!" Freddie called out brightly. Beth dropped her cigarette and ground it down with the heel of her boot. Lawrence continued to swing. Freddie made her way over to them, noting how the backyard, now that she took it in all at once, seemed barren and harsh. There once stood a grand old cottonwood that had been generous with its shade, but it sickened some years back and had to be removed. Freddie hadn't wanted to, but Ken had explained, not altogether patiently, that a dead tree could come down just like that in a windstorm, and land on the house. Freddie stood at the window and watched the men chop branches and saw off the thick limbs one by one. She hated it, yet couldn't turn away. Afterward, she sat forlornly on the stump, later removed at further expense. Ken suggested that she plant another tree, and they could watch it grow over the years. She wished she had, because even though Ken was gone, the tree would still be there.

Beth embraced Freddie. She smelled of shampoo and cigarette smoke. She was shorter than Freddie, even with the heels of her boots. Freddie and Ken often wondered how someone that petite could have come from them.

"You're early," Freddie said.

"I was lucky. The flight before wasn't full."

"Where are your things?"

"Inside. You still keep a key under the mat."

"I didn't realize."

"Not very safe."

"No."

Freddie looked at Lawrence. He'd changed a lot. For a moment, she couldn't remember the last time she saw him. Beth didn't bring him to the funeral. She hadn't come out during Ken's last illness, either. Two years ago, then? No, three. He probably didn't really remember her at all.

Beth removed her sunglasses and rubbed her right eye. She squinted in the light.

"Let's go in. Have you had lunch?" Freddie asked. Beth shook her head. She called to Lawrence.

"Hey! Move it!"

Freddie didn't like the way Beth talked to him. Children should be treated gently.

Lawrence let the swing slow, then jumped off. He ran to Freddie and squeezed her. Freddie picked him up with effort. He was big for five. She kissed his cheek. It was sticky.

Freddie made them both a grilled cheese sandwich. She expected Beth to object, because she was always watching what she ate, but she ate quickly, without comment. She asked if there were anything in the house to drink. She meant alcohol. Freddie had bought milk and juice for Lawrence, and a nice bottle of French wine she hoped Beth would enjoy with dinner. The manner of Beth's request meant it would be opened now.

Freddie put on a DVD of *The Magic School Bus* for Lawrence. She'd come across the show sometime back, and bought the entire series on Amazon. She figured that Lawrence watched a lot of garbage on TV, and could do with something educational.

"You're both looking well," Freddie said. That wasn't true. Only Lawrence looked well. Beth looked strained and uneasy. She was dark below the eyes. On her neck was what Freddie assumed was a hickey but might be a bruise. Freddie took the wine from the sideboard, glanced at Beth's picture, and put the wine on the table. She uncorked the bottle with some difficulty. Then she took only a little for herself. Wine made her woozy.

Freddie didn't ask how things were going at work. Beth didn't volunteer any information about that, either. She said she had something to tell her. Freddie hoped she was getting married. It had long been Freddie's dream that Beth would give up her sleazy life for a good man.

"I'm pregnant," Beth said.

"Heavens!"

"I just found out. This morning, in fact. I thought of canceling the trip, but knew you'd be pissed."

Beth didn't mind using bad language around her son. Her boundaries weren't very solid, Freddie realized. She'd never looked at her daughter's life in quite that way before, and it seemed to explain a lot.

"How far along are you?" Freddie asked.

"Not very."

"Is it his?"

"No. I haven't seen him for a long time."

They meant Lawrence's father, a rich businessman from California who used to frequent Beth's club. For a time he showered her with gifts, including a new car. Beth called up to brag how good she had it. Then he booked out when she told him about the baby. She never got a cent out of him.

"Is it Jerry's?" Freddie asked.

"No!"

Jerry was Beth's appalling boss. He had a record for tax evasion, selling drugs in his place of business, even laundering a little money here and there. He bribed local law enforcement to leave him alone.

"Then whose?" Freddie said.

"I can't tell you."

"Why not?"

"He's married."

"Oh my God."

Freddie prayed that Beth hadn't known that at the time.

Still trying to make her better than she is, hon?

"I don't suppose you'd relax your rule about smoking in the house," Beth said.

"No. And you shouldn't be smoking now anyway, or drinking, for that matter."

"Spare me."

There was never any point in telling Beth anything, but she had to try. *It's alimentary, my dear Watson, as in the alimentary canal,* the narrator's trilling, cheerful voice announced on the television. Freddie turned to look. The Magic School Bus shrank and took a tour of the human digestive system. It made Freddie queasy, but Lawrence seemed to be enjoying it. In that single instant, she had the desperate hope that he'd become a doctor.

"I was thinking about moving back here for a while. Just until I figure out what to do," Beth said. She meant about the baby. She had two abortions when she was younger. Lawrence was her third pregnancy. At the time Freddie was surprised, though pleased, that Beth decided to keep him. Later she thought Beth did so only so to get on the father's payroll.

"What about your job?" Freddie asked.

"I quit."

"Because of the baby?"

"It was time, that's all."

Freddie put down her glass. It wasn't so long ago that Freddie wanted

Beth home again. She thought if she were there, under her roof, then Ken might come around, that they'd work out their differences. Now Ken was gone, and Freddie realized with a sudden drop in her stomach, as if she were soaring down a hill, that she didn't really want Beth there. Mother love was one thing, but Beth had burned a lot of bridges in Freddie's heart. She was a flake. She had contempt for any sort of hard-to-reach goal. Ambition was bad. Living in the moment was good. You sucked if you cared too much about anything except having fun. *Fun, fun, fun!* That was Beth's mantra. *You and Dad never have any fun!* Freddie couldn't explain fun wasn't important compared to commitment, because that's what brought satisfaction, contentment, a sense of purpose. Beth was an intelligent person, but she was blind to the inner lives of other people. Except the men she titillated by taking her clothes off. Their lust was deep and complex, or so she assumed. But Freddie knew lust wasn't complex. Lust was as simple a thing as existed in the world. Beth thought that manipulating a man who wanted to sleep with her into instead spending money on her was a feat of delicate yet powerful ingenuity. Teasing was a high art, she thought.

"Well, it will be good having you here," Freddie said.

Beth nodded.

Freddie took her empty glass into the kitchen and rinsed it out.

Life is full of new beginnings, eh, Ken?

You betcha, sweetheart.

Five

1995

The first time Beth ran away was on her fourteenth birthday. Her celebration had been carefully planned. She was in a slump, and Freddie meant to pull her out of it. She invited her best friend, Sheila, a girl Freddie disliked for her sneering attitude about everything, but of whom Beth was very fond. They holed up for hours in Beth's room and experimented with makeup that made them both look like ghouls. Inviting Sheila had been awkward, because Freddie had to speak to her on the phone, something she never liked doing in the first place.

"So, like, she doesn't know you called me, right?" Sheila asked. She was chewing something, probably gum. Freddie often found her remnants on the underside of the kitchen table and stuck deep in her dining room rug.

"That's right."

"Hmm. Am I supposed to yell, 'Surprise' or something?"

"No. Just please come. And try to be on time."

"Yeah. Okay. Whatever."

As for the cake, Freddie was stumped. Beth was on a no-sugar kick, which followed her no-red-meat kick, and no-white-rice kick. It drove Ken nuts. Ken was a good eater. He believed that they all should sit down at dinner, and having Beth turn her nose up the food he paid for and which Freddie took the time to prepare, galled him. There was often yelling. Beth had held her tongue for years, but lately she didn't. She called him a fat pig, which earned her a solid slap after he chased her around the house, then caught her by the hair. Freddie tried to intervene, which enraged Ken. Freddie was sure he'd hit her, too. He didn't.

In the end Freddie made a simple yellow cake with a white frosting. Yellow and white. Easy, happy colors. And the candles were yellow, too. Fourteen, with one to grow on. She considered writing Beth's name in frosting, but she didn't own a pastry bag.

Beth came home from school every day by 4 p.m. At 5 p.m., Freddie knew she wasn't coming. She went into Beth's room, a place she seldom visited. She believed that if she gave Beth the privacy she constantly demanded, that in time she would pull out of herself and be more like the cheerful, fun little girl she used to be. On the pillow, pinned to a stuffed black and white bear she'd had since the age of three, was a note written in silver ink on red paper.

Dear Mother and you-know-who,
Time to hit the road. Catch you on the flip side.

Freddie called Sheila, and demanded information. Sheila played dumb. Freddie said something terrible might happen to Beth out there in a world she knew nothing about, and if it did, it would be on Sheila's head. Sheila figured she couldn't get in much trouble for keeping a friend's confidence, but she also figured that Freddie was right. Sheila thought Beth was naive as hell. She had tried to talk her out of leaving, in fact, though she didn't say so to Freddie.

Beth had gone off with a college boy she met at the mall. They were going to a bar first, to wait for the sun to go down, then they were heading out to someplace in Iowa, where this college boy lived.

"What bar?" Freddie asked.

"I'm not sure."

"Bullshit!"

Freddie never spoke that way, and Sheila was rattled.

"The Fuzzy Dice," Sheila said. "I don't know where it is, though."

"I'll find it."

Freddie hung up. She could go down there herself, but her tears and threats wouldn't mean much. She called Ken and told him where Beth was.

"Okay," was all he said.

When Ken said little, his mood was darkest. Freddie hoped he would go easy on her, maybe make a joke out of the whole thing.

Please let him keep his temper. Hello, are You listening?

She prepared Beth's favorite fried chicken and mashed potatoes. She set the table. She sat, waiting. The phone didn't ring. The light faded. Evening came on, and the house felt hollow. She sat on, in the dark.

Please.

She ate a piece of cold fried chicken. She drank a glass of water. She rinsed out the glass and put it away.

Eight o'clock came. Then nine o'clock. Her hands ached from being held so tightly together.

Ken's car pulled into the driveway. Two sets of footsteps came up the front stairs. The door opened, and Beth came in. She'd been crying. Ken went straight to the bedroom to remove his holster. Beth threw herself down on the couch.

"What happened?" Freddie asked. Beth said nothing. Ken returned.

"Go to your room, so I can talk to your mother," Ken told Beth. She gave him a look of pure disgust, and went. Freddie took Beth's empty seat. Ken got a glass of whiskey from the kitchen. Then he sat in his old leather armchair across from Freddie.

"Well?" she asked.

"They were in a car in the parking lot."

"Doing what? Or don't I want to know."

"Just sitting. The bouncer wouldn't let them in. College boy is really a sixteen-year-old high school kid. Beth told her friend a big, fat lie."

"She wasn't really running away, then?"

"She said she was. He said she wasn't."

"What took so long? It's been hours."

"Had to scare the shit out them, didn't I? So I drove them around. I told them about all the people I'd arrested, and what happened to them in jail. Said if she turned up pregnant, given that she hasn't reached the age of consent, schoolboy's gonna get slammed with a statutory rape charge."

Ken looked pleased with himself. He sipped his drink in a leisurely way, savoring it. Then he leaned forward when he saw Freddie was crying.

"Hey, it's okay. She's home now. I don't think they did anything," he said.

Freddie closed her eyes. She placed her hands palm to palm, brought them to her chest, and bowed her head.

"Probably not a bad idea, in case I'm wrong," Ken said.

Freddie continued crying. Her lips moved silently. Then she stopped and wiped the tears from her cheeks. Beth emerged from her room in her pajamas and bathrobe.

"I'm hungry," she said.

Freddie stood. "So, let's eat already," she said.

They went into the kitchen and tried to make the best of it. Freddie was glad no one brought up what had happened. To break the silence she talked about the garden she wanted to plant, then about how she'd made the cake from scratch instead from a mix, which took more time but was probably worth it. Beth opened her gifts. From Freddie was a sweater Beth had admired at the mall. Also from Freddie, but with Ken's name on the card, was a new purse.

Later, in bed, Ken held Freddie.

"It'll be okay," he said.

"What if it's not?"

"Didn't you ask God to take care of everything?"

"God doesn't work like that."

"Yeah? How's He work, then?"

"By rewarding the faithful with wisdom."

"Uh-huh." Then he drifted off. Freddie listened for any sound of Beth down the hall and heard nothing—only Ken's deep, regular breaths.

Thank You for this peaceful moment. May You grant us many more.

Soon she, too, was sound asleep.

Six

1995–2011

There were other episodes, sudden departures, planned escapes. Beth always came back, either with Ken, plucked from another scene of imminent downfall, or on her own when the thought of missing the relative comforts of home gnawed too hard. Yet Freddie always knew that one day Beth would go for good. And she did—two weeks after she graduated from high school.

Communication was sporadic. She was in Las Vegas working as a waitress, a cashier, for a while as a dog groomer. She called, asking for money, saying she couldn't stand the smell of wet fur any longer. Ken told Freddie he wouldn't allow her to send a dime. Freddie ignored him, and sent what she had. Beth took to calling only when she knew Ken wouldn't be home. Ken suspected as much. If he wanted to know how Beth was, he'd ask Freddie if there was anything new.

Freddie didn't think Beth's life in Las Vegas could be any worse than what she'd had at home. She didn't reckon the damage Ken had done her—how she would always seek comfort from the wrong men. Understanding that made Freddie pull away, into herself and her "meditations" as she came to think of them. She no longer actively prayed. God faded from view, and she was left with herself, her conscience, and a desire to give her life meaning.

With her withdrawal, Ken went slowly off the rails. He needed her affection, yet wasn't able to earn it by being a better person. He drank more, had violent outbursts against people he'd arrested, was suspended first with pay, then without. He took early retirement, and when he realized his pension was too small to really live on, he got a job as a private detective. That line of work suited him. He'd always been sort of a loner, a keen and harsh observer. Sometimes, in bad moments, he thought of how he'd watched Beth grow up, taking notes and not acting until forced. More than once he took out his nine millimeter and dispatched innocent prairie dogs.

The first diagnosis was a horror. Ken's prostate had to be removed, and though his recovery was difficult, he didn't complain. Freddie wept in private. She begged Beth to come visit. Beth refused.

Ken rallied, the prognosis brightened. They spoke of travel, home improvements, an easier life. With what money, Freddie didn't know. She had always lived frugally, and saved almost as much as she spent. Now Ken often longed for an indulgence. A flat-screen television she talked him out of. After that, a boat. Then he demanded a car, which she let him get. And of course, dear Pudgy.

She grew to enjoy his company, as she had in the beginning. Sometimes they were so comfortable being just the two of them that Beth might never have happened at all, a thought which both stunned Freddie and released a flood of guilt. One night, she shared this with Ken.

"You got nothing to feel guilty for. Me, maybe," he said.

"It just feels wrong."

"Why? Because you're having a little fun, after all these years?"

Just the other day they'd gone bowling. They hadn't bowled in years, not since Beth was born. Freddie enjoyed herself a lot. She thought it might be fun to join a league, but when she mentioned this to Ken, he said he didn't want to get used to a bunch of strangers. Freddie said they'd only be strangers at first. Later they might be friends.

"It's not that," Freddie said.

"What, then?"

"I just don't think she's happy."

"She's probably not. But that's her own damn fault."

While their talks about Beth had gotten more candid, and Ken had admitted he was a shitty father, he still had no sympathy for his daughter. The way he saw it, people got what they deserved. Beth didn't have to twirl around a pole. She could get a decent job and not be ashamed of herself. Beth wasn't ashamed of herself. Freddie knew that. Freddie wasn't really ashamed of her, either, only perplexed. Ken was ashamed. That was something he hadn't admitted.

"What?" Ken asked. He saw there was something on Freddie's mind.

"I was just thinking about my mother. What she'd make of Beth."

"She'd read the Bible to her."

"Maybe."

In a way, Beth was a little like Lorraine, at least in the depths of her defiance. Lorraine could never fit in. Neither could Beth. Freddie doubted that her mother would have been astute enough to see beyond Beth's lack of piety to the traits they shared in common. Her religion was always a barrier. You were either on her side of it, or you weren't.

"Come on, help me cook," Freddie said.

Ken took his place at the kitchen table. He drank a beer and worked on a crossword puzzle while Freddie boiled spaghetti. Ken liked it with sauce. They spent some time discussing which was better, hers or the jar from the store. That day, with the future teasing her heart once more, Freddie didn't have the patience to chop onions, garlic, and tomatoes. The jar was good enough. She broke the spaghetti in half, dropped it in the pot, and stirred.

"Look at you, with your busy hands," Ken said. His tone was affectionate. He was wearing his favorite sweater, the one with the suede patches at the elbows.

"You know what they say, about idle hands," Freddie said.

"That's how I first saw you. Remember?"

"I do."

Freddie had worked in a grocery store. She was the best checker they'd had.

"I would watch you from the dairy aisle. Had the best vantage point," Ken said.

"That must have been boring."

"It was your face. Your concentration. As if you were doing something completely different. Something really important, like saving someone's life."

"That's a silly thing to say. You're the one who saved people's lives."

"Protected them. Never actually saved one."

The banter was pleasant. The mood light. *This is all I ever wanted*, she thought. *All I really needed.*

Time passed. Freddie was grateful for the robust man she took care of every day.

Then the cancer returned. Ken's health began to fail, and the future closed down. Freddie tried so hard to pry it back open with optimism, hope, and relentless good cheer. In the end, though, her efforts gave way to the inevitable.

Seven

2012

The doorbell rang twice, and was followed by a rapid series of knocks. Freddie was at the dining room table paying bills. Beth and Lawrence were out somewhere, shopping maybe, or visiting some of the people Beth used to know who still lived in town. Beth said where they were going, and Freddie didn't listen. She realized she didn't listen to a lot of what Beth said—a defense mechanism developed over years of hearing harsh words and confronting ugly truths.

The knocking continued.

"Goddamn it," Freddie said. She made her way through the dining room, annoyed at the pain in her left ankle. It was there all the time these days. So was the ache in her right knee.

The man outside was a priest. She was used to seeing Jehovah's Witnesses on her porch, young men in pairs, all squeaky clean with an earnest look in their stupid eyes. And sometimes a kid saying he was putting himself through college and needed to sell some magazine subscriptions. The Girl Scouts came around, too. Never a priest.

"I'm looking for Beth," he said.

"She's out."

"Do you expect her soon?"

"I couldn't say." The priest shifted his weight. His gaze wandered down the street. His hair was black. He had a scab on his chin. He looked back to Freddie. It was clear that he expected to be let in.

"Is there any chance I could wait?" the priest asked.

"That wouldn't be convenient."

Pudgy strolled out from the kitchen, where he'd been sleeping in his dog bed in the corner. He sniffed the screen door, and stared up at the priest.

"Please," the priest said.

At the sound of his voice, Pudgy wagged his stumpy tail. Freddie decided to trust his judgment, and relented. The priest followed her into the dining room. Pudgy came, too. He lay down beneath the table. Freddie gestured to an empty chair. They both sat. Freddie waited for him to introduce himself. He didn't.

"How do you know Beth?" she asked.

"We live in the same apartment complex."

"You're a long way from home."

"Yes."

"Did you come all that way just to save her soul?"

The priest had trouble meeting her eye. He was clearly very ill at ease. Had Beth known he was coming? Is that why she took off?

"I think maybe she changed her mind," Freddie said.

"About what?"

"Seeking solace and salvation." That Beth would find religion didn't surprise Freddie at all. She'd see it as something new, worth a try, until she got bored with it.

The priest looked at her the way you'd look at a rude little child—with forced patience.

"Beth isn't one of my congregation," the priest said.

"I see."

A car drove slowly up the road. The priest turned his head toward the sound of its engine. His face tightened. The muscle in his jaw twitched. It seemed as if he were holding his breath. When the car was gone, he exhaled.

You thinking what I'm thinking, Ken?

You bet, sweetheart.

"Tell me something, Father," she said.

The priest looked her in the eye now.

"If I were to suggest that you and Beth are a lot more than friends, would I be right?" she asked.

"You're very perceptive. She said that about you."

"It's yours, isn't it?"

"Yes."

Freddie sighed and straightened the pile of bills she'd been slowly working through. What had once been Ken's job had become hers.

"You don't seem surprised," the priest said.

"When you've known Beth as long as I have, nothing surprises you."

"I'm glad you're so accepting." The priest offered a smile. Freddie noted how white his teeth were.

"My acceptance isn't what matters. What about the woman you married?" Freddie asked.

The priest stopped smiling.

"Guess you're not Catholic, then," Freddie said.

"Episcopalian."

"An Episcopalian who got bored with his wife."

The priest lowered his eyes. He took a white handkerchief from the pocket of his pants and patted his face.

"She's . . . ill," he said.

"You cheated on a sick woman?"

"Mentally ill."

"And you left her alone to come out here?"

"She's with her parents now."

Freddie watched him. He was looking at the surface of the table. Then he met her eye again with a gaze so piercing she was taken aback.

"Does Beth know all this?" she asked.

"I kept nothing back."

I'll say you didn't.

Good one, sweetheart!

"What sort of crazy is she?" Freddie asked.

"I don't think that's any of your business."

"Seems like an odd place to draw the line, given everything else you've already spilled."

The priest said nothing. Freddie massaged the knuckles of her left hand. She tried to picture him with Beth and couldn't. He was slightly built, not rugged at all, hardly Beth's type. But then Beth had had so many boyfriends when she lived at home—all sorts showing up at the door, with no common trait among them except that they were male and thought Beth was pretty. One boy had been nice, though. Stuart something. He was an athlete. His father owned a chain of gas stations. His mother was a secretary for some city councilman. They struck her as a fine, decent family, but Beth thought they were boring, and in time, she thought Stuart was, too. Stuart respected deadlines and rules. That was no doubt the problem.

"You know, it's quite possible that Beth's a little off her rocker herself," Freddie said.

At that, the priest gave a brief smile. "She's definitely out of the mainstream," he said.

Freddie realized that he probably knew all about her and Ken, and how Beth grew up. She didn't like being at a disadvantage.

"She ran away from you, didn't she?" Freddie asked.

The priest put his hands on the table, and clasped them together. "I begged her to stay. I said we could work it out," he said.

"You planning on divorcing your wife?"

"No."

"So, you offered to live in sin with her, is that it?"

"I told her I'd take care of her."

Freddie snorted.

"I'm not impoverished," the priest said.

"Maybe not, but you must not have been too persuasive, if she bolted like that."

The priest's expression darkened.

"And it's a good thing she did. What if your church finds out? Won't you be, what's it called . . . defrocked?" Freddie asked.

"I'm willing to take that chance. I love her very much."

Something in his voice softened Freddie just a little.

"And does she return your affection?" she asked.

"I thought so. But now, obviously, I don't know."

Freddie felt like letting him in on Beth's history with love. But again, he probably already knew. Maybe part of his attraction to her was all the unsavory things she shared about herself. Maybe part of him had needed to save her.

"What made you want to be a priest, anyway? The usual calling?" Freddie asked.

"I'm not sure God's call is ever usual."

"Probably not."

A car turned into the driveway. Beth and Lawrence were home. Pudgy lifted his big head, then set it down again.

"What do you go by?" Freddie asked.

"Call me Father Mark."

"Well, Father Mark, it seems like your lady love is back."

Freddie stood up, and went out the screen door to break the news to Beth. She didn't want any scenes for Lawrence to witness. She needn't have worried. When Beth heard that Father Mark was there waiting for her, she just looked terribly sad, as if all the joy in the world had suddenly disappeared.

Eight

Freddie relied on strict routines. Monday, clean house. Tuesday, volunteer at the animal shelter. Wednesday, shop. Thursday, visit the library. Friday, clean house again. Saturday, wash her hair. Sunday, sit and reflect.

Then her routines suffered, because she was suddenly surrounded by people. Not only did she have Beth and Lawrence, but also Father Mark every Thursday. He flew out, rented a motel room, came to see Beth, and returned to Las Vegas in time to give his sermon Sunday morning. How he juggled it all, Freddie had no idea.

Holly came in July. She was four years younger than Freddie but looked older because she'd been a heavy smoker for years. At fifty-eight people took her for seventy. Since Freddie didn't allow smoking in the house, Holly took herself to the back porch several times a day to light up. When Father Mark arrived on schedule, he and Beth claimed it for another tense conversation, which sent Holly out front, where there weren't any chairs. So she sat on the steps and complained about how uncomfortable it was.

Father Mark and Beth went out to dinner. Beth returned early, worn out. After she'd shut herself up in her room, with Lawrence once again glued to the television set, Holly told Freddie she had to get the bottom of it.

"I don't think this one has a bottom. Not that I'm going to find, anyway," Freddie said. They were out back again at that point. Even in the open air, Freddie hated Holly's cigarette smoke.

"Why doesn't she just tell him to leave her alone?" Holly asked.

"She must feel some sort of obligation, obviously. I mean, it's his child, after all."

"How the hell she did get involved with a priest anyway?"

"Didn't have the advantage of how we were raised."

As it always did sooner or later, their words turned to their mother, dead then for twenty-five years. She almost always had a Bible in her hand, and quoted from it more often than she ever engaged in actual conversation, except about the most mundane domestic matters, like saying it was time for bed, or that the dishes should be washed and put away.

At Joseph Swinn's camp in Coshocton, Ohio, Freddie, as the elder, had many duties. She collected the donations dropped into a pair of dented, brass plates. She brought glasses of water to the newly healed who had fainted with release and the power of the Spirit. She collected the tattered Bibles and stacked them in a wooden crate to be distributed again during the next sermon. Sometimes notes were found among the pages—desperate words written in pencil, often poorly spelled, on paper torn from grocery bags. *Save me!* And *Pleeze Lord Jeezus, pleeze!* Standing up there with Swinn, her black hair flowing down her back, often in a blue or green cape, Lorraine would read them aloud and howl about salvation.

Freddie and Holly wanted salvation, too, but a different kind. They were desperate for a normal life. When Freddie was eleven, Lorraine needed a change of scene and they came to Sioux Falls where she and Holly were able to attend school for the first time. They were teased by the other children because of their old, ugly clothes, and were often the butt of cruel jokes. Freddie and Holly ignored them and rose above it all, despite deeply wanting to belong. Wasn't that how they survived their mother? With deaf ears and hard hearts? Some people thought they were simpleminded because they had trouble expressing themselves. They'd never been encouraged to speak freely. Rather, they were told to remain silent and receive God's word. One teacher actually believed that Freddie was a deaf-mute, and suggested that she attend an out-of-state school for similarly afflicted children.

Holly ground out her cigarette in a small metal can she traveled with. The can once held mints. She looked out over Freddie's barren backyard.

"Why don't you plant something out there? It looks like a damn desert," she said.

"I prefer to think of it as a wilderness."

"'And your children shall wander in the wilderness forty years . . .'"

"Oh, not that long. They come back when they're hungry."

They laughed. Making light of their mother had taken a long time. Freddie wasn't sure what had made it possible not to cringe at the memory of her. Only time and perspective. And realizing one day, with both bewilderment and regret, that aside from her marriage and the home she'd made, she had never had passion for anything the way her mother had for the Bible. For a little while the realization made her feel empty and insignificant. Freddie had never held on to anything that hard. Maybe she hadn't needed to. Or maybe she just wasn't as strong.

She kept these thoughts to herself.

"What's that?" Holly asked.

"What?"

"Out there."

Freddie peered. The tiny round head of an animal appeared from a hole, then half its body, standing upright.

"Prairie dogs!" she said.

"I thought Ken shot them all."

"Obviously not."

"Are they on your land?"

"I don't know."

Freddie's property went on for quite a ways. There had never been a fence. Beth used to ride her bicycle over the hard-baked summer dirt until she was almost out of sight. After Ken died Freddie took to wandering out there, too, usually at night, with a flashlight in one hand and Pudgy's leash in the other. Pudgy liked to sniff and dig at the short, hardy brush. When she turned back toward the house, the same thought always struck her—how big and empty it looked. Ken's absence had done that, just as his presence had made the house feel small.

Holly went on watching the land. She sighed. Freddie didn't ask how things were going with Jack, though she'd been tempted to every day. Last Christmas, when they talked on the phone for a long time, Holly said that over thirty years of marriage had worn her out. There had been no updates on the subject since then. Freddie was afraid Holly would say that a divorce was imminent, and that she wanted to move in with Freddie. Freddie would use Beth as an excuse, saying she didn't have room. She was hoping Beth wouldn't suddenly announce that she was going back to Las Vegas. She didn't want to exchange one uninvited roommate for another. But that was silly. Holly had a beautiful home, and wouldn't want to give it up. Jack would do the leaving. Wasn't that how it worked?

You kept threatening to go, didn't you, Ken?

Had to, hon. You drove me nuts, remember?

Money was tight. They gave Beth private school, exclusive summer camps, art lessons, anything to bring her around. Freddie found a job bagging groceries. Ken was mortified. He never wanted her to work. It was against his principles. They fought. She took Beth and drove around awhile. Ken was silent when she returned. She worked for a week then quit. She thought Ken would be happy. He wasn't. He drank a lot. Beth acted up. Freddie couldn't take it anymore and got in her car one day and went off alone. She didn't go far. She ended up on the other side of town, just sitting, watching a train roll by. Ken was both terrified and furious. He retaliated with threats of finding his own place. Beth was the one who did that. Freddie blamed Ken for putting the idea in her head with all his talk of moving out. Ken said that Freddie was the one who left, even if that was only for an afternoon. She couldn't be found during that time. No one knew where she was. What defined abandonment more than that?

Lawrence appeared on the other side of the screen door.

"I'm hungry," he said.

"I could do with something myself," Holly said.

Freddie sat a moment longer, not because she thought Holly might get up and make sandwiches, but because she felt weighed down by her thoughts and memories.

No good looking back, is it, Ken?

Not when you still have things to look forward to.

What those things were, Freddie didn't know, only that they comprised the rest of her life.

Nine

Freddie told Holly she'd be back after lunch. She only did four hours at the animal shelter.

"Hardly seems worth it," Holly said.

Freddie hated going, but she made herself. It was her duty. She accepted the slot no one else wanted. Tuesday mornings were when the dogs and cats scheduled for euthanasia would die. She told herself the truth—that the animals taken to the back room were for the most part old and sick or unfit for adoption. Cats that had turned mean, or dogs that failed their socialization test and bit the plastic hand that got between them and their food bowls. Yet she hated to see them go. Some had souls better than those of the people she'd known.

The shelter was in a strip mall on the south side of town, which meant it was a bit of a drive. Freddie didn't mind. Time in the car meant time alone with her thoughts, and although those thoughts weren't very cheery, they were entertained in a quiet, uninterrupted atmosphere. Lawrence had had a bad cold for the last few days, and his mood suffered. Freddie's had, too, as a result. Beth didn't do much for him except pass him a box of tissue whenever she noticed that his nose was running a lot. Freddie, on the other hand, fed him chicken soup, gave him hot baths, read to him, and generally hovered. Holly was put out by Freddie's divided attention. She was put out by Beth, too. She rolled her eyes when Beth slept in. She sighed when Beth did her laundry in the middle of the night. Freddie hoped Holly would keep her annoyance to herself. She didn't want bickering. She wanted to keep the peace.

That peace, however tenuous, was aided a great deal by the suspension of Father Mark's weekly visits. Whatever had happened that night at dinner with Beth kept him in Las Vegas. At first, Beth was glum. Now she seemed relieved.

Freddie arrived at the shelter at 8 a.m. The girl who stayed overnight, Mary Ann, had brewed a fresh cup of coffee. She was a student in veterinary science and had an air of sorrow that was unrelenting. At first Freddie thought she must have a hard time putting the animals down. In time, though, Freddie realized Mary Ann's malaise had nothing to do with the animals. She was overweight. Her skin was bad. She talked about someone named Spencer that Freddie had assumed was a pet, but who turned out to be a vicious boyfriend who borrowed money and then wrecked her car.

Mary Ann looked up from her book.

"You look exhausted," she said.

"Do I? Well my grandson's been under the weather, and my sister's in town, too."

"All that would put me six feet under." Mary Ann never mentioned her family. Maybe they were dreadful.

"Anything up?" Freddie asked. She meant with the animals.

"Three dogs and two cats came in yesterday. All from the same house. Owner got sick, went in the hospital, didn't have anyone to come help. Said she couldn't take them back when she got out. Now, they're our problem."

At least they'd had a home once. They should be easy to place. The ones that weren't used to people fared badly. Only the babies made it. Pudgy was from a litter someone found in the yard of an abandoned house. The mother couldn't be socialized, and was put down. All her puppies found a home, though. Pudgy was the last one. Freddie had never been in an animal shelter before she adopted Pudgy. She went alone, the puppy meant as a surprise for Ken. The eagerness and love of all the animals moved her. She promised herself that one day she would do something for them. When Ken died, she volunteered. The best days were spent helping families choose the right pet. The worst days were saying good-bye to the ones no one wanted.

"I'll just go administer the last rites, then I'll take off," Mary Ann said. The dead animals would be wrapped in plastic and put in a freezer until they were collected for cremation.

Freddie went into the reception area and straightened the magazines on the table. She swept the floor, though it had been done the evening before. She stacked the outgoing mail on the counter. She changed the water in the white ceramic vase that held a bunch of wilted daisies, then poured out the water and threw the daisies away. She went back to say good morning to the animals. The cats were crated in the first room. They rubbed their bodies against the bars of their cages and purred madly. Maybe she should adopt one to keep Pudgy company. A cat might be good for Lawrence, too. He might learn a sense of responsibility.

That's exactly what she told her mother when she brought home a little orange kitten one day. They had moved out of Swinn's camp for the time being—there'd been some difference of opinion between him and Lorraine—and were living on the first floor of an old country house on the outskirts of Coshocton that had been divided into two apartments. The upper apartment was vacant, yet Holly and Freddie always thought they heard footsteps above them as they waited every night to fall asleep. Feral cats roamed the property, yet the kitten Freddie fell in love with was from town, one of several in a cardboard box tended by a little boy in front of the grocery store. Freddie named the kitten Marigold. Marigold was soon her constant companion.

Freddie wouldn't let anyone else take care of Marigold. Her possessiveness went unchallenged. Her mother didn't care for cats, and she avoided Marigold. Holly wasn't interested in her, either. She was only four then, and obsessed with her crayons, which she guarded carefully and wore down to the smallest stumps before begging for new ones. Freddie learned how to work the ancient can opener and to tolerate the stink of the fishy cat food. She learned how to clean out a litter box, a chore she despised and bore for Marigold's sake.

Marigold grew and scampered through the house. She made the large, empty rooms feel less scary when Lorraine was in town collecting money for Swinn. He had deputized her to stand on street corners with a sign that said Your God is Nigh. People threw coins into her can because they thought she was homeless. She sent the money to him every week, and never held back a single cent. Freddie didn't understand why they couldn't keep some for themselves when they had so little in the first place.

She asked her mother this one day. Her mother offered no answer.

She told Freddie to go out and mow the grass with the rusty, dull-bladed relic in the barn. Freddie did as she was told. When she returned, hot, thirsty, with bits of grass sticking to her shins, Marigold was gone. Her crate was empty. The litter box and cat dish were gone, too. Freddie was frantic. She wept and shook. Holly didn't know what was going on, and stayed out of her way.

By the time Freddie's mother returned, Freddie was all cried out. Her mother sat her in the kitchen, gave her a damp cloth, and said to pat her face. She stood over Freddie with her hands on the table. Her nails were filthy.

You have learned a crucial lesson today, she told Freddie. *Do you know what that is?* Freddie shook her head.

That you must love God, and only God.

But Freddie was hollow from grief, and there was nothing left in her to love with.

Ten

The manila envelope labeled "Your dear mother's effects" came to Freddie after Lorraine died. Every year, on the last day of Holly's visit, they took it down from the shelf in Freddie's closet. Space was cleared on the dining room table. The curtains were drawn so the faded photographs wouldn't grow even fainter in the strong summer sun, though in truth, they were never exposed for all that long.

Their grandfather, Olaf Lund, looked proud and firm. Their grandmother, Anna, was very beautiful. Her eyes were fierce, and suggested both passion and rage. Freddie was deeply curious about her. She and Holly met her only once, when she came with Olaf from Chicago to meet them. They took the train of their own accord. They hadn't been invited. Freddie was nine at the time. They were back at Swinn's camp by then. Anna inspected the tent they lived in. It had a wood stove for cooking, which gave warmth in the winter. She found it odd, the idea of living in a tent. Freddie said everyone there lived in a tent. There were only two permanent structures, a dining hall and a converted lean-to for cooking. Anna asked where they bathed. Freddie took her to another tent with two bathtubs, one for men, the other for women, separated by a rough blanket that hung from a rope down the middle of the space. Anna said the whole setup was no place for children. Lorraine said poverty was the way of the Lord. Olaf took the girls out for ice cream. When they returned, Anna was fuming, and said it was time to go. She gave Freddie a piece of paper with an address and telephone number, and told her never to lose it. The minute they were gone, Lorraine took the paper and threw it away.

The pictures they reviewed now had been with Lorraine all along. Freddie never understood why Lorraine had taken anything with her to remind her of a life she'd tossed out.

There were letters, written to the girls by Anna, that Lorraine never shared. Anna's words were surprisingly bland, as if she wanted to invoke no anger in Lorraine, whom she must have assumed would be the one reading them aloud.

The spring is later than usual here in town. My daffodils are only now poking through the ground.

One of our lodgers has a small white dog named Snowball. How apt that name will be, in a few months time!

I hope you enjoy the mittens I sent for Christmas.

There were no more letters after a while. By the time Lorraine decided that Sioux Falls was the place to be, Freddie and Holly, though still quite young, were pulling away from her hard. Lorraine was very active in a local Baptist church and was on the road a lot. Freddie and Holly were glad to have her gone.

Then one day they got a postcard saying she was taking up residence in western Missouri for an indefinite period of time. *Many souls to be saved here,* she wrote. Freddie finished high school and got a job in a grocery store. They lived in a tiny bungalow. Sometimes she went by there, when she needed a reminder of how far she'd come in life. It still had a desolate look, though it had been maintained fairly well over the years.

Beth and Lawrence were due back from the park. Holly's plane would leave in two hours. She seemed reluctant to leave; Freddie assumed it was because of the trouble with Jack. Freddie repacked the envelope, and put it away on her shelf. Then she took it back down and set it on the end of her bed. She didn't want it in her room anymore.

So, where?

Like I always said, hon, the dump's good enough.

She put the envelope in the basement near the water heater. Maybe she hoped the bottom would rust through and the place would flood, carrying the box and its contents away in a torrent of Biblical proportions. But then she'd have a mess to deal with, so she put the box on top of an old bookshelf she'd been meaning to refinish, out of harm's way.

☙

When she returned from dropping Holly at the airport, Nate's truck was parked in front of the house. She found him inside, chatting with Beth over a glass of beer. Lawrence was at the table, too, coloring. His shirt was dirty from the park. How like Beth not to notice.

Nate stood and shook Freddie's hand.

"Hope you don't mind my dropping in like this," he said. He looked happy and rested, whereas before he'd been strained and grim.

"Not a bit. I enjoy company," Freddie lied.

He offered her a beer from the six-pack he'd brought as a gift. Beer, a gift? *Oh, well, why not*, Freddie thought. She didn't feel like doing anything with herself right then. She wanted to relax after weeks of tension.

Nate said he was moving to Sioux Falls. He'd finally found his wife, when she stopped by the brother's house. Their conversations had been brief and pointless. They were getting divorced.

"Oh, I'm sorry," Freddie said.

"Don't be."

"I know how you feel. Sometimes you just have to get out of a thing," Beth said.

"Even if you still care," Nate said.

"Right."

How the hell had Nate and Beth connected so fast?

Didn't you always say she could charm the horns off the Devil?

Only by becoming the Devil herself, Ken. If you're going to quote me, you have to be accurate.

"'Course, my situation's a little different from yours," Nate said.

"I told him about the baby," Beth said.

"Oh, yes, we're all so pleased," Freddie said. She wondered what Beth said about the father. Maybe she said nothing. She was good at giving just a little and then holding back.

"Have you found a place to live?" Freddie asked Nate.

"Little hole-in-the-wall downtown. It'll do for now. I can hope for something better in time."

"And you're working?"

"I am. Driving a delivery truck."

Lawrence lifted his head.

"I like trucks," he said.

Everyone laughed.

Beth pushed away her glass. She'd only had a little over half of it. She stood up. She wasn't showing yet. She still had time to change her mind. She hadn't said if she planned to keep the baby. Freddie hadn't asked.

"Well, I'm off," Beth said.

"Where to?" Freddie asked.

"Seeing Gina. I told you, remember?"

Freddie didn't remember. Gina was a friend from way back.

"I'll watch Lawrence," Freddie said, as if there were a choice in the matter.

"Do you need a lift?" Nate asked.

Beth ran her hand through her hair, considering his offer.

"Well, if you drive me over, how will I get back?" she asked.

"Right. I didn't think about that."

"Thanks, anyway," Beth said. She smiled and kissed Lawrence on the head. "Be a good boy for Grandma."

Nate turned to watch her go out the door. He drank his beer.

"So," Freddie said.

"She's a lovely woman," Nate said.

"Yes."

Again, a silence fell.

"I just wanted to say thank you for the other day," Nate said.

"Oh, I didn't do all that much."

"You listened."

"Well, as I recall, you did a fair amount of listening yourself."

Nate nodded. He picked at a callus on his thumb.

"Looks like things worked out. You know, with your daughter and all," he said.

"For the moment." Freddie told Lawrence to go and watch some television. Freddie put his Crayons back in the box. She closed the coloring book. Lawrence had been working on a drawing of a house with a fence and tree—someone's notion of an ideal home, she supposed. She watched Nate out of the corner of her eye. His pants were pressed. So was his shirt. He'd pulled himself up and out of the hole his stupid wife had put him in. A man that could do that was worth something.

Freddie took her seat.

"When does your divorce go through? If you don't mind my asking," she said.

"Not exactly sure. A couple of months, I guess."

"She asking for alimony?"

"Not asking for anything—and not getting it, if she does."

Good for you, Freddie thought.

"Well, I probably ought to head out," Nate said.

"I hope you'll come and see us again."

"Oh, I don't want to be a bother. Some sad-sack guy going through a bust-up isn't much fun."

"Don't be silly."

What do you think, Ken?

You already know, sweetheart.

"Really, you'd be doing me a favor. See, Beth's going through something of a bust-up herself," Freddie said.

"Oh."

"Look, here's our number. You call us anytime."

Nate put the piece of paper Freddie had written on—torn from a corner of the coloring book—into his shirt pocket.

"And we'll make you a meal. Beth's a fabulous cook," Freddie said.

Now you're really stretching it, hon.

Freddie watched Nate drive off. He looked in his rearview and waved. She hoped he'd be back. He wasn't cracked, as far as she could tell. That put him head and shoulders above Father Mark.

Eleven

Nate, Freddie, and Lawrence were at the falls, enjoying a spectacular autumn day. Beth wasn't with them. She was shopping for new clothes. *Maternity clothes?* Freddie had asked. If Nate had been disappointed that Beth wasn't home, he hadn't let on. He had said the flowers in his hand were for Freddie, for all her kindness. Freddie had suggested that he wait, or come back later, but Nate had said there was no point in wasting a perfectly good day. Was she free then? And Lawrence, too, of course. Freddie liked a man who made lemonade out of lemons.

Nate was in a talkative mood. He was getting used to Sioux Falls. He didn't really miss Omaha all that much. He figured the winter ahead wouldn't be worse than what he was used to. Snow and cold didn't bother him.

Then he told Freddie that his wife had recently reclaimed her maiden name. He stared hard at the water.

"She's just wanting to move on, I think," Freddie said.

"She also changed her first name."

"From what to what?"

"Elaine to Bahira. Supposed to mean dazzling."

"Is she?"

"I used to think so."

A name was a deeply personal thing. To give it up and seek another was to change the way you saw yourself, the person you were, and the person you wanted to become. Though it was over forty years old, the memory was as clear as the sunlight around her. On her twenty-first birthday, Freddie filled out papers at the courthouse and changed her name from Faith to Fredrika. The new name sounded strong and fierce, and she tried to be both. It was difficult for the people she worked with at the store to call her something else; it was even harder for her to answer to it. She got another job, in a store where she wasn't known. In time, and with a lot of practice, she got used to being called Freddie. When she met Ken four and a half years later, she was more or less adjusted.

Then it was Hope's turn. She was less imaginative than her sister, and couldn't think of a good new name. Holly was Freddie's suggestion—taken from the Christmas carol "The Holly and the Ivy." Its cheerful, bright tune always warmed her. Holly seemed to take on the new name with less difficulty than Freddie had, or maybe she just pretended. Sometimes, in private, one of them would slip and call the other by her old name.

Freddie told Ken of her name change on their very first date. Ken said nothing; he just listened. Later he said that names weren't important, only souls. *What's on the inside*, he said to clarify, because she seemed taken aback. Ken had been raised in a generically Christian household where Easter and Christmas were celebrated along traditional lines, but church attendance was sporadic.

Freddie stirred from her reverie. Lawrence threw a leaf into the falls, and was disappointed when he couldn't find it again on the moving surface of the water. He threw in another and kept closer track. Next he tossed in a small stick, then a larger one. Freddie asked him to please stop and leave nature alone.

"I just can't understand it," Nate said.

"Women can be a mystery. My husband used to say so, anyway."

"Nothing to do with her being a woman. What I don't get is her obsession with this religion."

Freddie nodded. What could she possibly say?

"I asked her what it was like—what it meant to her, I mean," Nate said. He had Lawrence by the hand.

"And?"

"She said it was like sailing down the river of joy. Isn't that the biggest load of bull you ever heard?"

Freddie shrugged. She knew from observing her own mother all those years that joy—the attainment of it—was what kept her connected to her notions of the Almighty. Not joy by itself, of course. There was the power of persuasion, the instilling of fear and guilt. But joy had to be there, too, or the whole thing fell down.

Like a marriage, or a person's whole life, she thought. Religion wasn't a thing apart, only a mirror, some sort of reflective surface of the mind. The question was who came first, God, who created a race of faithful worshippers, or people, who moved out of their caves and needed a way to explain their existence?

Do you agree, Ken?

A hundred percent, sweetheart.

Twelve

Beth lived by certain principles: always have cash on hand in case your credit card gets canceled; remember the name of a cop you once met (circumstances undisclosed) so you can drop it if you're pulled over; tell a man whatever lie you need to if it's time to break free. Truth, after all, was a relative thing.

It was principle number three that had brought her back to Sioux Falls. Vegas had gotten old. So had dancing, Jerry's bullshit, and scuzzy guys trying to get in her pants. Father Mark was part of the problem. He kept talking about saving her, and not just her soul. He had visions of her living in a mid-century modern that they'd buy cheap and renovate together. He couldn't live there with her and Lawrence, obviously, but he'd spend plenty of time soaking up the domestic bliss. Under his influence, she'd eventually go back to school and finish her two-year degree in some useful field like bookkeeping.

When he said that, she laughed. *Me, a bookkeeper?* He looked stricken.

At first he'd enhanced her reputation at the club—*Hey, you're banging a priest? Way to go!*—but he soon became a liability. Jerry hosted a number of private parties at which Beth was expected to entertain important clients with lap dances, flirting, and flattery. Sometimes more. Father Mark often showed up and tried to haul her off. At one point, Jerry took Father Mark aside and told him to beat it, unless he wanted to find out that the "in" he had with God wasn't worth shit. Finally, Father Mark told her that he couldn't go on if she didn't leave her life and put in with him. Beth didn't like ultimatums, and she didn't like being held down. So she told him he'd knocked her up, hoping to make an end of it.

He was shocked, of course, though the idiot had never—NEVER—used a condom. He had assumed—HAD to assume—that a woman "of her kind" would be protected. His words, not hers.

Then he said that this was her last chance.

Really, for what, pray tell?

To become the mother you know you can be.

Unfair!

She wasn't negligent; she just didn't hover. She never left Lawrence alone unless she absolutely had to. She took him to the doctor when he was sick. She bought him new clothes when the old ones wore out. Okay, so she didn't sit and read to him, and sometimes he didn't get in the bathtub more than twice a week, but those weren't exactly crimes, were they?

At their last dinner in Sioux Falls he held her hand and leaned toward her with the dull-eyed look of a starving man. She told him she'd had an abortion.

She knew for a fact that he'd stood outside the two clinics in Las Vegas, holding a placard with a picture of mangled, fetal flesh.

Protect the life He has given you!

He went on holding her hand. He asked her to pray with him, right then and there. She took her hand back, and told him to stay the fuck away, or else.

Another of Beth's principles was to build an adequate lie. She told her mother she was pregnant. She took to bed from time to time. She told Lawrence he could look forward to a brother or a sister soon. She had him think about names. He settled on Andy or Sarah.

Only she couldn't lie to Nate. Something about him made telling the truth easy, maybe because he hung on every word.

He took her to dinner. She ordered wine. He asked her if she should. That's when she came clean.

"So, you never were?" he asked. He had ordered a large steak. At the end of the week, when money got tight, he'd probably be sorry for that. He didn't care. They were in a nice place, with wagon wheels on the walls and red vinyl booths.

"No."

"Maybe you thought you were. Maybe you weren't sure."

"I was sure."

The waitress brought his beer in a frosted glass. Beth had sangria. He thought she looked amazing in her teal blouse and silver earrings. As pretty as Elaine, who was her complete opposite. Elaine was dark-haired and full of self-importance, even before her conversion. Beth wasn't judgmental. Beth let things ride. Elaine would chide him for ordering meat. Beth said she liked a man with a good appetite.

"This fellow, this priest. How come you got mixed up with him anyway?" Nate asked.

"I felt sorry for him."

Nate drank his beer and studied the hollow of her neck. He wondered how he could get her to feel sorry for *him*.

"He came into the place one day and just sat. Looked dejected as hell. I mean, sorry-assed losers come in all the time. But he seemed worse off. I asked him if he was okay," Beth said.

"You didn't wonder what he was doing in a place like that? A priest and all?"

"He didn't have his collar on."

"What was his problem?"

"His wife. Found her wandering the neighborhood in her bathrobe. Must have been hard to see her like that."

Nate nodded. His wife never wandered around in her bathrobe. Only that stupid outfit. In the middle of the night once. With country boys whizzing past in their trucks, hooting.

Fucking infidels, she yelled back. He heard it from over a block away. Her statement summed her up perfectly: a profane American so pissed off that she'd forgotten everything she came from.

On the way back to Beth's, Nate asked her if she was ever going to tell Father Mark that the baby never was.

"I don't know. Maybe," she said.

Only if you need to hurt him some more, he thought. He didn't hate her for it. In the world she lived in, hurting people was sometimes necessary. The question was, why had she chosen that world over all the others?

‿

Beth let more and more days slip by before she told Freddie she had something to say.

"You're going back to him," Freddie said. She was blotting a stain on her blouse with a damp dishtowel. It was early morning. The light was thinning for the season, and the sun came later and later. Freddie had always enjoyed fall. Until last year. Ken died in November. She wasn't looking forward one bit to that anniversary.

"No, that's not it," Beth said. She'd been standing, and sat down abruptly.

"You need money."

"Will you please let me talk?"

Freddie breathed deeply to prepare herself.

"It's about the baby," Beth said.

"You mean the one that never was?"

The color rose in Beth's face. Beth stared at Freddie with narrowed eyes.

"Mom—"

"You've been here three months. Your tummy stayed perfectly flat. What the hell have you been playing at?"

"I didn't have any choice," Beth said. She was still in her pajamas, lightweight flannel with a pattern of black-and-white cows. Her hair was tangled.

"Bull."

"He wouldn't leave me alone! I thought if I told him I was pregnant, he'd turn tail and run. When that didn't work, I told him I had an abortion. That didn't work, either."

"Obviously. He still calls. You didn't figure on the fact that he's in love with you. Nothing you say or do will change that."

"He's not in love with me. He's just lonely and desperate, and reconsidering his life choices."

The wisdom of that statement surprised Freddie. Clearly, Beth had learned a thing or two twirling around her pole.

"Maybe so. But you should have dealt with him straight," Freddie said.

"Why? He didn't deal with me straight."

"Didn't tell you he was married?"

"Didn't tell me he was a priest."

Beth scratched her head and drank some of her coffee. Freddie brewed it a lot weaker than she liked.

"Would that have made a difference?" Freddie asked.

"Of course. I don't want anything to do with that crap."

"So, why did you keep at it after you knew?"

Beth looked uncomfortable.

"He didn't pay you, did he?" Freddie said.

"Jesus! What do you take me for?"

Don't say it, hon. Even though you're thinking it.

Beth bit her lip, just the way she did when she was little and had her back to the wall.

"Spill it," Freddie said.

"He's a great lay."

Of all the reasons! Well, good sex was important, especially to a young woman like Beth. She'd had the same need, once. Ken never let her down. Even when he'd had too many. Sometimes she joined him. That's how she got pregnant. A rainy night, sitting around the fire, and a few shots of whiskey in her. She didn't want kids. She was careful not to conceive. But that night . . . well, Ken was a hell of a man.

She wasn't happy when she found out. Though abortion was legal, it was very unpopular. Freddie didn't care. She made plans to go ahead with the procedure. Her doctor respected her decision. Ken did, too. In fact, it's what he wanted. He always said it should be just the two of them. At the last minute she changed her mind. She saw it as a chance to do something. To somehow leave her mark.

"And now you're tired of lying, and want to try telling the truth," Freddie said.

Beth nodded. Freddie's wide, soft face changed. She looked unhappy.

"What is it?" Beth asked.

"Lawrence."

"What about him?"

"He told me the other day how much he wanted a little brother or sister."

"Shit!"

"You didn't think of that, did you?"

Beth said nothing. She seemed smaller in her chair.

"Say you lost the baby. That it was an accident, and that accidents happen," Freddie said.

"You tell him."

"The hell I will. This is your game, you play it."

Beth flexed her fingers. Clearly the thought of making her child unhappy was upsetting.

She really seems to care. Maybe there's hope for her yet.

There's always hope, sweetheart. She'll never be the mother you are, though.

I thought you said I was a shitty mother.

Only when I was being an old grump. You're the best mother I ever saw.

Freddie knew Ken had really believed that. She just wished he'd said it while he was alive.

Thirteen

The child beside him cried incessantly. His mother kept apologizing. *His ears hurt, you know, from the altitude*, she said over and over. The child went on screaming, red-faced, unaware of the pain he caused anyone else, or his mother's obvious shame.

As the plane made its way east over the brown prairie, Father Mark reflected on the nature of shame. He should have felt it with Beth, and didn't. He should have felt it every time he thought of his wife, and didn't. Did that make him like this infant here? Lacking in morals because he wasn't emotionally or psychologically developed enough? Or had he simply moved beyond the weight of guilt?

To become a priest, he'd had to undergo a rigorous evaluation. Intimate questions were asked about his relationship to his parents and siblings, the love affairs he'd had, his attitude towards those in authority. The results were that he resisted subservience, but had a strong sense of duty—of wanting to shape not only others but also himself. His mentor, Father Lane, said it wasn't at all uncommon for people "of doubt" to be drawn to God. While the one in the pulpit was there to lead others and show them the way, he was also finding his own path.

Father Mark had recently contacted Father Lane and said his faith was being challenged, and that he was afraid of losing it altogether. Father Lane told him to take a leave of absence and to search his soul.

Beth told him the baby was a lie in a rambling phone call. She'd been drinking. She said she didn't want to see him anymore, that she was sorry, that he should forget all about her. Deep down, he knew she was right, that moving on was his best option. He also knew he was stuck right where he was until she told him it was all right, that *he* was all right. When Beth sent him away from Sioux Falls after the abortion hoax, he felt crushed yet ready to resume his duty toward his wife. They'd been apart seven months by then. She said she wanted to stay in Delaware with her parents rather than return to him. After the in-patient hospital stay, she'd had a say in where to go next. At the time, though Beth was very much in the picture, Father Mark had said he wanted her back in Las Vegas. Maybe he thought her presence would bring him around when his own will failed. It was her parents who put pressure on them both. They had the time and—how did they put it?—the "wherewithal" to help her with the daily struggles. He didn't. The truth of that was savage. He lost his bearings. Prayer couldn't comfort him. Only the pleasures of the flesh reminded him that the world was still beneath his feet. While he was fairly certain that Beth would withhold those pleasures now, he still wanted her near. She was the only one who made him feel in balance.

The child wore itself out and slumped soggily in his mother's arms. Father Mark was sad as he watched his small chest rise and fall. He had wanted a child. His wife had, too, before her diagnosis. She was schizophrenic. There'd been no sign of her illness in their early days, just her tendencies to overstate things and run down every argument to its vanishing point on the horizon. When the voices started, she said they were from things far away—a star, maybe, or a well deep in the ocean. As they came closer, they were urgent whispers from the Virgin Mary. She was to look for signs of the annunciation. She was to make herself ready for a golden arrow.

She'd been raised an atheist. When he told her he'd be a priest one day, she blinked and looked down. She said she was very much in love with him, and that he must follow his heart.

Her psychiatrist stated that her obsession with Mary stemmed from what Father Mark did for a living. Father Mark countered that the Episcopal faith did not emphasize Mary's role in the life of Christ—that was Catholic territory. The psychiatrist was unmoved. He said his wife's hallucinations were her way of coping with her own yearning for faith. Father Mark thought that was bull. He knew full well that her values were rooted in the natural world. Her father was a botanist; her mother, an astronomer. Science was their God, and he accepted that. Once, though, when alone with his wife—Lydia—he argued for God's existence in the perfection and balance of systems her own parents studied, documented, and discussed. Surely there must be plan to it all, if everything works so perfectly. What other proof did anyone need of God's presence? Lydia had taken a dandelion from the lawn they were sitting on at the time—the backyard of her parents' home—kissed it, and said, *Why can't the universe throw out brilliance?* He couldn't answer that question then or now. All he knew was that he felt God in the world each and every day.

His own theory was that the trauma of her infertility—she had scarred fallopian tubes from a pelvic infection when she was younger—had made her focus on mother figures. Yet he couldn't ignore the religious slant. It was possible that he brought to life a deep moral crisis within her by being overbearing.

Since his last visit early in the summer, the weather in Sioux Falls had changed. Sharp, cool air greeted him as he stepped through the airport's automatic doors. He had arranged for a rental car, which he'd have to exchange for something less expensive if he remained longer than a week. The motel he usually stayed at had raised their rates just enough that he'd have to find something cheaper there, too. One of his last sermons had touched on the sin of price-gouging in times of economic hardship.

As he drove, he assessed the land around him. The prairie had its charms, but his heart would always lie further west. The desert was a subtle, magnificent place, where tiny exquisite flowers bloomed for a short time every spring, and the shallow washes overflowed with sudden rain in winter. When he was a boy, Las Vegas was very different from how it was now. Quieter, a bit less flashy. Now it loomed. A lot of people who came into his church weren't locals; they were gamblers who'd suffered a crushing loss at the tables, or someone who'd just gotten married in one of the little chapels and had second thoughts that needed exploring in the quiet and dignity of a real place of worship. Sometimes the whores and exotic dancers came in. They always kept to themselves, away from the regular congregation, who gave them dark looks. He'd been approached several times about the wisdom of encouraging anyone to come and pray. At the monthly meeting of the senior committee the subject came up more than he liked, which was another reason he was taking time off and turning the pulpit over to his assistant, Father Jones.

The public statement Father Mark made was that his wife needed more of him than he could give while also continuing with his ecumenical duties.

The route to Beth's home was easy. She lived on the edge of town, which he had to think suited her. She often said that Las Vegas was too busy and loud, and that Lawrence needed a better environment. When he suggested once that what children really needed were good role models, she threw her flip-flop at him. She'd been at the pool, and her hair was dripping. The memory of Beth yelling at him in her bikini made him smile.

Freddie was on the porch, trimming her late-season geraniums. Father Mark expected her usual sour glance, but got none. She stared at him with disinterest, as if he were delivering furniture across the street.

"You look different," she said. Her shirt was smudged, her hair uncombed and in a tight mess around her round face. Beth said she was from Swedish stock, and Father Mark saw that now for the first time.

"No collar," he said.

"Give it up?"

"Taking a break."

Freddie cut the stem of a brown blossom that had once been white.

"Beth didn't say you were coming," she said.

"She probably forgot."

"Not likely. Probably just wants to avoid you, is all."

"She's got no need. I already know she made up the baby."

"That girl's candor begins to surprise me."

"Sounds like she's turned over a new leaf, living here with you. You're a good influence, I can tell."

Freddie snorted. She clipped a few more dead blossoms and let them fall to the porch where a small pile had collected.

"Not me. I never got her to do a damn thing. If she's changed her stripes, it's Nate's doing," she said.

"Nate?"

"Put my foot in that one."

Father Mark told himself that Beth didn't like being on her own. There was always a man around somewhere. Back in Las Vegas there'd been a constant stream of suitors, as he liked to think of them. It was easier than admitting that she was oversexed and hard to keep satisfied.

Freddie said Beth was inside doing her nails. That struck Father Mark as odd. Beth loved getting her nails done by someone else. She said it was therapy, a needed time-out. He imagined her telling her manicurist things she'd never tell a man, and enjoying the girl talk. Beth didn't have any women friends, as far as he knew, so those weekly encounters must have been a lot of fun for her.

That you can have any sympathy for people who've hurt you—I'll never understand.

Lydia told him that once. When she got mad at someone, she wanted him to be mad, too. She hated that he tried to see a situation from all sides.

You can't just float above it all, you know. Sooner or later you have to stand your ground.

Maybe that's why he was here. To declare himself once and for all.

Father Mark went inside. Pudgy lifted his head and stared at him. The sound of the television set drifted out from somewhere. Father Mark noticed that it was no longer in the living room. Probably Lawrence watched it so much it his grandmother let him have it in his room.

Beth was on the back porch, with her feet on the railing. She leaned forward, applying green polish carefully to her toes, which were separated with cotton balls. He wondered what Lydia would think of that scene. She tended to disdain women whom she perceived as vain, yet she was jealous of them, too. Maybe that's why Beth appealed to him so much, he thought. Beth was the anti-Lydia.

Beth's face was smooth and relaxed. Then her brow lifted when she saw him. An empty chair was on the other side of her. She allowed him to pass and take a seat. With only inches between them, he caught a strong scent of her body soap. She focused on her task and didn't turn his way. She could really concentrate when she had to. She said she learned to at the club. You had to ignore the catcalls and lewd remarks if you were going to be any good. The toughest customer in the place was the pole itself. It didn't let you mess up, and if you did, you landed on your ass.

"Have you come to scold me?" she asked.

"No."

"Why, then?"

"I'm taking a leave of absence from the church."

"That's a big step."

"Life is full of them."

She nodded. She dug some smeared polish off the flesh of her toe. Her bare feet struck him as tender, suggesting a vulnerability that he'd seen only a couple of times.

"Are you moving out here?" she asked.

"No." He knew that now.

"Where to?"

"Not sure yet."

Beth paused to regard her progress, then resumed applying the polish.

"So, you just came to say good-bye on your way to wherever," she said.

"Yes."

"I thought we said that on the phone."

"There are good-byes and good-byes."

"Hoping for a parting kiss?" Her smile, though brief, was utterly brilliant and gorgeous.

"I wouldn't presume."

Father Mark realized he needed a drink. If he asked for one, she'd give it to him. Then he'd stay longer than was wise.

"Well, you look good," Beth said.

"You, too."

He thought again about that drink.

"What's new with you?" he asked.

"Nothing."

"There must be *something*."

"Okay, my mother's being weird."

"In what way?"

"Lawrence lost a tooth, and she told him to leave it under his pillow for the tooth fairy."

"Sounds like something a grandmother would say."

"He doesn't believe in the tooth fairy. He told her so."

"And?"

"She told him it was important to believe in things even if you couldn't see them. And that if it couldn't be the tooth fairy, it should be something else. Anything he wanted, just as long as he believed."

Inside the house, the telephone rang. Freddie didn't pick up until the fifth ring. Her voice was audible, but not her words.

"Anything else?" Father Mark asked.

Beth shrugged. It was a familiar gesture. He longed for her again. He'd have to bear her telling him about the new man. His penance and recovery would begin there.

"There is, I can tell," he said.

Her eyebrows came together. She leaned back in her chair.

"Well, I suppose I should say I was a shit for lying to you, and all that good stuff," she said.

"You lied to a lot of people. Your son, your mother, and to a certain extent, yourself."

"Still preaching."

"Only speaking the truth."

That's what sermons were, really, parables of truth, he thought.

Beth finished her polishing. The green was pale, like jade. Father Mark stared out over the late-summer land. In the distance he could make out a number of prairie dogs rising from their holes, surveying the terrain much as he was, then ducking back down.

Beth replaced the lid of the nail polish, and dropped her feet to the dusty surface of the porch. She had on track shorts and a sweatshirt. She could be a girl in high school, worrying about who would ask her to the prom. Father Mark thought that's who she really was inside, not this brash, tough, world-weary woman. She got that way by being defiant, and she was defiant because ordinary life—the one most people lived—terrified her.

Freddie opened the screen door and leaned out.

"You guys need anything?" she asked.

"Who was that?" Beth asked.

"Someone your dad used to work with. Wanted to know how things were going."

"That's nice."

"He invited me to lunch."

"Oh, you should go."

Freddie shook her head and went back inside.

Beth plucked the cotton balls from between her toes. She pressed them into one big ball and tossed it out into the yard.

"Some bird will thank me. Bet those things are great nesting material," she said.

"You're a character, you know that?"

"Which is why you love me, right?"

"Sure."

She said they had enrolled Lawrence in kindergarten, but it was only part time. She was looking for a job tending bar. One place seemed interested, but they hadn't let her know anything. The problem was, they'd have to train her. Nate thought she should go to school and study something she liked. She didn't know what that would be, maybe drawing or taking photographs. Those were both things she once enjoyed. She didn't explain who Nate was, or how they'd met.

Father Mark picked up her hand and held onto it hard. She didn't object.

"Beth," he said.

"Yes?"

"Nothing."

"I really am sorry for the way I treated you."

"I know."

Her hand was still in his.

"And I know I was hard on you for not figuring the odds better. Guess I've always been a bully where bad gamblers go," she said.

"What odds?"

"Of saving me."

But he had saved her. Here she was, in her mother's home with her child, moving towards a decent future. He hadn't planned it that way, but the result was the same. He came on strong, and she bolted. The miracle was that she left it all behind, not just him.

He let go of her hand, and they sat a little longer on the porch. They were both lost in thought. She wondered about her feelings for Nate. He reflected on the nature of miracles.

Fourteen

The ringing of the telephone broke into a sleep so deep that Freddie at first couldn't remember anything. She moved her leg across the bed to nudge Ken awake so he could answer it for her. The phone continued to ring. Her mind cleared. The illuminated face of the digital clock by her bed said that the time was 3:12 a.m. *Beth*, she thought. *Beth's been in an accident.* But Beth was right there, across the hall, asleep. They had had dinner, done the dishes, and watched a movie before turning in.

Freddie lifted the receiver.

"Faith. Is that you?"

"Holly?"

"Faith. She's been here, Faith."

"Who?"

"Mother."

"What the hell are you talking about?"

"She came to see me."

Freddie said Holly had been dreaming.

"No. She was here," Holly said.

"Put Jack on."

"He's not home."

"Where is he?"

"Business trip."

Freddie was sitting up at that point, squinting in the sudden glare of the bedside light. Holly's words were slurred. She said that Lorraine had been in the house looking for something when Holly interrupted her.

"You know that's impossible," Freddie said. Her heart was racing. It had never occurred to her that Holly would get loaded and start seeing things.

"I'm telling you. She was here." Holly hung up. Freddie dialed her number. Holly didn't answer. Freddie was confused. Holly had sounded drunk, but she didn't drink as far as Freddie knew. Maybe she was living it up in Jack's absence, but that seemed unlikely. Lorraine had been a drinker, and so had Ken. Jack, too, could go overboard, but it was never Holly's way.

In the morning Freddie tried Holly's line again. There was still no answer.

"Maybe she's sleeping it off," Beth said. She was all dressed up in a matching jacket and slacks. Her hair was clipped nicely at the back of her head. For once, her makeup was modest. She was on her way to an interview at a family restaurant that needed a new hostess.

"I don't think so," Freddie said. She put her coffee cup back in its saucer. Beth had made the coffee that morning, and it was impossibly strong.

"Well, he probably drove her to it. Uncle Jack's a hairball, if you ask me."

Beth took her purse, which reflected her old style and had shiny beads dangling from the strap, and went on her way.

"Can you bring back some milk?" Freddie called out, but Beth didn't hear. The used Volvo she'd recently bought started, backed down the driveway, and took off down the street, with loud music pouring through the sunroof. Freddie shook her head. She showered, and drove Lawrence to school. Beth thought he should take the school bus, but Freddie didn't like the idea. Some of the children along the street had rough ways, and she didn't want him bullied.

When she returned, she looked up the number for the accounting firm Jack owned and called it. She was told he was out of town until the following Thursday. Freddie identified herself, and asked where he could be reached.

"It's a family matter," she said.

"Is there something wrong?" The voice was young, female, annoyed. Freddie realized in that instant that she and Jack were fooling around. Jack had a history of romantic liaisons.

"I'm planning a surprise party for his wife," Freddie said. She was given Jack's cell phone number. Freddie called it, got his irritating chipper voice mail, and left a message asking him to call her at once. Three hours passed before he did. He had no idea why Holly sounded strange. No, of course she wasn't drunk. She never drank to excess. The only change in her life was that he doctor had put her on a higher dose of hypertension medication. He didn't know why Holly hadn't told Freddie about her high blood pressure. They'd had two weeks together in South Dakota, so he assumed they would have covered pretty much anything of note. No, he hadn't spoken to Holly that day. He didn't usually call home every day when he was on the road.

"Well, maybe you should start. Something's going on out there. She's not answering the phone," Freddie said.

"She does that."

"What? Not answer the phone?"

"We had someone harassing us a few months ago. A lot of hang-up calls."

"Who was it?"

"How should I know?"

"That's what caller ID is for."

"We have caller ID. It always came in as a blocked number."

"So, change your setting not to accept blocked calls."

The silence on Jack's end suggested that he hadn't thought of doing that.

"Isn't there a neighbor you can ask to go over and have a look?" Freddie asked.

"Oh, for Christ's sake, Freddie. I'm sure it's not that dire!"

"Jack, trust me. I'm her sister. I have a sister's instincts, and something is wrong. Now go call someone."

"Jesus. All right. All right. All right." He hung up.

Freddie sat on the back porch and stared out at the flat ground. The prairie dogs weren't around today. She wished they were. Knowing they were there gave her a sense of companionship.

Beth returned, dejected. The restaurant had already filled the position. Some member of the owner's extended family went to head of the line and beat out everyone else.

"It's disgusting," Beth said.

"You'll have other interviews."

"There's a recession on, if you haven't noticed."

"Don't be snarky."

"What's the matter with you anyway? You're just been sitting here, staring at nothing."

"I already told you."

"Haven't you heard anything yet?"

"No."

"Weird."

Beth went inside to change. She would get Lawrence from school, and take him along on her dinner date with Nate. Freddie didn't want to be alone in the house, waiting for the phone to ring. In the daytime, it was fine. But in the dark, it was awful. Too many memories of lying awake while Ken was on night patrol.

I'm sorry, he's been shot. She always dreaded hearing that. Even after Ken told her that in that case, someone would come to the house and not bother calling, the anticipation of that call was agony.

Beth came out to the porch to say good-bye. She was back in her blue jeans and Vikings T-shirt, over which she wore a new sweater that zipped up in the front. Looking at her, it struck Freddie that Beth had changed since moving home. She was more mature and stable, at least in appearance. She still had moments when her tongue turned sharp and she accused Freddie of ruining her life. Just the other day she'd said, *If you and Dad thought I was doing so badly, why didn't grab hold of me and keep me close?* Freddie was shocked. Beth never wanted to be held back. All she ever wanted was to run. Now she made it sound like she'd been testing them, or crying out for help.

Do you buy it? Freddie had asked Ken.

Don't know, hon. Gonna have to think on that one.

When the air cooled, Freddie went inside. She knew she ought to make herself something to eat, but she had no appetite. Pudgy arrived from the living room, where he'd spent the afternoon on the couch. The pleading in his eyes touched her, as always. Dogs were simple, easy creatures. Freddie bent and scratched his head.

"You miss him, don't you? I know I'm a poor substitute," she said. She opened the cabinet under the sink where she kept his cereal in a large plastic box, and scooped some into his bowl. She added water. On cue,

Pudgy stood on his back legs and hopped after her, spinning around now and then as he went. She put the bowl on the back porch, and went inside.

She took out a carton of eggs, thinking she might scramble up two. She put the carton on the counter. The phone rang. She went into the dining room where she'd left the handset. It was the receptionist at Beth's dentist's office reminding Beth of her appointment the following day. Freddie hung up without saying a word. She put the receiver in the pocket of her sweater, and went back into the kitchen. She sat at the table. Pudgy scratched at the door. She asked him to wait a moment. Her heart pounded. Sometimes she wondered how much stress it could take before folding in on itself. Her doctor advised her to walk vigorously for thirty minutes a day, and to try to lose at least fifteen pounds. This was the same doctor who had said that Ken's cancer was completely treatable, even the second time around. Her heart slowed, yet a tightness remained across her forehead. She needed a drink. No point in denying it. There was a half bottle of red wine on the sideboard in the dining room. Since Beth's return, Freddie had taken up the habit of drinking wine, though not on a daily basis. Maybe she should.

The wine was slightly sour. Freddie didn't care. With a full glass in her hand, she let Pudgy in, and took a seat on the porch. She hoped the dropping temperature wouldn't chase her back inside, because she needed the fresh air and open view.

The telephone rang. It was Jack at last.

"Freddie, listen . . ."

"What's wrong?"

"Holly . . . she . . . she seems to have had a stroke."

"What?"

"She's okay. I mean, she's at the hospital. They don't think it's too bad."

"When the hell did this happen?"

"I don't know. Yesterday. No, today."

"And you found her?"

"No, I'm still in Cleveland. I called a neighbor."

"You're heading home, though, right?"

"First thing tomorrow."

"I'll come out."

"You don't need to. She's fine. Really."

"Bullshit. I'll be there by evening, or the day after, at the latest. Let me see to things here first."

"Freddie—"

She hung up.

Jesus Christ! No wonder Holly didn't answer the phone. She must have had the stroke sometime after she called Freddie that morning. But her speech had been slurred. Had it already happened? Or had there been more than one? Freddie wished she had the name of Holly's hospital. She could call and ask some questions. Jack must know. She should call him back, but she was too worn out. Wherever Holly was, she was in good hands.

Freddie went inside and dropped into a chair at the kitchen table. Pudgy was at her feet, sniffing her leg. The agitated sound of her voice had brought him from his roost. He wanted her to pet him. Freddie pulled her fingers into fists. She opened and closed them over and over. She was both scared and angry. Years of smoking had finally caught up with Holly. All the warnings and Freddie's begging her to quit had been in vain. Holly had always been stubborn and ignored facts and probabilities.

See what happens when you don't listen?

Holly's misfortune wasn't justice, only consequence. What it didn't explain was Lorraine's visit. The answer to that lay deep in the past, buried and unseen. It might be revealed in time, if they sought it hard enough.

Part Two

Fifteen

Freddie thought often of Anna. *A capable woman*, Lorraine might say. *But no interest in God.* Anna was her own person, Freddie was sure. Made up her own mind, just as Freddie did. About God, faith, and the rest of it. Anna's world was a thing of dreams, a blend of joy and countless moments of sorrow. *You had a hard daughter, too!* Freddie could never know the details, the truth of her years. But it was all there, housed with the keeper of time.

❦

In August 1920, two newlyweds descended the stairs of the railroad car that had brought them to Huron, South Dakota. They took in the hot, flat landscape, and realized at once that there was no lake. The husband, Paul Emile, had accepted the teaching position there because of the presence of a wide body of water that he would later learn was one of the Great Lakes, and considerably to the north and east of where he then stood with his wife, Anna. He had grown up on the shores of Lake Geneva. Living by water was necessary for serenity of spirit, he believed. Waiting for their taxi to take them into town, breathing the dry, dusty air, he thought the place he looked at was nothing like home. He was disappointed.

Anna wasn't. She was safe. What happened to her five years before would never happen here. The Turks had removed her family from their villa in Constantinople. They were not forced out into the countryside to die, as so many others were, because her father was a jeweler by trade, and not considered any sort of political threat, but into a far poorer neighborhood than they'd enjoyed before. The house they came to occupy was much smaller than the first, which had had a long stone balcony overlooking the Bosporus where Anna played as a child and later sat as a young woman dreaming of lands that lay beyond her line of sight. In time the only land she dreamed of was America, and she'd arrived. Now all there was to do was make the best of it.

They'd secured a cottage near the campus of Huron College. Whoever had lived there before had had a fondness for drink. Empty bottles were set neatly on the dusty windowsill. One bore the label "Uncle Oscar's Pick Me Up—A Tonic For Well-Bred Ladies." Anna removed the cork and brought the open vessel to her nose. All she got was a faintly floral smell. The bottle was nicely shaped—slender at the neck, wider in the middle, and then tapering again to the base on which it sat.

As she turned the bottle over in her hands, the tiny diamond in her wedding band flashed in the light. Theirs had been a Catholic ceremony, in a church on a narrow, quiet street. Paul had been so handsome in his long coat and combed-down hair. Only one of his five sisters, Marie, made the trip south from Le Lac, the Swiss village of his birth. Unlike her brother, she was short and thick, with a stubborn, sullen gleam in her brown eyes. Like a cow's, those eyes, Anna thought. Marie came to serve as Anna's maid-of-honor. It was not up to the bridegroom to choose who would fill that role, but Anna let him, to the pain and quiet sighs of her own two sisters. She let him do anything. She had waited a long time for a proposal. She was thirty years old.

She brought the bottle into the kitchen and put it by the sink. She lifted and pumped the iron handle until a stream of brown water flowed from the faucet. There was nothing to stop the sink with, so Anna released the pump. A list formed in her mind of things to buy in town, things she hoped the college would reimburse them for.

Paul had the same thought. He believed in counting pennies. The coat he'd worn at his wedding had been borrowed. Anna's ring belonged to his dead aunt, a fact he didn't share with her, though Marie obviously knew. He'd sworn her to silence. He told her she was such a big help to him growing up, though in fact she hadn't been. Marie was five years older than he, unmarried, and generally lazy. She served tea in a small establishment with pink-and-gold wallpaper that catered to better-off women in Geneva. She was also gullible, and susceptible to flattery. Anna wasn't. His praise and kind words were accepted without so much as a flicker in her black eyes. He loved those eyes. Her steel core made other means of persuasion necessary. Sex had proven to be the answer. He hoped she would soon be pregnant.

Anna continued her inspection of the house. There were two bedrooms: the one in front faced east; the one in back faced west. There were no curtains in either room. The bathroom was next to the kitchen. The tile floor was missing here and there, and the mirror above the sink was cracked. Anna examined her reflection in the mismatched glass. Her face split just above her mouth, so that above the line she was herself, with no way to speak, and below, she was only words. *I'll have to figure out what that means later*, she thought, and then forgot all about it.

Paul went to campus every morning promptly at nine, although courses wouldn't begin for another week. He wanted to become well acquainted with everyone in the French Department. The chairman had taken particular interest in Paul's doctoral thesis, written while he was an instructor at the American University in Constantinople where Anna was a secretary. The topic of Paul's dissertation was Denis Diderot and his philosophy of enlightenment. The chairman, Donald Plake, had never been to France. His son had died during the Battle of the Somme. In Paul Emile he saw a second son, someone his own might have become given time and opportunity. Professor Emile was no doubt highly cultured, Professor Plake had said during the staff meeting he'd held just hours before Professor Emile arrived in Huron. In person, Professor Emile exceeded Professor Plake's expectations. All that old world charm! The slight bow of greeting. The heels of his polished shoes always lined up side by side as he stood absolutely straight. He'd won a medal for marksmanship, Professor Plake told his wife. And it was so easy to picture him, his hand steady, nerves calm, not a drop of sweat on his brow.

In truth, Paul was given to bouts of melancholy that left him anything but steady and calm. He was a fearful man. He suffered from unnamed slights and insults, and took his misery out on Anna, sometimes refusing to speak, other times flying into a childish rage. Her own father had had an uneasy temperament. Anna tolerated Paul's bad humor. She was willing to bide her time and wait for the episode to pass, which it always did, most quickly after a soothing cup of tea and a little story she shared from her own past.

Her most recent tale was of a lost button. A small pearl button on her favorite blouse, held in place with fine silk thread. After leaving the house on the Bosporus, with their money all but gone, replacing that button was impossible. The finery she once enjoyed glimmered for a moment in her eyes, though Paul, sunk in despair over the sudden laughter from one his students—and on his first day in the lecture hall, no less—didn't notice.

Anna's only choice was to find a fake pearl button, easy to come by in any notions store. The man who sold it to her said it matched the others perfectly. Anna, with her damaged shirt in hand, agreed.

It'll be your secret, he said, as he put the button in a paper bag. But Anna wasn't sure. Her mother had sharp eyes, and the missing button was the very top one. So she removed the bottom button, sewed it where the lost one had been, and put the fake one in its place, where the shirt was usually tucked into the waistband of her ankle-length skirt.

Paul's spirits lifted a bit, as Anna said her mother never knew a thing. He liked the idea of concealment. He lived on it, in fact.

He was nearly found out the first week in Huron, when their neighbor marched in, pie in hand, to welcome them. Paul and Anna were unpacking. The afternoon was quite warm, hence the open front door. The neighbor stopped by the sideboard and said she'd never seen a candelabra quite like that. Paul explained what it was used for.

It belongs to my wife, he added.

Anna thought he was silly. It might have been important in Switzerland, or even in Constantinople, but out here, in the American West, who would care? Paul didn't relent. It had to be this way. He couldn't risk the college learning the truth, and taking issue with it. He said that his family had always practiced in secret. To their friends and neighbors they were strict Calvinists, which is what he'd indicated on his application for employment at the college.

So, the menorah became hers, and she the Jewess.

She passed because of her deep-olive complexion, black hair, and knowledge of Middle Eastern cuisine.

Sometimes she requested items from the green grocer, Mr. Norquist, that he didn't stock or even know. One such item was eggplant. She described it at length. Mr. Norquist turned red when she gave its size and the texture of its skin. He recovered himself by saying he didn't have goods just yet for the chosen people, but would see what he could do.

Another time she wanted grape leaves. *Must be another Jewish delicacy*, he told her. Anna didn't mention that grape leaves were, in fact, used in a Greek dish called dolma, because he wasn't being unkind, only ignorant. She wasn't mistreated, but regarded with curiosity, as an alien being.

She wasn't alone. There was a Jewish family in town: a husband, wife, and two boys. The husband repaired musical instruments. The wife painted miniature landscapes. One of their boys recited poetry; the other had a flair for baseball. She was often asked, *Do you know the Greenbergs?* When she said no, she was occasionally given directions to their home, as if she wanted nothing more than to connect with other Jews.

෨

Anna's neighbor, Britta Lund, lived one block over. Their backyards faced off across an alley. After the pie, they met again while hanging laundry. Britta's red hair lay in a long braid down her broad back. She towered above Anna, but then, everyone did. Anna barely topped five feet tall. She wore a size three shoe. These facts were later shared over a cup of strong coffee, after Britta called her a "tiny little thing." They were in Britta's spotless, stuffy kitchen. Britta explained that the window sash was broken.

"My husband got no time to fix it," she said with pride. Her husband, Lars, owned the town's hardware store. He'd just bought the property next door, and was expanding. Anna patted the perspiration from her forehead with a lovely linen handkerchief she'd embroidered herself. Britta admired it.

"I'd ask my son, but he's under the weather," Britta said.

"I'm sorry to hear that."

"He needs his rest, Olaf does."

Britta's gaze wandered when she said this. She took in her entire kitchen, it seemed, and settled on her plump, red hands, folded in her lap. She sniffed. Anna suspected that there were tears in her eyes. Her son must be quite ill, she thought. But no, because he was walking through the house just then, with a firm, strong tread. The front door opened and

87

closed. Britta lifted her head. Her eyes were clear. She sighed. She looked relieved.

Anna was quick to deduce from what she overheard around town that Olaf, who'd been in the war, just wasn't the same since coming home. Once a lively, cheerful young man, he now kept to himself. Before enlisting, he was often seen behind the counter of the family store, in a crisp white apron, weighing out nails and giving advice on saw blades. Now he was seldom there. He walked instead. Hours and hours of walking, followed by hours and hours of lying in bed. Britta wanted him to talk to Pastor Mueller. Olaf refused. Anna knew Pastor Mueller. Paul attended his Lutheran church. He'd chosen it because the Calvinists weren't represented in Huron. Paul was a bit sorry about that. He'd gotten so used to their ways, but thought the Lutherans were just as good, really. Sometimes Anna went along. People said it was strange for a Jew to attend a Christian service, and they speculated that perhaps Anna's husband was hoping she'd convert. When Anna heard that, she found it rich. She had begun to develop a cynical edge about the arrangement she'd had no choice but to accept, an edge made sharper after she learned about Olaf and the war, since Paul had sat out that same war on account of Switzerland's neutrality.

Olaf suffered from shell shock, but those words were not used. Like his mother's suggestion that he needed rest, other people spoke of him in terms of being overworked, exhausted, run thin. Anna couldn't believe that he was the only young war veteran in Huron who suffered so, and indeed, he wasn't. The difference was that other soldiers had someone pulling them along—a sweetheart, for instance, or a wife, sister, or mother. Always a female, Anna noticed. And since Olaf was unmarried and an only child, the only one who could fill that role for him was his own mother. Britta didn't want to interfere with his life, she said in a moment of surprising candor, once again over a laundry line.

"He will find his own way," she said firmly, pulling a pair of men's flannel underwear from the line and throwing them into her basket. She and Anna hadn't been talking about Olaf, but about the weather. Britta said that with the first cold snap they now felt on their cheeks, it wouldn't be long before the men would want to get out their cross-country skis and make sure they were ready for winter. When the snow fell hard, as it quite often did, Britta assured her, the only way to get around town was on skis. Olaf was a fine skier, she said. Once, as a young boy, he'd made his way all alone to a neighbor's out in the country to check on them after a blizzard. The family hadn't been seen in town, and had no telephone. So, off Olaf went, before anyone could gear up and come along, too. The family needed medicine for their daughter, who was down with fever. They were in Olaf's debt to that day.

Olaf crept into whatever conversation his mother had sooner or later, Anna realized. The husband, Lars, whom Anna had spoken to only at his hardware store when she'd gone first to buy picture wire to hang a portrait of her mother, then a new broom and dust pan, and lastly a rolling pin, didn't mention him at all, as if embarrassed—even disgusted—by his son's frailty.

❧

Soon Paul earned a reputation at the college for his teaching style and skill. He walked back and forth before the chalkboard, hands behind his back, head down, gazing at the dusty floor. His elegant shoes made tracks in that dust. His talk of man's rational mind made tracks in the heart of those green farm boys—and a few farm girls.

Religion—and the fear of religion is put aside!

Man must think for himself and find a reasoned balance, informed by the necessity of doing good—not for selfish motives, but only for practical gain.

The mind holds sway over all.

If they only knew that their professor was not himself a rational man! Anna couldn't help being bitter. She was lonely there in Huron. She missed her family. Her father had died some years before, and her mother sent imploring letters, begging her to come back. Anna replied that no return was possible, and told her mother to have faith in the Virgin Mary. Anna's own faith was no stronger than before, yet sometimes she removed her rosary from the green alabaster box that had been her wedding gift from an uncle she'd never met, and said a few Hail Marys. There was comfort in ritual, she discovered once more. Something Paul knew, too, given the peace, however temporary, that descended upon him after reading the Torah.

Professor Plake invited Paul and Anna to his home to celebrate Halloween. They had never celebrated Halloween. In Constantinople, the American University hosted a party every year, so they were familiar with the wearing of costumes. They recalled one young man who dressed as a bear and carried the head of his outfit under one arm when he got too warm. A woman in the style of Marie Antoinette lost her fancy wig in the fountain. Paul was nervous about attending the party. Groups made him uneasy. There were that many more chances to make a fool of oneself, he thought. He did so much better one-on-one. Anna told him to relax. He was doing very well. His students adored him. She'd heard nice things as she went about her errands in town. More smiles came her way just for being his wife. She could see him trying to believe her.

On the day of the party, Paul took to his bed. He was sick, he said, though his forehead was cool. He refused to eat. Anna tempted him with roast chicken, his favorite. Finally, he consented to take a bite. He propped himself up in bed and worried what would be thought of him for not coming to the party. Anna said she'd already phoned Professor Plake.

"I told him you were indisposed. He was very sympathetic," she said.

"You shouldn't have done that."

"Why not?"

Paul didn't answer. Anna watched him struggle with himself over the lie she'd told on his behalf. Part of him was afraid of being found out. Another part was ashamed. He would not resolve the conflict, nor make peace with it. He would allow it to torment him until it was replaced with the next crisis.

But did one allow oneself to be tormented by guilt, she wondered? Or was it the case that one simply couldn't avoid it? She never felt guilty herself. She merely regretted certain deeds and circumstances. And hardness of the heart. *Intractability.* That was not one of Paul's character traits. It was one of hers, and she was sorry she possessed it. She hadn't always. She began life as tenderhearted as anyone. Yet at some point, she became less kind. As a teenager, she saw the emotional cruelty her father inflicted on her mother. Then she saw what happened to her countrymen. Now she understood that her husband was a child, and rather than wanting to soothe and comfort him, she wanted to give him the back of her hand.

It's all right to get annoyed, she told herself. *You're still a good wife.*

She washed the dishes. A light was on in the Lunds' kitchen. Olaf stood before the window gazing into the night. Anna shut off her own light, so he wouldn't see her there, gazing back. He poured himself a glass of water and didn't drink it. He gripped the counter. Anna could see how hard he was holding it from the way his shoulders pulled forward. He hung his head for a moment, as if it had become too heavy to bear. Then he released the counter, stood straight, and left the kitchen. A moment later Britta appeared to wash out the glass, dry it, and put it in a cupboard. Her expression was grim. Anna knew how she felt. She also lived with an invalid.

❧

"But you *must* come. We always have the neighbors for a small celebration," Britta said. The Christmas season was upon them. Candles burned in windows. Wreaths were nailed to doors— including Paul and Anna's—and a tree lot stood behind the courthouse with evergreens from as far away as Wisconsin. Neither Paul nor Anna had had a Christmas tree before. The idea was thrilling.

"I understand if you might feel out of place. But believe me, no one will care that you're not Christian." Britta spoke in a low voice, even though they were alone in Anna's dining room, where the menorah with its burned-down candles sat on the sideboard. Each night of Hanukkah, Paul had made sure to have Anna draw the heavy curtains she'd made herself before he lit the candle and prayed.

"I can't imagine how I'll talk to them." Anna sipped her coffee. She was being wicked, and enjoying it.

"My dear! You mustn't worry. You get on well with me, now don't you?" Britta wore a pin with a blue stone that complimented her round eyes nicely.

"All right, then. I'll be glad to. I can't speak for my husband. He's often quite tired from teaching."

"But the college isn't in session? Surely he could rest up beforehand."

Britta was keen for a closer look at this fine professor. Word of him had spread. He was easily recognized in town, and sometimes people approached him to say how much their son or daughter was enjoying his course. Their words always brought his hand to the brim of his hat in recognition of the honor paid him. Women, especially, watched him as he came and went from campus to home on foot. He was a dashing, handsome man—there was no doubt. Anna wondered if she might find herself with a rival for his affection, then dismissed the idea at once.

As she had anticipated, Paul took to his bed again on the evening that they were due at the Lunds'. She knew it was her duty to stay with him, yet she refused. He sulked. She said she couldn't let their neighbors down, that Britta was counting on her. Paul turned his face to the wall. Anna knew that she would pay later. He would refuse to speak to her for several days, communicating his needs only in writing. Then he would be contrite, and buy her a little gift. These small (inexpensive) tokens of apology were collected on her bureau. A white vase, a silver pendant, a paper fan. Buying trinkets for his wife so often further enhanced his stature in the town. What a wonderful husband! How kind and loving! Some speculated, not always in private, that Anna was demanding and required frequent presents to keep her satisfied. One woman, the baker's wife—not Scandinavian like so many of the town's residents but a bulky Russian whose apron was always dirty—whispered to her husband that Jews were often that way.

Anna wore a red velvet dress she'd sewn herself with material she bought with leftover housekeeping money. Paul hadn't noticed her skimping—she was that skilled in the kitchen. She often bought day-old bread and used it as a crust over a pot of roasted chicken and vegetables the green grocer put on sale after two or three days. She spent a bit of money on dried spices—oregano and thyme—which were considered quite a luxury but were necessary to disguise the bland taste of food on the edge of going bad. It was worth the risk. She'd known luxury once, long ago, and sometimes she just had to have it.

She pinned her luscious black hair with two large mother-of-pearl clips. She draped her amber bead necklace, strung on sturdy wire, not string, around her neck. Lastly, she fastened her mother's cameo to her left shoulder. She was stunning, and she knew it. She didn't care if she put anyone to shame that night.

During her short walk, the falling snow collected on her hair. She found the snow exhilarating. She had never seen it before, and stopped to observe how it floated and swirled around her.

Britta took Anna's coat quickly, almost roughly. There was trouble in the kitchen, she said. The dinner wasn't coming out quite right.

"I hate to do this to you, on a night like this, but I don't know who else I can ask," she said.

Olaf stood at Britta's stove, mournfully basting a tired-looking turkey, which sat in an oval pan. He lifted the ladle slowly, and poured a greasy broth over its pimply skin. He was dressed for the evening in a black coat and gray wool slacks. His blond hair was combed down flat. When Britta said his name, he turned and looked down at Anna with cold blue eyes.

"Olaf, leave that thing alone, and let Mrs. Emile have a look."

Anna felt the color rise in her cheeks. Olaf put out his hand for Anna to shake. His palm was dry and rough. He held Anna's hand hard, almost painfully, crushing the band she wore on her right hand. (The ring was composed of seven connected ovals, each inscribed with the symbols of the Greek Islands. It had been a gift from a man who'd once been interested in her but eventually found her intellect too challenging—though the way he put it was that Anna thought she was "a little above herself.")

"Now go on, and talk to the neighbors. Your father can't do that all on his own," Britta said.

Olaf released Anna's hand. When he passed by her, she detected a clear scent of lavender soap. Anna turned her attention to the turkey. It had at least another hour to roast. She put it back in the oven, using two spotless white dishtowels to grab the handles of the pan.

"What else are you serving?" Anna asked.

Britta directed her to a bowl of puréed spinach. There was a platter of dried fruit, apricots and figs. Those were expensive, Anna knew. Britta had baked two pies and a cake for dessert. She had already put out a plate of crackers and a very bland-tasting cheese, which her guests had ignored, she said.

"Olaf can't tolerate the smell of strong cheese in the house," she explained.

"I see." Probably reminded him of rotting flesh, Anna thought.

"Do you think the turkey will turn out all right?" Britta asked.

"Oh, yes. There won't be a problem."

Britta drew in closer and said that she was overly nervous because Olaf had had a particularly bad day. One of the battles he'd been in had taken place on Christmas Eve, and the memories were pulling him down hard.

"Of course. I understand," Anna said.

She could see Olaf standing in the dining room alone with a glass of something in his hand. He caught Anna's eye. Then he was in the kitchen.

"Would you care for a glass of sherry?" he asked her. "We had it before the Volstead Act, don't worry."

"That would be lovely."

"For you, Mother?"

Britta looked stunned.

"Thank you, son. Yes, I would."

When he'd gone, Britta said, "I never saw him be so chivalrous with anyone. I think he's taken a little fancy to you." Britta giggled. "Let him down gently, won't you?"

"Of course."

That might be hard, Anna thought. Olaf was the most handsome man she'd ever seen. The way he looked at her made her feel like a gorgeous creature.

❧

Which is what he took to calling her when he slipped over to her house. His mother had to be out, or upstairs napping, for him to come. Otherwise, she might ask where he was going and why—he was that closely watched.

Anna served him coffee and biscuits, and listened to him talk. He didn't ramble. His thinking followed clear lines. While the war had changed everything for him, he wasn't ready to give up on life. He was tired of despair. He had decided that even before meeting Anna. She tried to discourage his affection for her, without success. He was clearly smitten, and said so.

"Maybe because it's, you know," he said.

"What?"

"That you're a Jew. I never met one before."

Anna stirred her coffee slowly with a small silver spoon—one of a set she had brought over with her.

"Drawn to the exotic, then, are you?" she asked.

"If the exotic looks like you."

He lifted her free hand and kissed it.

"You mustn't do that. I'm a married woman."

Olaf smirked.

"I've seen him, you know. Your husband," he said.

"And?"

"And nothing. I don't know what all the big talk is about."

"He's a hard worker."

"Do you love him?"

Anna went on stirring her coffee.

"Do you?"

"You are guilty of impertinence."

Paul's mood was splendid. He'd received his first evaluation from Professor Plake, and couldn't have been more pleased.

"I think come fall, you'll be married to an associate professor," Paul said. Anna watched him spoon more of her lamb stew onto his plate. He sipped his cider. She noticed a small stain on his shirtfront. She didn't mention it.

Anna pushed the food around on her plate. She set her fork down. She reflected on the New Year's resolution she'd made.

Be steadfast.

Paul watched her.

"You've got quite a glow to you this evening, Anna," he said.

"Have I?"

"Are you in the family way?"

Anna's heart beat loudly in her ears, like the tide of an angry sea.

"I shouldn't think so," she said.

"Oh."

She watched his mood darken.

"Are you sure you're really trying?" he asked.

"Trying?"

"You know."

"Yes, Paul, I'm trying."

Another time, Olaf talked about the war. He'd killed men—that was to be expected, that's what one was trained to do. He described stabbing a number of soldiers through the stomach with his bayonet. He'd witnessed terrible deaths, and terrible injuries. Amputations done right there, in the trenches, out of necessity. He wouldn't have minded losing a limb, he said. Not as bad as being left blind. He'd known many who lost their sight to explosions and shrapnel. It always struck him as odd that those men—all the men—needed their blindness before the war, not after.

They were in Olaf's kitchen that time. Britta and Lars were away for the day. They'd taken the train to Sioux Falls to meet with a different hardware wholesaler. *Better saw blades*, Britta had said. *Cheaper nails, too.*

"Sometimes marriage is like war," Anna said.

"How?"

"It can cause a sort of blindness."

Olaf drank his coffee.

"I'd suggest that being married might alter one's vision," he said.

"What do you mean?"

He looked amused—highly pleased with himself, in fact.

"He doesn't see you well enough, and you see him too clearly."

That Olaf had learned her secret without her telling it outright made her adore him even more.

༒

No note was left as to where they'd gone, nor why, but the town knew soon enough. Olaf cabled his folks and said not to worry. They were in Chicago, where he planned to go into the restaurant business. He'd told Anna in confidence that he'd made a little money on the black market during the war. It would see them through until they made money of their own. The restaurant would serve Greek and Armenian food, something Anna was naturally well versed in. Olaf had been shocked to learn that she was an Armenian, for they were a Christian people. Anna told him the truth. She hoped he wasn't disappointed. He wasn't. He didn't care what god, if any, she prayed to.

She took little away with her. Her jewelry, of course, and the prized alabaster box. A mixing bowl she particularly liked, decorated with blue stripes. A book into which she'd pressed flowers years before in Constantinople for luck.

She left her wedding band, which she'd known all along had belonged to Paul's aunt, on the base of the menorah.

Sixteen

1921

Chicago was like no place Anna had ever been. She was used to crowds and noise, as Constantinople had had plenty of both. What was different—and stimulating—was the diversity of people making their way swiftly down the sidewalks. The women in particular drew her attention. She had seen Africans at home, but they were usually demure, never calling attention to themselves. Here their voices rose in greeting, outrage, glee, always loudly, like music spilling from a lovely reed in their hearts. And the dresses they wore! Silks and velvets, embroidered with flowers and leaves in cheerful greens, blues, and whites; long coats with high fur collars; dainty patterned stockings and patent leather shoes with pearls for buttons. Seeing them made Anna ache. Money was tighter than she'd hoped. She would never say that Olaf had deceived her about his assets. She didn't ask how much money he had, nor did he volunteer that information. She'd gone away with him on faith and love, and she knew in her bones that they would have to carry her through the hard times.

And yet.

They lived in a cold-water flat on the sixth floor of a busy street, where the trolley kept them awake late into the night. Their rooms were at the back of the building, with a view down into a filthy courtyard overrun with stray dogs. Each floor had a laundry line that stretched across the courtyard and was anchored into the building opposite. Sometimes the residents of the two buildings disagreed about whose turn it was to use the line, which could be pulled in either direction. Often there was shouting in languages Anna didn't understand; sometimes objects were thrown, though Anna never saw the point in that. Nothing ever reached all the way across the courtyard; each object fell to the cement below, where it was examined by the dogs and for the most part ignored. One day, someone tossed out a pot, which clattered madly when it hit the ground. Anna quickly opened her window and peered down. Her eyesight was sharp, and she saw at once that the pot was a good one with a copper bottom. She scanned the windows across from her, trying to guess which one it had been launched from, but all the windows were closed, and the curtains were drawn. She scurried down the six flights of stairs and into the courtyard, where the smell of dog feces was strong enough to make her stop short. Seeing her, the three dogs present trotted off down the alley that connected the courtyard to the larger world. Anna picked her way carefully around broken dolls, a three-legged chair, piles of rags, rotting cabbages, broken glasses, a set of false teeth, and a bouquet of silk roses she would have liked to take with her and rehabilitate. She wrapped the pot in her apron, and returned the way she came.

Back in her apartment, she threw open all three windows to rid her nose of the stench she'd encountered below. Then she washed out the pot. She'd have to find some suitable copper cleaner to preserve the bottom. For the moment, she'd make a ratatouille in it. Chicago, unlike Huron, had all the vegetables and other ingredients that she required.

Olaf said he liked the dish, but she could tell he was distracted. He'd been out for most of the day talking to landlords about rental space for a restaurant. The prices were high—out of reach, really—and he was reluctantly coming to the conclusion that his dreams were being put on hold. Anna suggested that they kill two birds with one stone. They could earn money and learn about the restaurant business from the inside. She could work as a cook, and he could ask to be trained as a manager somewhere, as an apprentice, to be specific, which wouldn't pay but would be invaluable in no time.

He lowered his spoon thoughtfully and folded his hands on the tablecloth.

"You propose to support me?" he asked.

"Why not?"

"It's not fitting."

Anna straightened one of her hairpins. "Well, I don't think we should worry too much about what's fitting and what isn't, as long as we accomplish our goals."

Anna had always known that she was, at heart, a highly practical person. Olaf, she was sad to learn, wasn't. He was a dreamer. But, even so, he was considerably more solid on his feet than Paul had ever been.

Olaf agreed. Anna would look for work in a kitchen, and Olaf would beg to be taken on for free.

"Never beg," Anna said. "Just say you're eager to learn. Tell whomever you're speaking to that their reputation brought you through the door. Flattery works, you know."

"It never does with you."

"But I'm not a man, am I?"

He laughed.

"No. And thank God for that," he said.

Before Anna could look for a job, however, she broke a tooth. She'd taken to eating fresh prunes on a daily basis to keep herself regular, and one morning at breakfast she bit down squarely on the pit. She collected the pieces of her destroyed tooth and put them in a clean tea cup, knowing that they could never be put back as before. In pain, she wasn't thinking clearly. Olaf was out canvassing restaurants, and there no one to walk her to the dentist, who was several blocks away. She'd passed the office shortly after moving to the city, and made a mental note of its location.

She was given ether. As the dentist, a heavyset man with a German accent, removed the remaining fragments of tooth, Anna drifted away in a scrambled dream where Paul's stern and reproving eyes glared at her. The last time Anna had asked him for a divorce he had refused again, and now, in the dream, he told her she would never be free. She was moved to beg him, and this struck her as particularly odd, because the only time she had ever begged for anything was when she wanted the little watch fob her uncle had shown her at dinner. The fob was gold, and inlaid with small, oval, turquoise stones. She was just a child at the time, and it captivated her. She forgot her strict upbringing and cried until a servant hauled her upstairs at her mother's command. Then came a feeling of rising out of the dentist's chair, high above Paul. From her vantage point, Anna shouted, like the vengeful God of the Old Testament, that he would rue the day he defied her. At home there was a letter from Paul ordering her to return to Huron at once. The coincidence was a little unnerving, but she took herself in hand, and when her head had cleared, sat and wrote.

> *Dear Paul,*
> *Thank you for your letter. I have considered with great care your request that I return. However, as before, I am unable to do so. Olaf and I are embarked on a business venture, which occupies all of our time. I urge you again to understand that we intend to marry, and that your preventing us is at odds with your compassionate and humane nature.*

At that she put down her fountain pen—a lovely blue lacquered one Olaf had bought her when she saw it in a shop window, though she'd objected to the cost. Having to flatter Paul was unpleasant, and brought a feeling of abject helplessness that just then, with the aftereffect of the ether, made her despair. She tore up the paper she'd written on, and took the pieces to the back window and dropped them down into the courtyard one by one, like a poor imitation of snow.

Just as she was about to close the window against the afternoon's chill, the window opposite lifted and a robed figured appeared. Her eyes were the only part of her face that was visible. Those eyes were dark and menacing, like in Anna's troubled dream earlier that day. The woman was a Muslim, and the realization made Anna withdraw quickly from the window. For years she'd lived behind a steel wall in her heart where she refused to hate or fear the people who had murdered so many Armenians, but now, with her misery over her situation fresh and full of sting, she was both terrified and enraged. She stepped forward, with no specific purpose in mind other than to stare back, when the woman shrieked something in Arabic and threw another copper-bottomed pot out of her window. By the time it clattered to the ground, the woman had withdrawn and shut her window with a loud slam.

Anna went down the stairs even faster than she had the time before. She'd seen another window open, and a gray-haired woman was staring down into the courtyard with a look of desire, or so Anna thought. She collected the pot and returned to her apartment, light-headed from her haste, the drug, and the day's general ordeal. The socket, where her tooth had been, throbbed. The pot she held was sturdier than the one before, and she wondered why the woman was throwing it away. That evening, she prepared a lamb stew in the new pot. Olaf was delighted. His day had met with some success. He'd gone into a Greek restaurant, and said he was married to the best cook on the South Side of Chicago. The owner, Mr. Yanaki, had just lost his chef. Or rather, the chef had been fired for being drunk on the job. Olaf had persuaded Mr. Yanaki to meet with Anna, and see what might be worked out. Anna stared at him over the oilcloth on their table, her gum very sore.

"I can't cook for an entire restaurant by myself," she said.

"You wouldn't have to. There are other chefs who would work under you."

Anna didn't know if she had the ability to actually boss people around. The closest she'd ever come to that was long ago when her family employed a large staff of servants, and even then, she was generally terrified of them and kept out of their way. She thought of Paul, how he looked at her in her dream, and how she had shouted down at him, and decided she could handle the staff perfectly well, if the owner accepted her in the first place.

"You're not eating," Olaf said.

"I broke a tooth this morning."

"Oh, no! My poor darling!"

"It's all right. I went to the dentist."

"I thought you went shopping."

"What do you mean?"

"The pot. It's new. Like the other one."

Anna explained how she'd come by them.

"You don't think I'd spend money on things I don't need at a time like this," she said.

He was clearly embarrassed by the fact that that's exactly what he'd assumed. He hadn't said anything about it, though, and Anna softened at the thought of his not minding her spending money they didn't have if it gave her pleasure.

"I've had another letter from Paul," she said.

"And?"

"His mind is the same."

Anna got up and lit the gas ring under the coffee pot. They always had coffee after dinner. Then they sat in their tiny living room, lit only by one weak lamp, while he read the paper and she embroidered. It was a quiet, gentle life, she thought, and not at all bad.

Except for the money, and the dreams they needed to make come true.

She cleared away the cups and saucers and thought, *In this life we make there must be nothing to regret or grieve over.*

Seventeen

Mr. Yanaki's restaurant took over an hour to reach. The distance required changing trolleys twice, with a long wait between the first and second cars. Standing out in the winter wind in her thin coat didn't bother Anna nearly as much as the stifling heat of the kitchen. Only two small windows, set high in the tiled walls, allowed in any fresh air at all. They were opened with the hooked end of a long pole that Anna found difficult to manage. She gave up asking for help after the first day. The three sous chefs she commanded had trouble with English, and spoke to each other in Greek, often looking at her and smirking. They were all young men, probably in the same family, and how they were related to Mr. Yanaki she didn't know or ask.

The front of the restaurant had fifteen tables and two servers dressed in severe black jackets and slacks. The clientele was mostly shabby, but some were better off, with a bit of flash. The menu wasn't large. Three lamb dishes (roasted, skewered, shredded with potatoes and vegetables); the same number of chicken dishes, prepared the same way; two beef dishes (ground and skewered only); and a number of appetizers, including avgolemono soup, which Anna had trouble mastering at first but soon made brilliantly. Mr. Yanaki then shrewdly increased her modest salary. Though Olaf was willing to forgo any compensation, Mr. Yanaki had no place for him. Olaf persisted, and Mr. Yanaki reluctantly let him handle the seating arrangements in the "back room."

This was where liquor was served as quietly as possible. The police generally looked the other way, but every now and then they raided local restaurants and rounded everyone up. The room was a converted storage area accessible only from the alley behind the restaurant. Mr. Yanaki had decorated it lavishly with velvet drapes over the cold brick walls, several Middle Eastern rugs, and small, marble-topped round tables that only seated two at a time. A smaller, lighter menu was on offer, chosen daily from the main menu, served on fancy blue plates with gold rims, unlike the plain, heavy white plates the non-drinking diners were given, and ferried back and forth by a very tall, stately Negro named Josiah. Josiah and Olaf instantly clashed. Olaf stepped on the hem of a woman's gown after he'd shown her to a table, causing it to tear. Josiah called him clumsy and awkward. Olaf complained to Mr. Yanaki. He wasn't used to being insulted. Mr. Yanaki told him to pick up his feet or he'd dismiss him.

Late one night, after the main restaurant had closed its door and only a handful of hard drinkers remained in back under Josiah's watchful eye, Olaf went glumly into the kitchen to find Anna reading tea leaves for the two servers, Boris and Sven. The Greek kitchen help had left early, as usual, which meant Anna had had to clean up alone. Her hands were raw from washing dishes. Three large opaque light fixtures hung from the ceiling, casting a brightness on her black hair and plainly showing several strands of gray that hadn't been there only weeks before. Olaf was touched by those strands. He took them as proof of how hard—and willingly—she worked. They also reminded him of his mother, and he was taken with a wave of melancholy that shoved him clumsily into the wooden chair next to Anna. He didn't like city life. He didn't like their cramped apartment. And he didn't like this restaurant, most of all. Anna ignored him. She was bent over a small saucer, looking at an ugly clump of wet tea. Sven's red, sweaty face was tight with fear as she mused.

"She will be well," Anna pronounced.

"When?" Sven asked.

"You must be patient."

"A man only has one mother."

"Then pray for her," Boris said. He was sixty, at least, and his white hair was thick and wavy.

"I pray all the time. It's not working," Sven said.

"Maybe God doesn't find you worthy. Maybe you've committed some sin you haven't confessed, or accepted," Boris said.

He took a small silver case from the pocket of his jacket. He offered a cigarette to everyone at the table. Olaf declined. Sven and Anna each took one. It was Anna's first, though no one there knew that. Boris struck a match, and extended the flame to Anna's cigarette. She drew the smoke into her mouth, held it for a moment, and released it. A faint taste of wood and something sweeter lingered on her tongue.

Josiah's face appeared in the round window of the swinging kitchen door. He caught Olaf's eye.

"What the hell does he want now?" Olaf asked.

"Go and see," Anna said.

"If he wants me, he can come in here and get me."

"Oh, go on!"

The irritation in her voice stung him. He rose and left the kitchen.

"Come," Josiah said. Olaf followed him into Mr. Yanaki's private office.

"Sit," Josiah said. He took Mr. Yanaki's chair. Olaf sat opposite him, on the other side of the desk. There was no noise from the private dining room. Everyone must have gone home, which meant it was even later than Olaf thought.

Josiah pressed his hands together and regarded Olaf coolly.

"Well?" Olaf asked. He assumed Mr. Yanaki had charged Josiah with letting him go. He was thinking of an angry yet sophisticated comeback.

"A man who works for free needs money," Josiah said.

"Everyone needs money."

"That is true. And Mr. Yanaki has money. A great deal, locked here in his desk."

"How do you know that?"

Josiah didn't reply. Olaf became increasingly apprehensive.

"What do you want?" he asked.

"To help me commit an act that will free us both."

Josiah proposed that they break open the desk, share the money, then set fire to the restaurant. No evidence would be left, no sign of their work. Mr. Yanaki would assume that his money had burned up, along with everything else.

"You're mad," Olaf said.

"I'm anything but."

Josiah laid out his plan. Mr. Yanaki was involved from time to time with unsavory characters from whom he occasionally borrowed. It would be assumed that he'd fallen behind in his payments, and in retaliation, the restaurant was set ablaze. That, or some bad blood in the Greek community, perhaps. Mr. Yanaki had few friends. He'd been threatened the year before for not complying with some unspecified demand from a man named Stavos.

"You seem to know a lot about his affairs," Olaf said.

"I make it my business to keep abreast of things."

"And now you want to profit by it."

"Yes."

Olaf took time to consider.

"But why take a huge risk? Looks to me like you've got it pretty good around here," he said.

"Do I? Do you know what he calls me?"

"What?"

"His first-class nigger."

"Not that I've ever heard."

"Of course not. Only in private."

Behind the glass lenses of Josiah's gold-rimmed spectacles, his eyes took on a raw, almost hungry light.

"As tragic as that is, I still don't see why you're involving me in this. Why not do it yourself?" Olaf asked.

Josiah slipped off the white gloves he always wore, then removed his right hand. It was a prosthetic, a pale pink color. The manufacturer hadn't thought to supply people of his race, Josiah said. The hand he'd been born with had been blown off in the war.

"I've learned to do many things with my left hand, but some things require the use of two good hands. For instance, this drawer must be pried open, and one hand alone won't work," he said.

"You've tried?"

"Naturally."

Josiah reinstalled his fake hand, and tugged his gloves back on. He stood up and went to Mr. Yanaki's elaborately carved sideboard, where a crystal bottle held some very old brandy. He took two glasses from inside the cupboard, and brought them along with the bottle back to the desk. Olaf watched him carefully. He carried the glasses in his left hand, and pressed the bottle to his chest with his right. He poured them both a drink. Olaf had never tasted brandy before. He didn't think much of the flavor, but enjoyed the warmth it left in his throat very much.

"Additionally, when the authorities determine that arson was the cause, then Mr. Yanaki will suspect me," Josiah said.

"Why you, and not all those other people who want to do him harm?"

"Because we quarreled recently. Rather viciously, I'm afraid."

"About what?"

"It doesn't matter."

Josiah sipped his drink. Olaf thought about the brandy they were drinking, and how much it must have cost. Then he thought about the money locked away in the that desk, and how Mr. Yanaki said, flat out, that he couldn't afford to pay Olaf while he learned the ropes.

"So, you must not only be my assistant, but my alibi. You'll say I was with you, that we went for a late coffee, after closing the place up tight for the night," Josiah said.

"And why will he believe me?"

"Because you're white and he likes your wife."

Mr. Yanaki did like Anna. Olaf had seen that on many occasions.

"And in order to get you to be my alibi, I'll have to share the money with you," Josiah said.

"How much is there?"

"I'm not certain, but at least fifteen thousand dollars."

"My God!"

"Apiece."

Olaf knew there was no way he could pass it up. But how would he explain the money to Anna? He put this very question to Josiah.

"A relative back in the old country died and left it to you," Josiah said.

"You think of everything."

"I have to."

"And when is this great blaze to be?"

"Tonight."

"That's impossible."

Josiah poured them both a second brandy.

"It must be. Mr. Yanaki plans to move the money into a bank soon. Maybe even tomorrow."

Olaf would go into the kitchen and send everyone home. He'd say that Josiah had agreed to show him how to keep the books, as part of his continued training in the business of running a restaurant. He would call a cab for Anna, so she wouldn't miss the trolley and come back to wait with him. As for Sven and Boris, they lived close enough and would walk easily. Then they would lock all the doors but the one to the alley. The fire would be set just there, in the office, the fault of a cigar some late-night reveler had left, Josiah would suggest later. He would accept the blame for not having made sure it was extinguished properly before leaving for the night.

Anna was perfectly happy to go on her way alone, and in a taxi, because she was exhausted. Boris and Sven had already left. Anna had cleaned up the tea leaves, cups, and saucers. She told Olaf she was proud of him for being willing to put in the extra hours, and she apologized for speaking sharply before. He helped her into her coat, and wrapped her heavy scarf around her neck. He held her purse while she pinned her hat to her hair.

"Can we afford it?" she asked.

"What?"

"The taxi."

"Yes. It's fine."

They walked through to the restaurant's front door. A woman's glove lay on the floor. Anna picked it up. The glove was pale purple silk with a rim of fine lace, and a pearl button clasp. Anna held the glove lovingly.

"Imagine, losing a thing like that," she said.

"Yes."

"What should I do with it?"

"What do you mean?" Olaf was anxious to get back now.

"What if the owner comes looking for it? Should I put it in Mr. Yanaki's office?"

"I'll take it and put it on his desk with a note."

"That's a good idea. He'll see it there first thing, I imagine."

"Yes."

He accepted her parting embrace. He waited at the door while she got into the taxi. When the taxi had gone, he locked the front door. The shade in the glass was already lowered for the night. The curtains in the front windows were also drawn. From the street the whole place would look quiet and empty.

Josiah was where Olaf had left him, at Mr. Yanaki's desk. He had a screwdriver and a hammer. He held the screwdriver in his left hand, and attempted to grip the hammer with his right, without success. Olaf took both tools from him.

"I thought you said you couldn't manage these," he said.

"Just proving my point."

Olaf wedged the screwdriver into the top seam of the locked drawer. He hit the handle hard with the hammer. They listened. The only sound was the quiet tick of the grandfather clock, and a faint hum from the electric lamp on the desk. He struck again and again. Pieces of wood splintered from the drawer, but the drawer itself stayed fast. He put the blade of the screwdriver into the lock, and hammered away. A faint cracking sound came from the drawer. Olaf pulled on the handle, and the drawer slid open.

The drawer contained a number of papers and ledgers. One of the papers appeared to be a letter to someone named Eleanor, in Mr. Yanaki's hand. *Surely you can understand my predicament*, said the very first line. Josiah removed the papers and ledgers, and dropped them on the floor. He reached his good hand, now gloveless again, into the far back of the drawer. He brought back a large envelope, tied with string. He broke the string with his teeth. He emptied the contents of the envelope onto the desk's blotter. The bills were tied together with more string. Olaf used his pocketknife to cut the bills free. Then they counted the money three times, each arriving at the same figure: forty-two thousand, one hundred and nineteen dollars.

"It's not equally divisible," Olaf said.

"You can have the extra dollar."

"Don't mind if I do."

How to secure the loose money, so it could be safely tucked into the pockets of their overcoats? Josiah told Olaf to go to the kitchen, and get the ball of string Anna used to bind the legs of her roasted chickens. They would retie their respective bundles. He said not to forget his overcoat from the hook in the hall because he wouldn't have a chance to go back for it. Olaf went. The lights from a passing automobile swept the darkened room. He stopped, because the automobile had stopped, too. The headlights shined straight through the glass above him. Then the automobile turned and went back the way it had come down the street.

When Olaf returned to Mr. Yanaki's office, Josiah said they didn't need the string after all, because he'd found a number of empty envelopes they could put their shares in. Again, they counted slowly and carefully. Each had two full envelopes. Olaf's overcoat had deep pockets. He put one envelope in each pocket, then folded the coat across the back of Mr. Yanaki's chair. Josiah went into the lavatory, and returned with a metal can. He'd hidden it on top of a shelf where the cleaning supplies were kept, a place no one would look. He poured gasoline onto the desk, and over the rugs. He even splashed some on the heavy velvet drapes. Some got on his trousers and he swore.

"You'll want to change those first chance you get," Olaf said. His heart beat hard. What if the fire didn't consume the entire restaurant? As soon as he dropped the lit match he'd struck from the box Josiah had in his coat pocket, that concerned disappeared. The flames were sudden and overwhelming. Olaf stood for a moment, transfixed. Josiah tossed the empty can onto the blaze, and pulled Olaf by the sleeve. Olaf grabbed his coat, and went to the office doorway, where they stopped and looked back. The fire was eating everything in its path, and the smoke burned their eyes and throats. They went quickly to the alley exit. They made certain no one was scuttling up the narrow passage between the buildings. They walked briskly away without speaking. Then Josiah said to slow down. They had to be sure, he said. Soon the sound of the fire bell reached them. They doubled back cautiously, to find a growing crowd in front of the one-story building where the restaurant stood. Flames had broken through the windows. Olaf had a queer feeling, and realized that up until then he'd been in a kind of trance which reminded him of the seconds before going over the top, when any kind of thought became impossible to bear. Now his mind raced, but not fearfully. He felt elated, almost like celebrating.

Later, he told himself. *Plenty of time for that later.*

Eighteen

As Olaf had expected, he was interviewed by the police about the fire. His well-combed hair, worn suit, and the way he made direct eye contact presented him as an honest, sympathetic former employee. What a grievous loss for Mr. Yanaki! No, he could think of no one with a grudge. Yes, he'd been a very kind and fair man to work for. Did Olaf know the whereabouts of another employee, Josiah Smith? He seemed to have left the city with no forwarding address. Olaf thought Josiah was a fool for having done that. Nothing looked more suspicious than simply disappearing. Olaf said Josiah once mentioned having family somewhere down south. Georgia, perhaps. Josiah had never spoken of his family, but Olaf saw no harm in throwing the police firmly off his trail.

Anna didn't ask where the money came from. The lie Josiah suggested Olaf tell her was never spoken. He said only that he'd had some good fortune. He hoped she'd think he'd won it gambling, because that made him seem like a desperate yet very romantic character. Anna knew perfectly well that the money was connected with the restaurant fire, though she wasn't sure how. She thought perhaps someone with a grudge against Mr. Yanaki had hired Olaf to burn the place down, but again, she didn't ask.

All she said was that it must be kept safe, and not left lying around their apartment.

Olaf gave up the idea of owning his own restaurant. He wanted to buy a boardinghouse, instead. A boardinghouse seemed like a good bet. A lot of people came through Chicago looking for work. There would be a steady demand for lodging. Anna would cook—only if she wanted—and others would be hired to clean.

Anna wasn't sure she liked the idea of living with strangers. Olaf promised that they would have their own quarters away from lodgers, and remodeled any way she liked. He thought it likely that they wouldn't have to carry a mortgage, which Anna said was a lucky thing, given that neither of them had any source of income.

They wanted out of the South Side, and looked in a middle-class neighborhood not too far from the lake. Prices were high. Olaf once more became discouraged. Then he found something suitable that needed sprucing up. They'd have a chance to put their own touch on it, he said.

Anna imagined a place in very bad shape, and she was right. The house, though large and with grand proportions, needed paint, new windows, new floors throughout, not to mention the plumbing and electrical repairs. She told Olaf to get estimates for all the required work. Then, they'd see.

The deal was transacted. Men were hired. Work was begun as soon as the weather warmed. Anna and Olaf went each day to observe the progress. She packed them a small lunch of delicious food—fresh breads, fine cheeses and fruits, and even wine, which was easy to obtain even though it was illegal. Even with buying the property outright, there was a great deal of money left over. They bought a car. Anna had a fur coat, which she kept hidden under the bed. The cash went into the bank, except for several hundred dollars, which Olaf stashed in a metal strong box. He wouldn't chance losing it to fire the way Mr. Yanaki had. They had made no friends in the city, and there was no one to ask about their sudden change in fortune.

One day, the Muslim woman who'd thrown the pots out the window into the courtyard came to Anna's door. She was with another woman, also veiled, who spoke broken English. The neighbor was Fatimah. The other was Aalia.

Anna's throat tightened as she looked at them. Perhaps not enough time had passed. Her memories were still sharp. From the small window of the home she'd been made to occupy, Anna would watch women come and go in the harsh Mediterranean sunlight, their robes lifted by the breeze, coated with dust. Sometimes trash was thrown at her front door, then the sound of feet hurrying away, up the alley. Eyes were always on her when she went about her business. Sometimes ugly words—*Kalb! Kalb! (Dog! Dog!)*—reached her ears.

This was another country, though. Anna was no longer a dog. She invited them in.

She served them tea from a new set she'd purchased from Marshall Fields. Neither woman commented on the quality of the bone china, or the way the sterling silver spoons, also new, clinked pleasantly as they stirred in their lumps of sugar. They didn't speak after their initial greeting until Anna prompted them.

Aalia said that Fatimah was married to a very old man she was in slavery to. She waited on him hand and foot. He was more or less an invalid who never left the apartment. Aalia was her unmarried cousin. The three had come to America together. The old man was paid a substantial dowry by Fatimah's parents for taking her off their hands. The cousin, considered unmarriageable at twenty-five, was part of the deal. The dowry had been in kind, not cash. The expensive pots, hurled from the window, were part of it. There were some loose diamonds as well as several strings of pearls.

Anna asked why they were living in such a terrible place, if they had that sort of riches. Aalia said the husband refused to part with the jewelry. The cash the women spent on food came from a very small bundle he'd brought over with him. The bundle was dwindling, and there was almost nothing left. Fatimah had begged her husband to sell one of the diamonds. For her trouble, she'd been beaten with a cane. She pushed up one black sleeve to show the bruises.

Anna didn't understand why she was being told all of this.

"Take us with you," Aalia said.

"What are you talking about?"

"You have money. You won't be here for long. Take us with you."

The coat had been seen through the window the times Anna wore it. The car was noticed, too.

"Then what will you do, with no money of your own? Escaping with no money is no escape at all," Anna said. Her own words made her feel rueful. The comfort of all the money they now possessed only sharpened the memory of coming to this huge, cold city with so little.

The women looked at each other. It seemed as though Fatimah might cry. Her eyes, all that was visible of her face, gleamed.

"We will steal the box. But you must help us sell its contents," Aalia said.

"And if he calls the law? Then what?"

"We will say he is . . . demented. Forgetful. He is a very old man, after all. With barely the strength to stand."

"But strong enough to hit."

"Yes."

Anna asked why they had left home at all. A man that age, why should he start over in an unknown world?

He was supposed to meet a nephew there in Chicago who had set up an import/export business. A rug merchant. A seller of Middle Eastern goods. He had promised to help the old man establish a new life for his remaining years, to be spent in luxury and comfort. There was another family debt involved in this arrangement—Aalia wasn't certain of the details. Some quick whispers between her and Fatimah revealed that Fatimah had once accepted this nephew's advances while betrothed to her husband. Then the nephew left home, made his way in America, and agreed to avoid further scandal and judgment by the family by helping the man he'd wronged. So far, though, the nephew hadn't presented himself, leaving the three isolated and on their own.

Anna looked deep into her empty teacup and let her mind wander over the world, from her ancestral home, to Huron, to that stinking flat she'd soon leave. Then it wandered to the souls she'd known: her own long-suffering mother, her righteous, blustering father, and Paul, proud and terrified by turns. Any woman's fate came down to a man, she realized. Unless she had enough money to either show him to the door or go through it herself.

Anna stood and opened a squeaky drawer in the table by the stove. She removed a brown bottle. She told the two women that it contained laudanum, which she'd been given after her tooth extraction but never took. It was said to have a bitter taste, so it must be mixed with honey, then added to strong tea. It would make Fatimah's husband sleep hard enough so that they could take the box, and whatever else they needed, and leave.

Fatimah shook her head.

"She's afraid," Aalia said.

"The future is always frightening in the abstract. The thing to do to is make it concrete. Here, take it. We've moving out the day after tomorrow," Anna said.

After they left, Anna wondered if she'd done the right thing. But they could prove useful, she thought. Two pairs of willing hands would go a long way toward making the boardinghouse attractive. And once it began to receive lodgers, there would be laundry to do and meals to cook, rugs to beat and furniture to dust. The women would go on their way soon enough, once they felt they'd repaid Anna for her help. But until then, she intended to get every ounce of work out of them that she could.

Nineteen

1922

Aalia and Fatimah proved to be hard workers. Tireless, in fact. And they worked in silence, which Anna appreciated. Not hearing them speak meant she could think her own thoughts as she pleased. Those thoughts were usually about the progress of the renovations, which was slow. Workmen were lazy and unreliable. One plumber and his crew disappeared to take another, larger job, promising to return as soon as they were available. Anna fired them on the spot. Olaf was furious. He had had trouble finding people in the first place. Anna said having people who came and left before finishing a job was no better than having no one at all.

Aalia and Fatimah were charged with keeping the place clean enough so that some residents might be enticed to move in before the painting had been completed and the floors re-sanded. Anna wanted to start collecting rent. Olaf didn't think they should rush. He was having too much fun to care about the future. He spent freely, which made Anna worry. Every week he came home with a new suit, or new shoes, or a piece of jewelry for her. She begged, then ordered, him to slow down, and take careful stock of their cash. Olaf was downcast. He had waited all his life for a windfall like that, and now that he had it, he meant to enjoy himself. Soon he was spending more and more time in speakeasies, drinking French champagne and eating oysters, while Anna remained at the boardinghouse, overseeing what must be done. She didn't tell him she was pregnant. She wanted him to make his way back to her on his own.

The spring was stormy and late. Aalia and Fatimah, though successful in their theft of Fatimah's husband's jewels, lived in fear of discovery. Their plan was to pay off their debt to Anna for giving them a place to stay and then go to New York and disappear. There had been no discussion of how many more weeks of work Anna required. She secretly hoped that they would remain permanently, since she was feeling sick most of the time now. They guessed her situation. She was heard throwing up in the hall bathroom several mornings in a row.

As the renovations entered the final phase, Anna's mood suffered. She had endured a number of life changes in only eighteen months: marrying, coming to South Dakota, leaving Paul for Olaf, arriving in Chicago, moving to the boardinghouse, and becoming pregnant. Yet now, with a regular, orderly life on the horizon, she wasn't sure she wanted it. She thought she might hate the future and its bland consistency. She had considered doing away with the pregnancy. A doctor could be found, with the money she now had. Then she changed her mind. This child might be her only chance at motherhood.

One night Olaf came home badly beaten. There'd been an argument at one of the clubs he visited; insults were exchanged and punches were thrown. He didn't name his assailant. Anna didn't want to know the details. He took to their bed for days on end, even after his bruises had faded, as if he couldn't bring himself to rise. The sight of him rankled Anna. Harsh words formed on her tongue. But she said nothing to him.

Instead, she picked on Fatimah. Anna told her to remove her veil. Aalia no longer wore hers, though her hair and body remained concealed.

"She cannot," Aalia said.

"Nonsense. She's in America now. There's no need to think that you have to hide yourself away. At least not here, in this house."

There were four lodgers by then: two spinsters, a college student, and a traveling shoe salesman whose circuit had him in Chicago several times a month.

Fatimah refused, and Anna let it go. She was overcome with fatigue. She lay down on the plush couch in the office where she managed accounts; it seemed preferable to going upstairs and crawling into bed next to Olaf.

Later that same day a man in a heavy wool coat came into the front yard. He yelled in Arabic, and Anna knew at once he was there for Aalia and Fatimah. She opened the door and told him to shut the hell up.

"You! You, missus! I want my women!" the man shouted. He was young, and ridiculously handsome.

"I don't know what you're talking about. I'm the only woman here."

The man shook his head. He looked up at the house appraisingly.

"Nice. Lot of new work here," he said.

The shutters had been painted and rehung. The windows had been reglazed. Siding had been replaced in a number of areas. The entire front porch and stairs were new. Two low mulberry hedges bordered the slate walk on either side.

"Leave," Anna said.

"No, missus. I want my women."

Anna stood on the porch, hands on hips. The man picked up a small stone and threw it at her, missing her by inches. The aim was perfect. He could have hit her had he chosen. Another small stone bounced off her knee, with surprising pain. Her dress that was day thin, but a thicker cloth wouldn't have mattered. The man grinned. He spun in a circle, arms raised to the gray, scudding clouds. He was in possession of some delicious joy that showed in every part of him except his black eyes. They were empty. He stopped smiling. His face became hard. The wind lifted the hem of his coat. His trousers had a band of black silk running down the outside of each leg. A dandy, Anna thought. The Arab thug was a dandy.

He hurled a third stone, gotten from where Anna didn't know. He must have had it with him all along, she decided, as it struck her squarely between the eyes. She felt a solid tap, followed by her lurching backward over a low wooden bench where she sometimes liked to sit.

The blood was warm on her face. She got to her feet, and dabbed herself with the fine lace handkerchief she kept in the pocket of her apron. Her forehead throbbed almost exactly in the center. This man was practiced. He'd done this before.

And Anna had seen it before, in the country outside Constantinople. She couldn't remember why they'd gone there—to call on a friend, perhaps, someone considerably worse off than they after the Turks took over. A crowd was gathered, and Anna wanted to know what was going on. The driver of their hired car warned her to not go and look, to not get involved in any way. Anna ignored both him and her mother, who pleaded with her to stay safely there with her.

A young Muslim woman was being stoned, probably for cheating on her husband. The woman wasn't tied, because there was nowhere to run with the crowd massed all around her. There were only men in the crowd, but some women stood apart, looking on. The ground was rocky, and there was no lack of stones. They were thrown in absolute silence, slowly at first, and then faster and faster, hitting the woman with thuds that made her reel and waver, just as Anna had done on her own front porch moments before. The woman's hands covering her face were bloodied at once, then her face was streaming, and she was on the ground. The circle of men closed in on her, until she was no longer visible, and continued their hail of stones. When they stopped and pulled apart, Anna knew that the woman was dead.

"I will give you money, and then you must leave," Anna told the Arab man in her front yard. She went into the house, where Fatimah and Aalia were in the kitchen, standing by the stove, clutching each other. Anna motioned for them not to speak. She went upstairs to her bedroom, where Olaf had managed to sleep through the entire encounter. She removed a box from the top shelf of the closet, took what she needed, went swiftly down the stairs and onto the front porch.

"I have it," Anna said.

"I am grateful. But I must prove to myself that the women are not here."

The man came up the walk, then climbed the stairs and stood very close to Anna on the porch. He was quite a bit taller than she was, which made holding the barrel of Olaf's service revolver to his throat a bit awkward. Anna cocked the trigger—she'd practiced with the gun before—and told the man that if she ever saw him again she would kill him on the spot.

"They are not here. Do you understand me?" Anna asked.

The man nodded. The color had drained from his face. His breath was sour.

"They have never been here. I'm an Armenian. Do you expect that I would shelter trash like you beneath my own roof?" she asked. The man didn't answer. Then he started to speak, and Anna pressed the muzzle of the gun more firmly into his bearded neck.

"Now go away, and don't come back," she said. The man stepped back. He looked down at her with hatred and fear. *If he lunges, shoot,* Anna told herself. Then she wanted to shoot him anyway, even if he did what he was told. She could say he'd attacked her. Her wound was evidence enough of that. She'd tell the truth, that she kept him still with some story about going inside to get the money he wanted, but went for the gun instead. People might wonder why he tried to commit a robbery in broad daylight. She'd say he'd come to the house before looking for someone, and so knew that she was there alone at that hour, with her invalid husband upstairs. The police might recognize Olaf's name. They'd remember how during the interview about the fire he said he was broke, with the clothes to prove it. His being there now, an owner of a newly renovated house, with a fine car in the garage, might very well arouse suspicion. They should have left Chicago, Anna realized. As big as it was, it might not be big enough to hide them forever.

The man backed down the stairs and left across the yard. Anna watched him go. She locked the gun, put it in her apron, and went inside. She told Aalia and Fatimah it was time to sell one of their diamonds, and give her half as payment for what she'd just done.

Twenty

Freddie's own mother was less of a mystery to her than Anna was, though when Freddie reviewed what Lorraine had actually shared of herself, it was little. Born in Chicago, 1922. Raised in a boarding-house. Left at a young age and never went back. Right around the time that Freddie was taking stock of her own name (then still Faith), she asked Lorraine about the origin of hers. Lorraine said it was the region in France her father had loved most during the Great War, Alsace-Lorraine. Freddie liked that idea. It meant her grandfather was a man who made something good out of something bad.

In truth, Anna and Olaf chose to honor a dead aunt. Lorraine believed she was cursed. Her name was ugly and fell harshly on the ear. So did her mother's voice. Anna's words were to be obeyed. To fail to do so meant getting slapped. By the time Lorraine was five, she'd learned how to perform a canny maneuver whereby she leaned back swiftly to avoid the palm of Anna's hand. She didn't need to see the slap coming. She could sense it a good seven to eight seconds before it arrived. Her mother was enraged most by discovering that an order had not been carried out. Olaf told Lorraine again and again that the best thing to do was follow instructions. Lorraine soon gave up. There was no pleasing her mother, and she learned to avoid her as much as possible.

In a boardinghouse, that was easy. There were many places to be by herself. When she ventured into the two parlors, which served as common sitting rooms, the lodgers accepted her presence without interest, though one, Miss Hollister, always smiled and said hello. Miss Hollister gave piano lessons to the better-off families who occupied the grand homes lining the lake. Sometimes she brought Lorraine with her so she could have company on the trolley ride. It was 1929. Lorraine was seven. She didn't like sitting silently through someone else's lesson, especially since Miss Hollister's pupils were young, like herself, and played very badly. The tortured, stumbling melodies stayed with her on the long trip back home. Sometimes she couldn't shake them for days, and took to humming something she made up just to drive the sound from her brain. The humming was frowned upon by her mother, who told her she sounded like a simpleton.

One day, Lorraine found that she couldn't sit still, no matter how hard she tried. Miss Hollister's pupil was a fat, miserable-looking boy, who swung his legs as he sat next to her on the shiny black piano bench. He, too, looked like he wanted nothing more than to jump off and escape the cool darkness of his enormous house. Although Lorraine had visited the home a number of times before, she took special note of its lavish furnishings. The marble staircase seemed cold and impersonal. Her house—the part she occupied with her parents—had rich rugs on the floors. Here the sofa was covered in silk. Lorraine had recently learned from Mr. Burress, another frequent lodger, that silk came from worms. Mr. Burress enjoyed reciting what he assumed were little-known facts. His remark at table that particular evening had gone unanswered. Lorraine wanted to hear more, but she was afraid to say so. It made Lorraine uncomfortable to think that she was sitting on the labor of worms, and she began to consider worms in general, with a growing sense of unease.

So, she stole herself away. Just slid off that fancy sofa, which the fat little boy's mother had called a "settee," and stepped softly out of the room, down a long tiled hallway with heavy pieces of furniture lining the walls along with a number of oil paintings of old people who stared down at her with frank disapproval, into an antiseptically white kitchen, and through the screen door into a fabulously lush green garden. A winding brick walkway led to a stone building with stained glass windows. Lorraine wondered if it was some sort of fantastically rich and luxurious playhouse for the little boy, whose name she suddenly remembered was Thomas. If the playhouse were indeed his, why did he look so unhappy all the time? Maybe he'd done something bad, and had been forbidden to enjoy himself there for a specific period of time. Lorraine's mother always put a time limit on her punishments, her strange way of trying to be fair, Lorraine supposed. *You will have no ice cream after dinner for one week. You are not allowed to play with your dolls for another two days.* That second interdiction was impossible to enforce, because it meant coming unannounced into Lorraine's room at random moments. Anna was always busy in her tidy home office, going over accounts and paying bills. And Olaf couldn't be bothered with something so trivial as whether or not his daughter was playing with her dolls, most of which he'd gotten for her. He'd recently bought a furniture store and spent a lot of time there refinishing pieces and selling them at prices so high that people automatically assumed their inherent value.

As Lorraine approached the stone house, she was overcome with a profound sense of peace. It looked like the sort of place where nothing awful could ever happen, where you could be safe and happy. The doorway was a tall arch with two heavy wooden doors. The doors were open. Inside there were benches on either side of a central aisle that led to a little stage with a podium. The stained glass windows facing her let in bars of red and blue light. They were beautiful. It was like looking inside a dream. *May I?* Lorraine asked whatever spirit ruled there. *May I put my hand in the light?*

An old woman in a long black dress knelt in front of a red velvet rail. She was like a crumpled piece of paper.

Is that you, Miss Dormand?

But that was impossible. Miss Dormand was long gone.

A spinster heading west to Seattle, she had needed a few weeks recuperation in Chicago. Her deep cough said why. The hand that flew to her thin lips was dressed in white silk. *I am recovering from a slight illness, as you can see.* Another cough, longer than the last. *Your establishment has been highly recommended*, she told Olaf. Her bag was of rough material, burlap perhaps. Olaf sized her up in that way he had, one quick look up and down, and led her to the "dormitory," a large room with four single beds lined up like pencils on the first day of school, and placed her by the only window, which overlooked the long driveway. He explained the arrangements—the bath down the hall, breakfast and dinner served in the large room he'd indicated on their way to the back stairs. As they passed the kitchen, he nodded to Aalia and Fatimah (the "crows," he

called them, then confided that this was his wife's peculiar term). All the
while Lorraine crept swiftly behind them. Miss Dormand wore a gold
necklace around her scrawny neck, and Lorraine was drawn by its glint.

At the sound of Lorraine's step on the stone floor, the old woman
turned her head, peering into the brightness let in by the open doors.
Lorraine stopped. The old woman got slowly to her feet and approached
Lorraine. Her face sagged, but her eyes were bright.

"You must never interrupt someone at prayer," she said. Her voice was
soft yet firm.

"What are you praying for?"

"The soul of my late husband."

"Is this your church?"

"My chapel. Our family chapel, I should say."

"Oh."

The woman put her hand on Lorraine's shoulder. The hand felt as
light as a leaf. She said it was time that they both be getting back to the
house. The woman pulled the pair of doors closed behind them, then
inserted a large iron key into the lock in one of the doors and turned it.

"I cannot stand the thought of any sort of defilement on holy ground,"
the woman said. Lorraine didn't ask her to explain what she meant. They
walked slowly, with the woman's hand once again on Lorraine's shoulder—not out of kindness, Lorraine realized, but to steady herself.

During her stay Miss Dormand had declined, and wasn't expected to
recover. Anna had ordered her removed to a hospital. Olaf wouldn't hear
of it. The Christian thing would be to let her stay put, and hire a nurse
to care for her. Anna refused. *I will not have anyone dying under my roof!*

In the end, Anna let Olaf have his way. He told her she was becoming
a cruel woman, and it made her stop and think. Aalia offered to serve
as nurse. She said, in English that was becoming easier to understand,
that she had sat with her own mother in a similar circumstance. Aalia
said Miss Dormand could last many weeks, which indeed she did. When
Miss Dormand slipped into a coma from which Aalia knew she would
never awaken, Aalia removed the gold cross and gave it to Lorraine. How
she gleaned Lorraine's interest in it, Lorraine didn't know. Aalia seemed
to sense things, rather than observe them outright. She was alone there
now, since Fatimah had recently gone to New York. Her elderly husband
had died the year before, and she had no more to fear from him, nor

from the nephew, who was never seen again. Aalia had had the chance to go with her, but chose to stay. After Miss Dormand had been taken away, Aalia and Lorraine went through her things. She left very little, only a small number of clothes and a little journal bound in pale green silk that Lorraine read eagerly, though she knew it was wrong to do so. The entries were about the weather, the sky seen from the train window, a cat named Isabelle who kept her up at night where she used to live. The last thing she wrote was, *Soon you will find me in His kingdom.* Miss Dormand must have known what lay ahead. Why had she chosen Lorraine's house as the place to die? The adults had their own ideas, of course, all anchored in logic and practicality. Miss Dormand simply couldn't travel anymore, and this was as far as her failing strength would take her. Lorraine had a different thought as she and the old woman made their way back into the dim light of the fat boy's mansion, where they were met by Miss Hollister, who looked flushed and cross.

Miss Dormand had been sent by God so Lorraine could receive His word. When she hadn't listened, He had brought her there, so she could discover the chapel, and the splendid serenity within.

Twenty-One

1933

Anna hated winter. It was a season of disappearance. The light went away, taking with it color, warmth, and people. Streets became empty and silent. The house fell silent, too, less from the season than from the loss of fortune. Everyone was out of work. There were no jobs. Prosperity was not right around the corner.

Olaf had been warned. He played cards with a group of men, one of whom followed the stock market closely. On the day it happened, he telephone Olaf and said to take his money out of the bank. Olaf didn't ask why. He didn't want to take the chance of not acting. Now, eight thousand dollars sat in a safe in Anna's office. She was glad it was there, but didn't want to touch it. The problem was that they had fewer and fewer lodgers. They weren't making much money, and so sometimes she had to open the safe to get to the end of the month.

The approach of the holiday season only deepened her gloom. Paul had finally given her a divorce several months before so he could remarry. She hadn't told Olaf that she was free, since she intended never to marry again. It wasn't necessary. She was as secure as she ever would be, given that she had complete control of their affairs. She couldn't help wondering what Paul's new wife was like, and if she minded that he was a closet Jew. Maybe Paul had given up his religion and converted. Anything was possible in this crazy world, wasn't it?

By mid-December they were down to one lodger, Joseph Swinn. Swinn was an itinerant Baptist preacher from Ohio who covered Illinois and parts of Missouri. He came to Chicago to find converts among the down and out. He didn't have much success, he confided to Anna one morning as he sipped his lukewarm tea—the only nourishment he allowed himself that time of day.

Anna wasn't surprised. City people suffered as much as country people did, perhaps more, but they were far more wary. Swinn had had bottles thrown at him for trying to bring Jesus into the hearts of drunks and derelicts. It was a test of faith, he was sure. And he was determined not to fail.

One morning, Aalia brought out a plate of day-old biscuits. She still wore a head scarf, but no longer prayed three times a day and had, in fact, retired her frayed rug. As she set down the lovely blue china dish—Anna still had all of her fine housewares from better days—she met the level gaze of Joseph Swinn. Anna watched him, and decided immediately that she would allow no attempt on Joseph Swinn's part to convert Aalia. He'd tried that with her, and was told that if he wanted to remain under her roof, he'd best save his fine words for strangers.

But the look in Joseph Swinn's eyes did not show a man on the hunt for new souls. Nor did it show fear or revulsion at so foreign a person. What Anna saw there was lust.

"Will there be anything else?" Aalia asked Anna. Her accent was heavy. Joseph Swinn was charmed. He smiled and cocked his head.

"A Levantine princess," he said. Aalia smiled. Joseph Swinn was both young and handsome, if a bit rough and seedy around the edges. His shirt cuffs were worn. The collar wasn't clean. His fingernails were lined with black. Anna had suffered seeing them hold her fine china. They were further evidence of how badly the whole world had fallen.

Aalia looked a moment longer at Joseph Swinn and then withdrew.

"Do you think she knew what I was talking about?" he asked Anna.

"I should imagine so. She's highly educated." Anna knew that Aalia wasn't highly educated, but it sounded good.

"You're very broad-minded, having her here," he said.

"Am I?"

"Please take no offense, Mrs. Lund. A broad mind is a sign of God's grace."

"Yes."

At dinner a few days later, Joseph Swinn said that he'd be on his way again soon. He had failed in Chicago.

"These are the times that try men's souls," he said. He sliced into the lamb chop Anna had broiled earlier. He seemed to like it. She always did well with lamb.

"Perhaps many people have more important things on their minds than God," Anna said. Olaf nodded. He, too, liked the lamb and was blotting up the gravy with a thick crust of bread.

"Nothing is more important than God," Lorraine said. She didn't like lamb, or any sort of meat, and was attacking a particularly large boiled potato.

Anna stared at her. Lorraine seldom voiced an opinion about anything. She was eleven, a strange child, always in some sort of trance or reverie. She gave the impression of being pliable. In school she was apt to be persuaded to get involved in pranks, and was punished by her teachers when she confessed. Sometimes she even took the blame for things she hadn't done, on the grounds that the other child couldn't handle the consequences as well as she could. Anna was afraid of what might happen when she got older, and was grateful that she was homely and unattractive to boys.

"And where do you practice your faith?" Joseph Swinn asked Lorraine.

"In my room."

"I see."

Anna and Olaf looked at each other. Anna stood up and lifted Lorraine's plate from the table. Lorraine sat for a moment, her heavy knife and fork still in her hands and poised above the lace tablecloth. Then she followed her mother into the kitchen, still holding her utensils. Anna told her to sit down at the small wooden table and finish her meal.

"She hasn't been well," Anna said when she rejoined Olaf and Joseph Swinn.

"Under a strain," Olaf added.

"She's a remarkable sensitive girl," Joseph Swinn said. He had finished eating, and was hoping Anna would offer him coffee, as she usually did. That evening, she declined.

Anna and Olaf repaired to their private study, a lovely, quiet place. That time of year, the fire was always lit. Anna poured them each a sherry. Olaf sat in a wing-backed chair and put his feet on an ottoman that was finely embroidered by Anna's own hand. She sat in a smaller chair, her feet on the Persian rug. She removed the velvet house slippers she'd taken to wearing with fewer lodgers about, and stretched her feet towards the warmth of the grate.

"Is it his doing, do you think?" Anna asked. She meant the fervor of Joseph Swinn.

"I shouldn't think so. She has spent very little time in his company."

"Why, then?"

Each of them realized at that moment that their daughter was, at heart, a simple child, not particularly gifted or special in any way. She was a disappointment, and now a concern.

"These things happen," Olaf said.

"Maybe she's lonely."

"And turned to God?"

"Why not? People do."

Olaf sipped his drink. Anna admired the firelight on his hair, which had very little gray. At thirty-eight he was still beautiful. That he no longer stirred her heart would never change that.

"You should have seen how many converted, out there in the field," he said. His gaze hardened as he looked into the past. "Some would come out strict atheists, and in not too long a time, they were praying with all their might."

"That's different. They were under duress. Staring right at death, every day."

Olaf sighed. The memory was still difficult. Even now, fifteen years later, he wasn't able to really put the war behind him.

After a long moment he said, "Well, I suppose there are worse things. Maybe we should take her to church."

"Which one? Catholic or Lutheran?"

"I wouldn't feel right in either one."

"Exactly."

The sound of Aalia washing dishes in the kitchen reached them. The clock on the mantelpiece chimed that it was seven in the evening. A sudden, sharp gust of wind pressed against the night-black windowpane. Olaf and Anna thought about their daughter, her calm and quiet ways, her wandering gaze, her lack of interest in the world she occupied, and feared for her.

Twenty-Two
1936

As always, any time spent on a trolley left Anna in poor spirits. The pinched, anxious faces; the worn, dirty clothes. All those people and their problems were like a river of gray water that flowed on and on, yet never met the sea, never found release, was never set free. A child in a frayed coat sat next to her with a comic book open in her lap. She was engrossed in the flying characters before her. *I bet you wish you could do that*, Anna thought. *Better to escape life than see it for what it is.*

There was no escape for Anna. She was a facer of facts. She no longer loved Olaf, though he had his own place in her heart she'd never cede to another. Her child was a creature she couldn't fathom. The fortune Olaf had secured through crime had shrunk substantially, despite Anna's economy and vigilance. At forty-six, she wasn't young. Those were her private woes. The world had its own. Europe was sinking under the weight of its growing madness. Reason had taken flight. Fear and hatred lived in the hearts of more people every day.

Out the window the cityscape worsened. Anna chose this neighborhood because she wouldn't be known, though in fairness, she so seldom ventured beyond the pleasant confines of her few immediate streets, that she was unlikely to be recognized anywhere.

The little girl next to her didn't move when Anna's stop came, so Anna had to step over her. Her coat caught on the point of the little girl's boot, and tore when Anna yanked it. If she believed in omens, she'd have turned back then. Being stubborn had its disadvantages, to be sure.

Her destination was two blocks over. The spring wind smelled of flowering trees. A lone dog trotted down the middle of the cobblestone street, its tongue lolling from its long black face. Another omen? Oh, why not? Signs were everywhere, if you just cared to look.

The stone steps were smooth, the floor inside worn, with a missing tile here and there. The darkness took her a moment to reckon. She found a seat and waited her turn. Around her the silence was broken by whispers. Only a handful of other people were present, yet their quiet voices were magnified by the cavernous space.

She patted her forehead with her handkerchief, though the air inside was cool, even chilly. She fell into the uneasy events of a few days before. Paul's face was older and more refined, his eyes tired and dark. She was struck by how his voice hadn't changed. His wool suit was well cut. The lid of the gold watch he consulted was engraved with his initials.

He had come to ask her forgiveness. The bar they were in was noisy, so they'd taken a booth at the back, against a brick wall. She considered the way her sherry caught the dim light, and seemed to make it brighter. She said she had nothing to be forgiven for. He said he had put her in an impossible position. Anna couldn't help feeling rueful. What about the new wife? Had he done the same to her? He didn't take her question badly. On the contrary, he explained how he had embraced his faith and encouraged his wife, a local farm girl who'd been smart enough to go to college and get into one of his classes, to convert. Was there now a rabbi in Huron, someone she took her instruction from? Paul said he'd engaged the long-distance services of a rabbi right there in Chicago. His wife had been successful in her conversion, and had changed her name from Mary to Miriam.

"So, you are happy, then," Anna said. The sherry in her glass went on glowing.

"No."

"Because you need my forgiveness?"

"Yes."

She drank her sherry, hoping that she would then glow from within.

"Paul. It doesn't matter now, after all this time. You have your life, and I have mine."

He pushed his glass of brandy away.

"And yours makes you happy?" he asked.

"Of course."

"Then why did you come?" He took her hand.

"Don't be a fool!" Anna reclaimed her hand.

The waiter asked if they would care for another drink. Paul looked at Anna, awaiting her reply. Anna shook her head. The waiter went on his way.

"I made a mistake, Anna. What I asked of you was unspeakable. It was my fear that drove me," Paul said.

"A fear you have overcome."

"For the most part."

"And your . . . moods. Do you still have those?"

"Not so often."

"So, you're saying that you've changed."

"Yes."

The sherry inside her didn't brighten her heart; it just made it heavy and sick.

"Paul—"

"Leave him. Give us another chance."

"You must be joking!"

"No."

"What about your wife?"

"She's my wife in name only, Anna. We do not share a bed. We never have."

Anna brought the palm of her hand to her forehead.

"But why did she marry you, and then convert to your religion if she . . . has no intention of giving you children?" she asked.

"She wanted to get away from her family. Religion meant little to her. It didn't matter what rituals she practiced, or when."

"And you accepted the hollowness of that? The pretense?"

Paul cocked his head.

"Yes. Which led me to see the folly of my previous one," he said.

Anna leaned back and closed her eyes. A dull ache had settled above her left eye. She had trouble taking it all in.

"It's impossible," she said.

"Please. Promise me that you will think about it."

She expected him to embrace her as they left and went their separate ways. He merely shook her hand warmly then tipped his hat.

That was four days ago. She hadn't been able to take a deep breath since.

The door of the confessional opened, and a young woman came out. Her high heels clacked across the floor. From the tight fit of her dress, it was easy to guess her sins, but then appearances could deceive. Anna stood. The rosary rattled in her pocket. She'd turned back at the last minute, as if pulled by a string, to the bottom drawer of her jewelry box.

I might need this, was all she thought.

She went to the door, opened it, and went inside. There was a smell of perfume, from the previous occupant, no doubt, overlaid with cigarette smoke and garlic. Anna sat. She didn't cross herself. The priest's window slid open.

"Forgive me, Father, for I have sinned." Anna's voice sounded strange in there, amplified and harsh.

"How long has it been since your last confession?"

"I don't know."

"What do you wish to confess?"

Anna considered. The list was long. The priest waited. Anna glanced at him. His face was mostly hidden, but she saw that it was old, with folds along the jaw.

"I have caused unhappiness," she said.

"What, and to whom?"

"My ex-husband."

The priest shifted in his seat.

"I know divorce is a sin," Anna said.

Silence.

"On top of the sin of causing him unhappiness."

More silence.

"Please understand, I left him because of the pain he caused me. Pain I couldn't bear. I should have borne it. That was my duty."

Continued silence.

"I gave my pain away when I should have suffered it."

The priest cleared his throat.

"And now he wants reconciliation," she said. Her voice quavered. Her heart pounded. Her hands ached from clenching them.

"There are obstacles to this reconciliation. He is married, but in name only. I am not married, and live in sin with the man I left him for," she said. "We have a child." She sat up straight. Her breathing slowed. So did her heart. How simple it all sounded, now that she'd spoken the words. *There's freedom in that alone*, she thought. *The power of plain truth.*

The priest stirred on his side of the screen. Anna had forgotten him for the moment.

"You must find your way back to God," he said. He murmured out her penance. The confessions of her youth stood before her then. An easy way out for wrongs, some small, others not.

Not back to God. To myself, she thought.

Anna patted her face once more, then put her handkerchief in her leather handbag. It was made of crocodile. A lavish gift to herself in a moment of despair. She re-pinned her hat. She still wore her hair long, though the fashion was not to. She left the confessional. The darkness of the church was the same. So was the dusty, broken floor, the smooth steps, and the steel-colored sky. Now it was her heels that sounded on the street stone, echoing sharply in the open air.

She made for the trolley stop, wondering if she'd see the little ragged girl again. Of course she wouldn't. She was long gone by now.

The rosary made no sound when Anna tossed it in the gutter. All she heard was her own footfalls and the steady thump of her heart.

Twenty-Three
1938

Change wasn't always sudden. Sometimes it was slow, subtle, and horribly seductive. Like the gradual progression of an illness, perhaps. You come to believe that it's nothing that wasn't there all along. You make allowances for the loss of function. It's only Time itself, you think, doing what Time does, which is to whittle away what was once strong and firm.

Such was the change Anna observed in Olaf. For so long he'd been glum, not interested in much of anything. The failure of his furniture business he took personally, despite Anna's saying over and over that the broader world, and its lack of money, was to blame. He wouldn't have it. He believed that somewhere out there people were making money, living the good life, and that he'd missed his chance through some personal flaw. A spirit of defeat was with him always, as if there were no point in getting out of bed in the morning.

Then the spirit lightened. Once in a while Anna saw him smile to himself, as if remembering a moment of happiness or something funny. Though they had grown far apart, and no longer shared a bed, Anna wanted those memories to be of her, and of the life they once led, before her heart grew cold, and her attitude sour.

Lorraine also seemed lit from within. Anna assumed she was happy at no longer having to go to school. At fifteen, her academic performance was so poor that she'd had to repeat not one but two grades, so Anna pled special circumstances to the school district, and Lorraine was allowed to permanently withdraw. Those circumstances were, in essence, that

Lorraine was too simple to handle a classroom setting. No one thought to put her through any sort of testing or assessment. Her odd demeanor under the probing eye of her teacher was enough.

Anna thought she could complete Lorraine's education herself. She had her sit in the dining room between meals. She begged her to pay attention. Lorraine tried to comply.

Democracy is not a new idea. It was practiced by the ancient Greeks.

The President is elected not by the people themselves, but by the Electoral College.

Successful farming is based on a system of rotating crops. Failure to do so is what resulted in the Dust Bowl.

The Nazis are gaining power through intimidation, propaganda, and an assault against Jews.

Our Lord was a Jew, Lorraine offered.

Anna decided that Lorraine might be better served if she were given a list of books to read. She went to the local library and borrowed *Bullfinch's Mythology*, *A Tale of Two Cities*, and the *Federalist Papers*.

The books sat on Lorraine's shelf, undisturbed. Anna gave up. She'd been foolish to think that her child would be interested in anything worldly or temporal. Yet Anna still felt the need to connect with her somehow. Maybe she was at fault. Maybe Lorraine had turned away from her because Anna hadn't given her enough love. Anna wanted to correct that. She wanted to be kind.

Lorraine had magnificent black hair, which she let flow as it would. Anna bought her a set of exquisite mother-of-pearl combs, and wrapped them in lavender tissue paper. Even someone with her head in the clouds would be brought down to earth when she saw those! And this was only the beginning of the warmth Anna would show. There would be movies and walks in the park. She would invite Olaf to join them. They would behave as a family ought to behave. And they would be happy.

One evening, Anna went to present her lovely gift. Lorraine's room was empty. Her coat and hat were gone, as was her suede purse in which she carried a few coins and a small compressed copy of the New Testament, a gift from Joseph Swinn on his last visit. She didn't have a house key and wouldn't need one. The back door was right next to Aalia's room, and Aalia would let her in, as she no doubt had done many times before.

Anna confronted her.

"How long has this been going on?" Anna asked. After all these years, Aalia's room had taken on a bit more luster. There was now an attractive cut-glass lamp she had found at an estate sale, and a watercolor of a marsh framed in gold hung above her bed.

"I don't know what you mean."

"Yes, you do. Where does she go? Whom does she meet?"

Aalia looked at Anna with defiance. She no longer wore the abaya, and dressed as any woman would. Her hair was short and crimped. There was polish on her nails. Her shoes had thin, shiny straps. She complained about her workload and did less and less, which meant Anna sometimes had to hang laundry with pins that splintered her fingers.

"She looks for the Spirit," she said.

"What the hell is that supposed to mean?"

"If you do not know, I cannot tell you."

But she did, even though Lorraine was paying her to keep quiet. Lorraine helped herself to the cash box on a regular basis. She never took very much. Anna knew about the missing sums—she was meticulous in her accounting. She assumed it was Olaf who was lightening the box. He went out in the late mornings on occasion; Anna assumed it was to a racetrack.

Aalia had more to say. When Joseph Swinn was in town, he took Lorraine with him to give the word of God to drunks and whores, women on the stoops of buildings with babies at their breasts, drug addicts clinging to lampposts, and anyone who just sat and wept. Those they persuaded followed them to an old hardware store where Joseph Swinn preached. The owner was someone he'd supposedly saved, yet who still charged a nominal rent for the use of the space after hours. Coffee was served, along with whatever food they could find, quite often from Anna's larder.

Anna didn't understand why Aalia broke her silence in favor of candor. Was she so fickle that her swearing to keep Lorraine's secrets—and taking her money—meant nothing when confronted? No, it wasn't that. She wanted her words to wound. She wanted the upper hand. Over time she had grown angry and cruel, but why?

One morning Aalia brought Olaf a cup of coffee he hadn't asked for. He nodded thanks, but didn't look at her. Only when she left the room did Olaf gaze at the doorway she had just passed through.

Anna went to her private study, locked the door, and sat for hours, until she was surprised by the glare of late afternoon through the lace curtains she once thought were so pretty, but which now seemed cheap and old-fashioned.

Aalia did her shopping mid-morning, and left just before Olaf did on the days when he went out. They'd been at it for a long time, clearly. Anna hadn't seen it. Nor the collusion between Lorraine and Joseph Swinn. They sat at her table and conversed as long-time acquaintances, nothing more.

She began a letter to Paul, then destroyed it. There was no going back. She hadn't replied to his request when he'd met her in Chicago two years before, and she hadn't heard from him since. Surely he had made peace with his situation.

She put her face in her hands. Her breath was hot against her palms.

Why are you punishing me? Is it because I turned away? I had no choice. You know that. My heart could never truly receive You!

She dropped her hands and lifted her head.

Talking to God was sign of a madness she refused to indulge in ever again. No matter what.

Twenty-Four

1939

The river was wide and slow. Its bank was hard and cracked, which meant the water had stayed right where it was for a long time, and not flowed over. The summer had been dry. Farmers were desperate for rain. The sky was a blaze of blue and white, and Lorraine longed for the shade of the willow trees she saw in the distance.

The bus ride had left her skirt wrinkled. Her mother scolded her for wearing it, but that was just a dream, because her mother didn't know where she was or why she had gone to Ohio. Nor did she know that she would never return. Aalia urged her to leave a note, lest Anna bother her for information. Aalia, too, had her own travel plans, which included Olaf, though she made no mention of this to Lorraine. Lorraine wrote a few words in her crooked, uneven hand, gave the paper to Aalia, then begged her to come with her.

"The way of the Lord is the only true way. You'll see for yourself," she said.

Aalia shook her head. She was through with God—any God. So Lorraine went alone, with a small suitcase and a tiny amount of money, leaving the only home she'd ever known for a blessed calling.

In Indianapolis she got off the bus and boarded another one bound for Coshocton. She knew there was a more direct route, but Joseph Swinn had been explicit in his instructions. Later Lorraine learned that changing buses cost less. It also took longer. He wanted her to have a lot of time among strangers to watch the passing land and reflect on the gravity of the path she was now undertaking.

The cynical voice in her said that it was he who was reconsidering. She heard this voice often, and knew it was the Devil speaking. Doubt was the Devil's tool, and must be broken with faith. Her faith was strong. Her faith was unwavering. She entertained no more cynical thoughts as she bounced, hot and thirsty, along that bumpy road.

At the station in Coshocton she was met not by Joseph Swinn, but by a young woman who recognized Lorraine at once and approached. She was short, barely up to Lorraine's shoulder. Her skin was pale, almost translucent. She was slightly purple below the eyes. Her teeth were crooked and yellow. Below her velvet cap her cropped red hair stuck out in a way that said she never bothered with it. Her name was Nora, and she was one of Joseph Swinn's "helpers." Lorraine felt a hot bolt in the pit of her stomach at the realization that Joseph Swinn had dispatched someone else to fetch her. Then she told herself that God's work was often time-consuming, and that he was certainly ministering to someone in great need.

This thought sustained her the rest of the way. The car they rode in, with Nora at the wheel, dated from the late teens. It whined and lurched, and sent out black smoke. The seats were worn, and Lorraine had to unhook the sharp end of a spring from the fabric of her skirt. She'd been told to dress simply, without stockings, which she'd have to remove in any case. Even so, Lorraine was uneasy being barelegged. Her hose were torn and dirty at that point, and glancing down at them, she felt ashamed.

The camp came into view. One large tent, surrounded by a number of smaller ones; an outdoor fire with a metal grate and large black pot, which gave off a lovely smell of pork, or so Lorraine guessed; two old, battered cars parked to one side, and a recently erected outhouse. All of this was a test, too. Joseph Swinn knew well the life Lorraine had had in Chicago, the luxury her mother indulged in.

Lorraine got out of the car. Nora reminded her to take her suitcase from the backseat. She was led to the large tent, which had a podium and rows of plain, wooden chairs. Lorraine wondered how those had been transported. One would need a truck for that.

You have such a fine, practical mind, Joseph Swinn told her back in Chicago. Feeding the saved in the hardware store wasn't easy. Lorraine had to find a small electric burner on which to heat soup. It was simple enough, with the jewelry she took from Anna's box. A slender pin with two small sapphires had gotten the burner, then a coffee pot, plates, utensils, and new shoes for Joseph Swinn. The theft went undiscovered, as Lorraine knew it would, because her mother seldom wore jewelry anymore. Gaiety and cheer had left her. While she knew her mother was unhappy, and she prayed for her, she also knew that Anna's gloom was a gift from God for the furtherance of Joseph Swinn's ministry.

The tent had a bad smell that Lorraine recognized as human sweat, yet it was empty. Against one of the posts holding the dingy canvas in place was a broom whose bristles were bent and broken. Lorraine put down her suitcase, took the broom, and swept in useless strokes back and forth. The dust only moved from place to place over the rough wood planking that comprised the floor. After a while she put the broom back where she had found it. No one had come into the tent after her. There was no sign of Joseph Swinn. Once more, she feared that she was being misled. This was another test she mustn't fail. There was nothing to do but take a seat, bow her head, and pray.

Dear God, I am your humble servant. I have come only to serve and worship you. I beg only to partake of Your glory and goodness.

Her mind wandered. Her mother would be reading her note by now. *I have gone where I am summoned. Good-bye.* Would there be tears? Probably ones of anger, not sorrow. And from her father? Surely none. In some ways, he had hurt her even more than her mother had. He was physically present, but that was all. Lorraine remembered when her voice would cause his eyes to lift from the newspaper or book he was reading and meet hers with happiness. Then, one day, he didn't look up, but kept on with what he was doing, a strange heaviness about him. That was when she first heard God's voice.

Do not grieve the loss of earthly love, for you have Mine forever.

She'd been in the kitchen, pouring herself a glass of water, something she always did when upset. The glass fell from her fingers. Aalia looked at her sharply, swore in Arabic, and chased her away with a broom.

A hand pressed lightly on her shoulder. It was Joseph Swinn, at last. His coat was new. So were his trousers.

"You've come," he said. Lorraine stood. She was full of light, and would rise and float away, if not for the weight of his hand now in hers. She went on looking up at him, not wanting to move and knowing she had to.

"Nora will take your things to your tent. You may have a few moments to prepare, if you like," Joseph Swinn said.

Lorraine shook her head. She was as ready as she'd ever be. She removed her hat, because she didn't want it to get ruined. Then she chided herself for that vanity.

Lorraine followed Joseph Swinn out of the tent and down a dusty path through parched, low-growing bushes. Sometimes the path wound through shade, most of the time not. When they reached the river, there were a number of people there whom Lorraine knew at once all belonged to Joseph Swinn. There were nine women and two men, of all ages. The oldest was a woman with long white hair. The youngest was a teenage boy in shirtsleeves who looked as though he'd been working on something, a car engine, perhaps, because his hands and forearms were spotted with black. They were there to bear her witness, and she was afraid.

Fear not, for the spirit of the Lord is with you.

At the water's edge, Joseph Swinn didn't hesitate, but waded slowly into the river. Lorraine wanted to tell him to mind his new clothes, and then understood that this was all a part of offering yourself up to God—not caring about finery. She should have worn something nicer. Her best dress was black silk with small pearls down the front. It was in Chicago, among the things she'd instructed Aalia to do away with, preferably into the good hands of some charity (yet she knew that Aalia had always admired that dress and would no doubt make it her own).

Joseph Swinn reached out to her. She hesitated. She was afraid of water. She always had been. In Chicago one summer, her father took her to the shore of Lake Michigan and brought her to the edge of the waves. The immensity of that wide, blue surface terrified her, and she struggled against his grip. He remonstrated with her, calling her a silly child. Maybe that was when he lost interest in her, when she failed to control her terrible fear.

She was trembling now, and dizzy. If she fainted, she'd die there in the river. Maybe Joseph Swinn would stand by and watch the last bubbles from her mouth rise and break on the sunny surface.

She stepped into the water, and found it surprisingly cold. All the time on first one, then another bus, and in Nora's rattling car, she'd longed for something just this refreshing, but now it made her tremble harder and clench her jaw. Joseph Swinn pulled her to him. The water was above her knees. She wanted to focus on him but couldn't. She needed him to say it was going to be all right. He drew a long, deep breath, let it out, and lifted his hands to the flawless sky.

"Truly, truly, I say to you, unless one is born of water and Spirit, he cannot enter the kingdom of God. That which is born of the flesh is flesh; that which is born of the Spirit is Spirit. Do not marvel that I said that to you; You must be born again."

With that, he put his hand hard against her and bent her backward. Her knees gave, and she descended into the water. Then her face was below the surface, and her eyes were still open, seeing only light, muted and diffuse. Her ears rang from the cold, and everything spun. She was aware that she wasn't breathing and needed to, yet she remained absolutely still. Seconds passed. The pressure in her chest gained strength. If he didn't pull her up soon, she would inhale the muddy water all around her.

Joseph Swinn hauled her to her feet. The warmth of the sun was welcome. River water had gotten in her nose and throat and she coughed. Joseph Swinn ignored her discomfort.

"And Peter said to them, repent, and let each of you be baptized in the name of Jesus Christ, for the forgiveness of your sins."

The congregation sang a hymn. Lorraine didn't know its name. She pulled away from Joseph Swinn, and made her way with great difficulty to the bank. The mud beneath her feet was soft and slippery. She'd removed her shoes beforehand, and wished she hadn't, because she might tread more easily. When she reached dry land she sank, exhausted, still breathless, soaking wet and freezing. The singing continued. Gentle hands were on her. She despised their touch. She wanted to be left alone. She was a sinner who couldn't find redemption. For her, there was no salvation, only the desire for physical comfort—a dry dress, warm food, and a soft bed. Then she was led away, aware of nothing but the sound of her own weeping.

Twenty-Five

For a few days, Anna kept Lorraine's note in the sleeve of her white cotton dress. Then she put it inside a book of verse she was reading. She closed the book and sighed. With a cool, fresh handkerchief she patted her face, which was always damp. The hottest summer for the past ten years had all the guests demanding electric fans in their rooms, except for Miss Waverly, a retired schoolteacher who'd been living with her sister until "difficulties arose." Miss Waverly had a fear of catching cold, and demanded that anyone employing the use of a fan keep his or her door firmly shut. Baking had been impossible, which meant buying bread. While there was more money coming in now, Anna still didn't like it. She tried not offering her usual rolls and biscuits, saying that as soon as the heat broke, they'd reappear. Mr. Jackson, a car salesman who'd relocated from Minneapolis, said he very much would appreciate something substantial at table to help him digest the cold soups and salads Anna instructed Aalia to prepare and serve.

After a few more days, she put the note in her jewelry box. She noticed the missing pieces at once. At first she thought Aalia was to blame, but realized that made little sense. Aalia still had the bulk of the diamonds she'd brought to America, plus whatever savings she'd accumulated from her wages. That Olaf might have added to her nest egg made Anna's hands shake with rage. She wouldn't be able to tolerate the situation much longer, and prayed that it would resolve with a minimum of disruption to her and the house.

Lorraine was in love with Joseph Swinn, though she probably wasn't fully aware of it yet. She was seventeen and stupid. The disloyalty of that thought caused Anna little pain. Truth was truth, after all, and Lorraine was no more intelligent or gifted than God had made her just because she was Anna's daughter. What did pain—gall—Anna was that Lorraine had done exactly what she wanted, or had found what she wanted, to be precise. Wherever she was, and whatever idiocy she was engaging in, she was happier than Anna was then, in that steaming house, with a cheating husband and a servant who'd turned against her.

Anna and Olaf didn't speak of Lorraine. Anna said only that she'd gotten a note. She asked the new servant she'd hired, a tall, thick refugee from Poland named Rochl, to help her clean out Lorraine's room. Rochl was Aalia's replacement. Aalia hadn't yet given her notice, nor had Olaf informed Anna as to when they'd be leaving. Anna decided that the matter should be moved forward, no matter what. When she stopped and thought about not having Olaf near, especially then, with her only child gone, too, it was as if the room she happened to be looking at grew dark and much smaller. Then she told herself that she would make a new life for herself one way or another, as she always had. It was 1939. There were opportunities then for women that had never existed before. She was forty-nine years old and felt strong and healthy. And she was still a handsome woman. Sometimes the eyes of her gentlemen boarders told her so. Love, should she seek it again, would surely come her way.

Lorraine's room was on a corner, and full of light. Her pampered life was evident everywhere. The canopy bed had fine hand-embroidered linens. The furniture was solid cherry and maple. The dresser had exquisite china and crystal figurines that Lorraine had admired once, long ago, and which Anna had bought for her, thinking she hungered for them. A small antique writing desk stood below a south-facing window. Lorraine must have sat there at least once, because there were a series of crosses carved in its polished surface. It was Aalia's job to clean that room. She had never mentioned the crosses, but then that wasn't the sort of thing she'd think was important or unusual. Rochl carefully folded Lorraine's many dresses, stockings, and even her underthings, so that they could be given away to charity. She put her dolls, figurines, picture books, and a silhouette done when she was only four into a wooden crate that Anna would later ask Olaf to move to the cellar. It was possible that Lorraine might one day wish to reconnect with her childhood, though

Anna already knew, as she watched Rochl work, that she wouldn't. Anna wasn't sure she'd take her back, even if Lorraine asked her to.

What sort of mother am I?

Anna had loved Lorraine once, of that she was certain. She wished her no harm now, and success at whatever she applied herself to. But she didn't like her as a person. Maybe she never had. And maybe Lorraine, sensing that dislike as children will, turned inward to protect herself.

Anna sat down suddenly on the bed. Rochl asked if she were feeling entirely well. Anna said she was fine. Rochl continued with her chores, made lighter now with a sweet tune she was humming that reminded Anna, quite unreasonably, of her own childhood. Rochl was a Jew, and whatever songs she'd learned as a child wouldn't have had anything to do with the melodies that floated around Anna's large house on the Bosporus. It didn't matter. Music was music, the same in any language.

Like love, but only if you remember how to speak it.

As Anna had hoped, Rochl's presence in the house spurred Aalia to give her notice. She came to Anna's private study one evening directly after dinner. Anna cordially invited her to sit down.

Aalia looked grave.

"I am sorry for the grief I have caused you," she said.

"Grief? There's been no grief."

Aalia looked at her hands. She wore a brown knit dress that seemed too warm for the season, but then the part of the world that they were both from had been hotter than this.

"I will pay your wages through the end of the month," Anna said. She poured herself a glass of sherry. She offered none to Aalia, though she knew Aalia had taken up the habit of drinking from time to time. *How far you've come from your Muslim ways*, Anna thought. Oddly, she didn't seem all that much happier for it.

"You are generous," Aalia said. Anna waited for her to continue. She didn't. Then Aalia lifted her head.

"Do you hear again from Lorraine?" she asked.

"No. Do you?"

Aalia shook her head.

"Sometimes I fear for her, out there, in the wilderness," she said.

"I don't worry about her. Why should you?"

"But you are her mother!"

"I *was* her mother, you mean."

"Once a mother, always a mother."

Anna stared at her coolly. "Once a wife, always a wife," she said.

Aalia flushed. She stood up. "I must collect my things. I take the train at ten this evening," she said.

"So soon? Well, yes. You must have a number of things to see to."

Aalia offered her hand. Anna shook it. Then she was alone again in her room for an indeterminate amount of time, during which she consumed three more servings of sherry. She might have slept. When Olaf shook her shoulder gently, she realized her head was on her desk. For a moment she could neither remember the day nor the circumstance. She must have cried earlier, because there were dried tears on her face.

"You've heard," Olaf said. He sat in the chair Aalia had used earlier.

"Yes."

"I've made arrangements. We leave first thing tomorrow."

"You mean tonight."

Olaf's thick eyebrows, which were still blond, lifted in confusion.

"We cannot get a train to Huron before morning," he said.

"What are you talking about?"

"The telegram."

"What telegram?"

"My mother is ill."

Britta's cheerful round face came into Anna's mind. Neither she nor Olaf had seen her in all the years they'd been gone.

"But what of Aalia?" Anna asked.

"She is going to New York."

"And you will join her later, then."

"No."

"You . . ."

"It's been over for months, Anna. I thought you knew."

There'd been no sign. Or if there had been, Anna just hadn't seen. She had stopped looking.

"But, you love her," Anna said. She had never asked him that before.

"I thought so once."

Anna pressed her fingers to her forehead. Her shoulders were sore, and her mouth was dry. She hadn't eaten since breakfast. No wonder the sherry had hit her so hard.

"You turned me away, Anna. I was desperate," Olaf said.

Anna nodded. There was a great deal more to discuss, but she didn't have to ask if he still cared for her, because she could see in his eyes that he'd never stopped.

"You will come with me, to see my mother?" Olaf asked.

"Yes, yes, of course."

"Good."

Then he left her alone, drunk and bewildered, searching for a way forward.

Twenty-Six

The compartment was stuffy, the air stale with the smell of cigarette smoke from previous passengers. Anna fanned herself with a magazine she'd bought at the station, a woman's magazine with a long article about how to decorate on a budget and another on contributing to the overseas war effort by knitting socks and sweaters for refugees. Olaf sat opposite her, arms folded, eyes closed. The rocking motion had soothed him. He was anxious about his mother's condition, and also about seeing her again. His father had died two years before. He'd taken the news with little interest. He was closer to Britta. Anna knew that they had corresponded over the years, and although no visit was ever made, Britta had urged, sometimes begged, to see him. Now there was no choice.

Anna considered her years with Olaf. After the fire she withdrew because she didn't want to admit how much she'd profited by his crime. Then she simply forced herself to stop thinking about it. There were enough reasons from then on to lose touch—his drinking and the violence in the speakeasies, his taking to his bed and giving up on his furniture business. She told herself he had a weak character. Now she could no longer avoid asking herself if he'd failed because of her, because she'd withheld her love.

Olaf opened his eyes. He stretched out his long arms. He consulted his pocket watch. He was dressed in a linen suit that would be badly wrinkled by the time they arrived. He said he was hungry. Anna said they'd be serving dinner within the hour, and that if he couldn't wait, he could have one of the little cheese sandwiches she'd made that morning.

He took it and a bottle of lemonade they'd bought at the station along with the magazine. They also bought a set of lace handkerchiefs for Olaf's mother, both thinking it was probably a useless gift for a sick woman.

They had never shared many secrets, even in their first days. Expressing love wasn't the same. Love was a common ground, but not an inroad into another's soul. You had to be able to really talk to someone for that to happen. Love needed words, not just deeds. Maybe from words came trust, and from trust, redemption.

"I was hoping we could have a little talk," Anna said.

"About Aalia?"

"About the fire."

Olaf's eyes met hers.

"That's a peculiar subject at a time like this," he said.

"Perhaps. I'm still curious, though."

"Why? You weren't before."

That was true. He'd wanted to speak of it, more than once, and she always stopped him.

"No matter. Please," she said.

"What exactly do you want to know?"

"Who struck the match?"

"I did."

"Who poured the gasoline?"

"Josiah."

"You were equally guilty, then."

Olaf looked at Anna.

"If you like," he said.

"Were you surprised?"

"By what?"

"That you did it at all. That you were capable of it, I mean."

Olaf's eyes were impossible to read.

"I did things much worse than that in the war. And Mr. Yanaki was a criminal. That was illegal money he had. He didn't earn a cent of it. He was laundering it through his restaurant for some very dangerous people."

"I see."

"If you want me to feel guilty, after so many years—"

"No. I don't want that."

What did she want then? To know all about Aalia—as he rightly suspected—only she wasn't brave enough to put the questions to him. Clearly it took practice, this art of open conversation.

"Do you miss Lorraine?" she asked.

"Yes and no. It was so very hard to talk to her."

"Indeed."

Olaf had tried. He asked her about her dolls, which were all named for Biblical characters. He took her to his furniture store and showed her the pieces that were being refinished. Her writing desk had come from there, the one she later marred with crosses. Anna would watch Lorraine listen to him, her eyes always elsewhere, never on his face.

"After a while I gave up," he said.

"I did, too."

A father could be distant. That wasn't so unusual. But mothers were supposed to stay close. It was their duty.

"Anna, what's wrong?"

Anna lifted her face from her hands.

"I was just trying to imagine her, where she is now, and what she's doing," she said.

"She's with that scoundrel, Swinn."

"I know that, but how does she spend her days? Where does she live? All of that."

Again Olaf shrugged.

"I dreamed of her," Anna said.

"Oh?"

The landscape was vivid, cut with blocks of yellow and green. Lorraine walked past some trees where a number of people were eating at a table out in the open. The food on the table was from Anna's own hand—eggplant dishes, lamb, grape leaves—along with wine and sherry. The diners enjoyed their meal. Lorraine sang them a song in a clear, high voice. The diners clapped. Lorraine bowed. Her dress had a red velvet sash about the waist. It was a beautiful dress, and she was beautiful in it. *I go into the world through you*, Lorraine told the people at the table, but it was Anna's own words, saying them to Lorraine from the shelter of the trees.

"Dreams are funny things," Olaf said.

"We are still connected, she and I. Nothing can change that."

"It needn't be changed."

They went to dinner, and spoke of other things. Neither mentioned what seeing Huron again might be like. Both thought of Paul. Anna didn't know if he still lived there or had moved away. The college would know. She could make inquiries, if she cared to.

Over coffee, Anna took Olaf's hand.

"It will be all right, this visit," Anna said.

"I hope so."

"What ails her? I don't believe you said."

"She had a stroke."

"Oh, dear!"

"And she has not regained the use of her right side."

"My heart goes out to her."

"That's kind, Anna."

They returned to their compartment, the air still stuffy. They dozed, upright. They could have arranged for a sleeping compartment, but neither had the courage to mention it. They'd have had to share the bed. Anna wished then that they had. As the night deepened, and Olaf leaned into his corner, Anna went to him and sat close enough to feel his heat. She laid her head gently against his arm. How solid he felt! She slept and dreamed she was standing in a wide field of waving grass. Again Lorraine was present. Anna waved to her over the distance between them, and Lorraine waved back. *Can the lost ever be found?* Anna called. She heard only the wind in reply. Lorraine turned, walked away, and kept walking, although Anna yelled her name again and again. The call that they were arriving soon in Huron awakened her. Olaf had his arm around her. He was looking out the window. Anna sat up straight. She removed her hat, and took a compact from her purse. The compact was gold-filled, with small seed pearls on the lid. She stared at her reflection. She looked like a woman hollowed from the inside out. Her blouse was wrinkled. She hoped the hotel would provide her with an iron. Both of their outfits could do with a good, firm press.

The town had grown. The hotel was new, with a wide, carpeted staircase. The banister was highly polished and smooth under Anna's hand. Their room had a double bed. Olaf asked if she minded. She said she didn't. He suggested that they wash up and change and then look in on his mother.

The taxi drove them down streets that were once sparsely populated.

There were homes everywhere now, it seemed. With green lawns and flowers, which Anna didn't remember from before. Imagining the men and women living there, and tilling their little bit of soil made her restless. *So much work left to do!* As they entered her old neighborhood, Anna's stomach dropped. She passed the house she and Paul had shared. She strained to see the name on the mailbox before the taxi turned the corner. *Simonson*, it said.

The Lund home was little changed. After a closer look, it seemed that none of the furniture had been replaced, the rooms hadn't been repainted, even the curtains—heavy green velvet—were as Anna remembered. The hardware store the family had owned was sold when Olaf's father died. Evidently the proceeds hadn't been enough to allow Britta to improve her surroundings. Or perhaps she'd saved it all and forbid herself to spend a penny. Maybe there was a healthy amount in the bank downtown. Olaf, as her only living heir, would receive it. Anna chided herself for counting that imaginary sum.

They expected to find Pastor Mueller in the house. It was he who'd summoned them.

Mother ill, possibly dying. She is in the care of her congregation. Come with all Godspeed.

The woman at her bedside gave her name as Greta. She looked Anna sharply up and down. Anna was certain that her reputation among Britta's circle was poor. She was the older woman who'd run off with Britta's son and abandoned her husband. Anna didn't care. She went straight to the foot of the bed and stared at Britta. She was propped up on several pillows. The long braid she'd always had, and which Anna suddenly remembered with an odd pang, trailed over her shoulder and breast. On the table by the bed were a number of small bottles, containing medicine, no doubt. The room had a chemical smell overlain with something sickeningly sweet that Anna realized was coming from Britta herself. It was the same smell Miss Dormand had given off in her final days. It was the smell of death.

Olaf put his hands gently on Anna's shoulder, and moved her aside. He asked her and Greta to leave them alone for a moment. Anna and Greta withdrew into the kitchen, which was no longer the bright, clean, welcoming place it used to be. There were dirty dishes in the sink and a pot of cold food on the stove. Anna opened the icebox. A cooked ham sat on a nice china plate. How the hell was Britta supposed to eat ham, given the damage the stroke had done? Greta watched Anna move about the room. Anna ignored her. She removed her coat and hung it on the back of a chair. She found an apron from Britta's pantry, and set about washing the dishes. Every now and then she peered through the window over the sink into the kitchen of what had once been her home. A young woman was feeding a baby in a high chair.

"Would you like me to dry?" Greta asked. Her Scandinavian accent was strong.

"Up to you."

Greta removed dishes one by one and rubbed them vaguely with a blue towel she took from a drawer.

"It is good that you've come," she said.

"Yes."

"She is dying. We are sure of that now."

"We?"

"The doctor. All of us taking care of her. We had hoped for a recovery, but it is not God's will."

"No."

Greta gave Anna a hard look, but said nothing. They went on working in silence. When Anna had washed the last glass, she removed her apron and put it back in the pantry. She went into the living room. A stack of mail had been collected on the coffee table. She sat on the sofa and looked through the pieces one by one. They were mostly bills, some overdue by the yellow invoice visible through the transparent return address window.

Greta joined her.

"I must return to my home now. Inga will be along soon," she said. Anna was annoyed. She hadn't anticipated having to wait on anyone else's schedule. Greta went to the hall closet. She put on her hat, some ugly velvet thing with a fake flower.

"And there is something else you must know," Greta said.

"Yes?"

"She promised the church five hundred dollars upon her death."

"Did she, now?"

"She is a most generous woman."

"And you'd like me to make sure you get it."

Anna studied Greta as she fussed with her hat before the hall mirror. When it was properly placed, she turned one way, then another, to make sure. Her reflection was firm yet not unkind.

After she left Anna went to find Olaf to tell him what she'd learned.

Twenty-Seven

To save a man from the Devil, you had to let the Devil enter you first. You had to breathe the fire he exhaled, cover yourself in the ash he left in men's hearts. You had to taste evil in order to cast it out.

The first lesson was in liquor. Lorraine had smelled it many times on the breath of men in the street, but she'd never taken a single drop herself. Joseph Swinn told her to sit down, and clear her mind. They were alone in his tent, which he shared with no one. Lorraine shared hers with Nora, and another woman, Magda. Like Lorraine, both of them had come from families where religion was either ignored or seldom practiced. Lorraine believed this fact proved that the absence of faith made a terrible hunger in the soul.

Now, once again, she sought to feed that hunger, although she was frightened at the idea of drink. Joseph Swinn told her that she would lose herself in the liquid she was about to swallow. She was not to fight or resist. Her faith would be tested more than it ever had been before.

"Are you ready?" he asked her.

The air was still. Crickets chirped in the bushes and dry grass. On the table was a bottle of whiskey and two glasses. Joseph Swinn intended to join her in the testing of her faith.

"Yes."

Lorraine's hands were clammy. She felt unwell. The food there at the camp often disagreed with her. She would have preferred spending the evening on her cot, reading scripture and praying. She also needed to wash her underthings, and thought that she wouldn't be able to do so now. Nora had offered to do that for her. Lorraine declined. She didn't like Nora. Nora had presented her earlier that day with a bottle of aspirin. Everyone had to go through it, she said. Joseph Swinn referred to it as "baptism by sin." Nora called it "baptism by hangover." Nora never stilled her sharp tongue. Some of the things she said shocked Lorraine and made her wonder how Joseph Swinn allowed her to continue on with the camp. Then she learned that Nora came from money, which she shared liberally. She was paying for their food, bad as it was, and to keep the car running, as well as the cattle truck they all rode into town to preach at the fairgrounds in the evenings on Sunday and Wednesday. She paid for the notices that they diligently handed out around Coshocton, many of which were instantly crumpled and thrown to the ground. There was talk of building an actual church with dormitories where they could all live, and draw an ever-growing congregation. Of course, Nora's money would be very useful there, too.

Joseph Swinn bowed his head. Lorraine did, too.

"Oh Lord, I bring Your humble servant, Lorraine, so that she may prove herself worthy of Your great mission. Grant her the strength to take in the Devil, and to cast him back again into the flames of Hell. Amen."

He poured them both a drink. Lorraine lifted the glass to her nose. She wanted to gag. She sipped the whiskey. It burned her lips, tongue, and throat when she forced herself to swallow. She put the glass down. Joseph Swinn ordered her to continue.

"It's only one shot," he said. Lorraine didn't know what he meant. She went on sipping. After a moment the burn in the throat was less painful, and a slow warmth spread in her stomach. Joseph Swinn drank his right down. He grimaced a little, but not in a way that said he was in distress. He put his empty glass on the table, and wiped his mouth with the back of his hand.

Lorraine wasn't making much progress.

"Just take it all at once. Hold your nose if you have to," he said.

"My mother drinks sherry." Lorraine didn't know why she said that. Maybe the liquor was already taking effect, although she felt nothing, only the warmth that was now reaching her face.

She did as she was told. She wasn't able to take it all, and some spilled down her chin and then her throat. Joseph Swinn laughed, and passed her his handkerchief across the table. As she patted her skin, she picked up his smell on the cloth, sour and sharp. The bathing accommodations in the camp were rudimentary. There was one bathtub, a sign-up sheet, and a large pot with which to pour in heated water. Because the tub was deep, there was never more than two inches of water in the tub. Lorraine mentioned to Nora that bathing there come winter might be difficult. Nora said by the time winter came around, they'd be living in the Taj Mahal.

At least that's what Lorraine thought she'd said. She couldn't remember her exact words at the moment. Only the smirk Nora made. Nora wore a ring on her left hand, a large red stone. A ruby, she'd told Lorraine. *Pigeon-blood red.*

"Have you seen Nora's ring?" Lorraine asked Joseph Swinn.

"Naturally."

"Do you think it's beautiful?"

"Yes."

"I think it's vain."

"A thing can be both vain and beautiful at the same time. Especially a woman."

Lorraine wondered if Joseph Swinn was in love with Nora. Nora was pert and energetic. She laughed easily. She seemed to find many things funny. Or rather, she just didn't take anything too seriously. Even when Joseph Swinn preached, she was looking somewhere else. Sometimes she was clearly bored.

Joseph Swinn poured Lorraine another drink.

"No, thank you, I couldn't possibly," she said. That's what the lady lodgers in the boardinghouse sometimes said when pressed to take a second serving at table. Sometimes those same ladies would later be found in the kitchen, raiding the larder. Lorraine's mother had had to put a lock on the icebox. The ladies were just pretending not to be hungry so they wouldn't be seen as gluttonous. Gluttony was a sin, after all. One of the original seven.

Joseph Swinn smiled at Lorraine.

"You are a fascinating blend of so many things, my child," he said.

"I'm not your child."

"I speak for God, and are we not all his children?"

Lorraine nodded. She knew he was making fun of her, teasing her. She had been teased before, in school.

Lorraine, Lorraine, has no brain.

Lorraine lifted her glass and put it back on the table. She felt like laughing, but knew she mustn't. Joseph Swinn had another glass for himself that Lorraine didn't remember seeing him pour out. He drank it.

"I remember your family," Joseph Swinn said.

"Yes."

"They were well-bred. As are you."

"I don't know about that."

"They are people of means, to be sure."

Lorraine shrugged.

"And while they might not have the insight to appreciate your courage and bravery in taking on this arduous task, I have no doubt that their deep love for you would make them quite willing to help you, should you need it."

"What help do I need?"

Joseph Swinn leaned back. He was flushed. His eyes looked sick. A moment before they'd seemed normal, then Lorraine realized that she hadn't been looking into his eyes at all, only at the table, her own hands, and the drink that needed to get inside her.

"There are so many challenges to doing the Lord's work. The world of men turns on money. Though it is surely the root of all evil, it is necessary to accomplishing the task at hand."

Lorraine sipped her drink. It was easier now.

"What about Nora?" she asked.

"Nora may be leaving us soon."

"Oh? Why?"

"Her commitment has wavered."

"Did she tell you so?"

"It came to me in a dream."

As Lorraine forced herself to drink down her second glass, Joseph Swinn spoke more of his dreams. Some, of course, were the ordinary nonsense every man entertains in sleep. But others were messages from above, some clear, some more difficult to decipher. Most recently he'd walked the length of a wide field, eyes on the ground, looking for a box with a golden lid. The box held a truth he needed, an answer to a question he hadn't yet asked. He experienced a growing sense of unease. He thought he might be looking in the wrong place.

"What do you think it means?" Lorraine asked.

"That I believe I am capable of being led astray."

Lorraine felt the liquor. It made her both strong and light, like a beautiful voice raised in song, or a river rushing over rocks.

Joseph Swinn's expression was strange.

"What is it?" Lorraine asked.

"I'm thinking of my wife."

"Oh."

"You didn't know I was married."

"No."

"Are you unhappy?"

Lorraine shook her head. She wasn't anything, just then.

Joseph Swinn said his wife was a decent, plain woman, but her heart couldn't hold God's love. She fretted over daily life. She lacked confidence in good outcomes. Her outlook was often negative.

"Sounds like my mother," Lorraine said.

"Your mother has no faith."

"She's a Catholic. *Was* a Catholic, I mean."

"Ah. It's often the papist who is first to depart God's cause."

Joseph Swinn went on about his wife. She didn't want to live in the camp. Her duty was to stay home, she said. And to raise their children.

"You have children?" Lorraine asked.

"Four."

"Oh."

"You sound surprised."

"It's just . . . well, it's hard to imagine . . ."

"Me, in the act of procreation?"

She met his eyes. They were hungry and flat like an animal's, like the stray cat that came around her home in Chicago and howled for a bowl of milk.

"I may be God's servant, but I'm also a man," Joseph Swinn said.

The room tilted. Lorraine laughed. She stood up. The tilting worsened.

"Oh," she said. She went on laughing. Joseph Swinn laughed, too.

"You feel him, don't you? You feel the Devil now," he said.

"I feel something."

"Welcome, Devil!" Joseph Swinn slapped the rough surface of the table. The glasses jumped. Hers fell over. Joseph Swinn got to his feet. She couldn't tell if he wavered or not.

"Come," he said. She followed him out of the tent. The air felt cold against the flush of her skin. He led her down the path toward the river. She hoped he didn't think she needed to be baptized again. The moon was out. She hadn't realized it was full, then she wondered if he'd waited until this particular night for her trial. Didn't Satanists worship the moon?

"Joseph—"

"Quiet. We're almost there."

A moment later he stopped at a clearing. The river carried the moonlight in ripples of silver. There was a voice coming from the camp behind them. Magda was giving orders to Cedrick. At sixteen, he was only a year younger than Lorraine. There were no other teenagers in the camp. It could have been a bond between them and wasn't. Lorraine heard random words—*coffee pot* and *motor oil* and *shampoo*. She giggled. Maybe Cedrick was to put motor oil in the coffee pot. Or add shampoo in the truck instead of motor oil. The ground lurched under her. Joseph Swinn had her around the waist.

"Now you must declare that the Devil has no hold on you," he said. His face was damp with sweat. She shivered. Her dress was thin and not new. Nora got it for her in town, she didn't say where. Probably from some church or other giving away the clothes of someone who'd recently died.

"Declare," Joseph Swinn said.

"I declare."

"More."

"More what?"

When she felt his mouth on hers, her second lesson in Devil-casting began.

Twenty-Eight

It had been clear from the outset that Britta would not recover, yet Olaf continued to believe in the possibility for many days, until Anna offered one of her stern rebukes.

Face facts!

She wanted to get back to Chicago and go on with her life. The little time they'd had there in Huron had filled her with a great restlessness. First, it had been necessary for them to leave the hotel and move into Britta's house after Britta's church women informed them that they would no longer be able to tend to her.

"It is best. She needs the comfort of her own kin at a time like this," that unctuous ass, Greta, had said. Anna scoffed. They only wanted to be let off the hook. So much for their godly goodwill. A nurse had been employed for bathing and dealing with bedpans. Her name was Martha. She was blunt, efficient, and did not sleep over.

Next, Anna went to the college to ask about Paul, and learned that he'd taken a teaching job back in Switzerland. The woman who gave her the news hinted that his departure had not been entirely amicable. *Had a bit of trouble with the department chair*, she said. Anna asked if that was still Professor Plake. Indeed it was.

Anna paid him a visit. He said he remembered her, though she could tell from the vagueness in his eyes that he didn't. She barely remembered him, though as she sat for a moment, his younger self returned to her. Now he was elderly and distinguished, without the buoyant zeal he'd once possessed. He was candid about Paul's bad luck. He'd gotten involved with a student, and the results were typical. Accusations, threats, tears.

"His wife had left him, you see," Professor Plake said.

"His second wife, you mean. She was a student, also, I believe."

"Yes."

"And when was that?"

"Oh, years ago now. I don't exactly remember."

The professor's secretary brought in a tray with tea. She set it on the professor's untidy desk.

"Of course, that was devastating for him. Though, at the time, I couldn't help thinking that it was for the best," Professor Plake said.

"How so?"

"The wife was odd. Pleasant enough, I suppose. But there was something off. As if she wasn't really there."

"I see."

Professor Plake turned and looked at the tray of tea things. Then he ignored it. Anna was glad. She didn't want to be offered anything.

"I was sorry to see him go. He was more than a colleague. I liked to think he was my friend. And I, his. I was greatly distressed by his parting words."

"Which were?"

"That I was anti-Semitic."

"Why did he say that?"

"Because I told him once that he was overly sensitive about his faith."

"After he admitted to which faith he had."

Professor Plake removed his glasses and polished them with the end of his tie.

"Indeed. He comes to us as a Christian, then years later he says, quite casually, that his wife is converting to Judaism for his sake."

"You must have been taken aback."

"Not really. We all knew he was Jewish."

"How?"

Professor Plake shrugged.

"Mannerisms. Attitude. His competitive nature in particular," he said.

Anna snorted. "No wonder he thought you were anti-Semitic."

"I was merely being observant. I knew a number of Jews when I lived in New York. They have their own ways, just as any group of people does."

Professor Plake put his glasses back on. He looked around the room, as if surprised by the clarity of what he now saw.

Anna squeezed the gloves she'd taken off and put in her lap. Through the tall, dusty window of the professor's office she could see the small quadrangle in the center of the campus. Class must have just let out. There were students everywhere, walking alone or in small groups. They looked young yet not carefree. The world weighed upon them. The future was eclipsed. Only the promise of war could be counted on.

She became aware of Professor Plake studying her.

"I hope I haven't upset you with my candor," he said.

"Not at all."

"Then you won't mind my saying how odd I find it that an ex-wife would be so curious about the fate of her ex-husband."

Anna said she really must be going. Professor Plake stood, and shook her hand.

"Lovely to see you again," he said.

It was a short walk back. The air was full of early fall, and Anna thought her coat was too heavy. She stopped and unbuttoned it, then took it off and carried it over her arm.

At the house, Olaf was running the vacuum cleaner around the living room. Anna motioned for him to turn it off.

"I was going to do that this afternoon," she said.

"I just felt like doing something."

He'd worked up a sweat. His expression was fierce. Anna saw then how much watching his mother suffer upset him.

"Where's Martha?"

"The druggist's."

"Is your mother asleep?" Anna asked.

"Yes."

"I don't see how, with that racket you're making."

Anna nudged open Britta's door. She was now on the main floor, in what used to be Lars' office. Wrestling the double bed had been impossible. They'd had to disassemble it, while Britta lay on the couch. Olaf had carried her down. Later he said it was the oddest thing, carrying his mother like that in his arms.

Because she used to carry me, he said, when Anna delved a little deeper.

Britta lay as she always did, on her back, her head to one side. She was getting weaker every day. The doctor, an energetic young man, came by each morning to examine her. He'd suggested moving her to the hospital, but Olaf wouldn't hear of it. His mother was going to die right there, in the same bed he'd been born in.

Britta opened her eyes slowly. They took a moment to find Anna's face. She seemed not to recognize her. Then Britta lifted her good hand and beckoned. Anna sat in the chair by the bed.

"I want to see Pastor Mueller," Britta said. Anna could hardly make out her words, the slurring was so bad.

"All right. I will telephone him." The pastor had come by only once since Anna and Olaf had taken up residence. Anna feared that he might remember her from all those years ago when Paul demanded that she go with him to church. He didn't seem to. Instead, he told her how well she was serving God by being present for Britta in her time of need.

"No, don't do that, just tell him . . . tell him . . ."

Britta's chest rose and fell, lifting the thin fabric of her nightgown.

"Yes?"

"He won't get a penny."

"You've changed your mind?"

"Privilege of a dying woman."

"May I ask why?"

"Because he . . . he's . . ."

Somewhere behind the house a dog barked frantically. Anna had heard it over the last several days. She thought it must have been abandoned, and was calling for help. Britta turned her head a little in the direction of the noise.

"When the dog barks, the soul departs," she said.

"Don't be silly."

Britta managed a small smile.

"Old Swedish folktale," she said.

"Nonsense."

"Maybe. Maybe not."

Then Britta was asleep again.

Over dinner in the kitchen, Anna told Olaf what Britta had said.

"Perhaps he pressured her into agreeing," he said.

"Preying on a sick woman."

"And one with so little."

"Oh?"

"Only about eight hundred dollars, according to the bank."

They sat together, listening to the wind and the occasional bark of the desperate dog. It was a large animal, judging by the depth of his voice.

"What about the house?" Anna asked.

"She put it in my name after my father died. Wise, under the circumstances. They might have tried to coax that out of her, too. Anyway, I spoke to someone at the assessor's office. They list its value at around thirty-five hundred dollars."

"You will sell it."

"Of course. Unless you want us return here and take up residence."

"Would you like that?"

"I would hate it."

"Settled, then."

Anna washed the dishes. The young woman occupying her former home was doing the same. Olaf tried to get Britta to eat some soup. She wouldn't.

"That makes a whole day without food," he said when he returned from her room.

"It won't be long now."

He sat. The wind rose.

"I wonder if a stroke affects the mind," Olaf said.

"It affects the brain. Is that what you mean?"

"No. The mind. The memory."

"Any bad illness can do that."

Anna's sister had written pages about the strange things their mother said while she was dying, conversations with people who never existed, wild flights of fancy. One in particular Anna remembered.

Some day, when men travel the stars, they will find blood.

Anna hoped that when her own time came, she would be completely rational.

"She asked how the grandchildren were," Olaf said.

"Whose?"

"Ours, of course."

"Poor thing."

"I said we had only a daughter."

"Well, then."

"She was vehement."

"Wishful thinking on her part."

"Maybe."

That night Olaf slept on the couch again, so he could be near his mother. He slept hard, with dreams unrecalled, until Anna shook him awake just before dawn to say that Britta was dead.

Twenty-Nine

The donation to the church hadn't been made, per Britta's express wishes. Even so, the funeral had been well attended by Britta's congregation. Anna thought then that their concern was genuine, not mercenary. She and Olaf returned to Chicago in an optimistic frame of mind. They'd agreed to reconcile. At the moment, Olaf was resting in their bedroom. Anna was in her office. She opened the letter from Lorraine, which had arrived in her absence.

I speak only the Lord's command, Lorraine had written. Then she asked for one hundred dollars.

"Little brat," Anna said.

Soon, though, she sought a softer turn of heart and words that wouldn't wound.

> *Dearest Lorraine,*
> *How pleased I was to hear from you!*

Anna put down her pen and began again, on a fresh sheet of her engraved stationery.

> *Lorraine,*
> *It occurs to me that you know little of my experience with faith, and*
> *I thought perhaps now was the time for me to share with you what*
> *I can only call an "up-and-down" journey.*

Anna tore up that piece of paper, and pulled out another fresh sheet.

I was raised a Catholic. I went to a parochial school in Constantinople and was taught by nuns. They were both loving and cruel. I was a small child, and often bullied. Some stood up for me, others said God was testing me, and that I would be made stronger. I stopped believing in the power of God when I saw the suffering of people every single day. We are endowed with free will, or so the teaching says, but those who suffer do not have the privilege of exercising their free will. And if their suffering is a call to action on the part of the rest of us, a chance to find "the better angels of our nature"—
she knew Lorraine wouldn't recognize these words as belonging to Abraham Lincoln, and considered striking the quotation marks—*then it seems to be that God is guilty of grave inefficiency.*

The face of Sister Sylvia came back to her for the first time in over forty years. Sister Sylvia had been born in England, the daughter of an investment banker. She knew comfort and luxury. At seventeen, she married a man in the British Army. She was pregnant. Her father bought her new husband's commission, and they went out to India. The travel was too much, and she miscarried. Within only a few months, her husband died of fever. Sister Sylvia was commanded by her father to return to England at once. She got as far as Constantinople before realizing that what awaited her in the green hills of Devonshire was a life she despised. She came to the door of the convent, and threw herself on the mercy of the sisters.

Sister Sylvia was fervent in her devotion to God. She was also an expert in human nature. No one could put anything over on her. No one could maintain a false innocence under the intensity of her gaze. She liked to remind her students that she was well versed in the ways of the world, and that they would do well to heed her words, which were simply to trust God.

Sister Sylvia loved beauty in all its forms, for beauty was the surest sign of God's hand. Yet ugliness, too, had the power to elicit a deep love of God. One must revel in all aspects of the creation, she said, in order to find one's way.

Anna loved Sister Sylvia, and Sister Sylvia loved her. She was murdered by the Turks for refusing to leave the convent walls. Anna's cynicism about God began with her death. Were she there, in her sunlight office, perched in the upholstered chair opposite the desk, her blue eyes twinkling, she'd say that Anna must travel any road, however twisted or treacherous, to allow God's grace once more into her heart.

To Anna's lingering rage over the Sister's fate the Sister would say, *Death is nothing. Only life.*

For as much as Sister Sylvia abided by Church doctrine that salvation can be found in death alone, she worshiped the hard, filthy, gorgeous world she stood in.

Anna thought of writing all that out to Lorraine. She didn't. She wrapped a five-dollar bill in a blank sheet of stationery, which Freddie found years later in a beautiful alabaster box in Holly's home, where she'd gone the day after Holly's stroke.

Part Three

Thirty
1975

The grocery store where Freddie worked was in a part of town Officer Ken Chase routinely patrolled. He went in one day to buy a roll of paper towel. He explained that someone he arrested that morning had been sick in the back of his cruiser. Freddie said he should buy some bleach, that paper towel alone would be worthless. He did as she suggested. He came back the next day for milk and eggs. After that it was for hamburger buns.

"I'm having a cookout. Would you like to come?" he asked. Freddie fascinated him. Her hands were big and strong, although she was slightly built. She was tough-talking and blunt, but there was something frail, almost childlike, behind the words that he wanted to know more about.

Freddie declined. She said he could save himself a lot of unnecessary trips by making a more complete shopping list. He didn't come back for several weeks. When he did, he asked her out again. She agreed. It was summer, and they were having sandwiches overlooking the falls.

"Tell me all about yourself," he said.

"Nothing to tell."

At that point, he became direct in his questions. He wanted to know how old she was (twenty-five and a half), if she had a steady (she didn't), if she lived alone (she lived with her sister). The mention of Holly led him to ask about her childhood.

"What was it like, growing up?"

Freddie stared at him. She had never been asked that, and had no idea how to answer. That he wasn't in uniform unnerved her, as if she wasn't quite sure who he was without the badge and holster.

"Come on, tell me anything. A formative experience," Ken said.

He seemed like a nice person. Anything she shared might drive him away, though. *Better to find out now*, she thought.

Just that morning, Holly, who still struggled with her name, had heard from Lorraine in a brief, unexpected phone call.

I pray for you all the time, was all Lorraine said. She didn't ask to speak to Freddie. Holly had been baffled, then uneasy. Freddie tried to assure her by reminding her that their mother was always unpredictable. Holly went off to her job at the bank a bit more relaxed. Freddie knew how to prop her up. Thinking of that, she was drawn back in time to the story she then gave Ken.

When she was ten and Holly was six, Holly developed a fever. The rustic Baptist camp outside of Coshocton where they lived didn't have a thermometer or baby aspirin, or hot water bottles. The camp members were stoic about their miseries, except for their leader, Joseph Swinn, who complained of headaches when the Lord's voice had fallen silent in his ears.

"You mean, like revival meetings, and all that?" Ken asked.

"Yes."

"I'm sorry, go on."

Holly lay on her cot in their family tent, shivering and calling for her mother, Lorraine. Lorraine had been away for nine days by then, on her route through rural Ohio with Joseph Swinn. The girls had not gone with her, as they typically did. Freddie didn't remember exactly why. In Swinn's absence, the camp was under the jurisdiction of his assistant, Nora, who was unmoved by Freddie's concern. She told Freddie to find a washrag, wet it, and dab Holly's forehead.

"Sounds like a real Florence Nightingale," Ken said. Freddie didn't know who that was, nor did she ask.

All of Freddie's dabbing did nothing. Holly needed help going to the outhouse; she refused to eat, or even to sip water. That first night, Freddie climbed into her cot with her to keep her warm. In the morning, she was no better. Freddie shook Nora awake. Nora asked her what the hell was the matter. Holly needed a doctor, Freddie said. She must be taken into town at once and seen right away. Nora sat up. Her head sat heavily on her neck in a way Freddie had come to recognize. Nora had had too much to drink the night before. While she tried to comfort Holly, there'd been the sound of music playing, laughing, even a bottle breaking in the building that housed the kitchen and two wringer-style machines.

Nora considered the situation. It would do no good to have Holly become so ill that she'd land in the hospital. Hospitals were expensive, and while she knew perfectly well that Joseph Swinn had a lot more money that he pretended to have, most of it was kept in a safe-deposit box in Coshocton, and that she herself could pay the bill, but the cost would be a topic of concern and criticism. Then, there was also the chance that Holly could die. That would be even worse. They could bury her there, on the land that Nora owned (the other camp members, including Lorraine, thought it was the property of the First Baptist Church of Lexington, Kentucky, Joseph Swinn's hometown) but someone might say something inadvertently during a revival meeting, or in town, anywhere, and then the police would be all over the place like white on rice. So Nora got unsteadily to her feet, took three aspirin from a bottle she kept in her locked makeup case after she'd ordered Freddie to wait for her outside, dressed, belted down a cup of cold black coffee, and went to Freddie's tent.

At that point in the story, Freddie paused. She looked straight at Ken.

"I bet you think I'm making this up, don't you?" she asked.

"Why do you say that?"

"It must sound weird, that's all."

It did sound weird, very weird, in fact. He wasn't about to say so, though.

"Not compared to some of the stories I've been told. Remember, honey, I'm a cop," he said.

She wasn't sure what to make of the term "honey." She'd never been addressed that way before.

Nora drove them in her car—her private, personal car that she didn't use for camp business. Freddie remembered the huge tailfins, the leather seats, and the push-button console. She was ordered to sit in the backseat with Holly, which required shoving the front passenger seat forward because the car had only two doors. Nora said that if Holly got sick in the back of her car there'd be hell to pay.

The doctor's office was on the first floor of his home. The smell of fried chicken came from somewhere in back, where the fat black woman who'd opened the door had gone once they were inside. Nora had carried Holly. Her face showed the strain and dislike of having her so close. She sat in a chair with Holly slumped in her lap, while Freddie looked the place over. There were plants in copper pots on stands with curved legs. The rugs were black and red and white, with fringe. The dining room across the front hall had a glass chandelier with fake candles in it. Or maybe the candles had been real—it was hard to tell. Finally, the doctor came through a door and told Nora to bring Holly inside. Freddie was told to wait. Freddie wanted to go, too, but the doctor's nurse, a stout woman with gray hair and a thin black mustache on her upper lip, said she had to take some information from her.

You're old enough to do that, aren't you? the nurse asked, not very nicely.

I'll tell you what you need to know, Nora said, but the doctor, assuming Nora was their mother, said she'd best stay with Holly during the examination.

The nurse wanted to know Holly's name.

Hope, Freddie said. That's when Freddie explained to Ken that they'd both changed their names. He wanted to ask why, but didn't.

First and last name, the nurse said.

Hope Full.

The nurse stared at Freddie

And your name? the nurse asked.

Faith Full.

Ken laughed. "That's quite a sense of humor for a little girl," he said.

"I wasn't trying to be funny. Our mother always said that was our last name."

"You're kidding."

Freddie shook her head.

"What last name did she go by?" he asked.

"Lund."

The nurse asked for an address. Freddie didn't know what to say. She never realized it was possible to have an actual address. Any mail was picked up once a week from a post office box in town. She didn't even know the name of the long, winding road the camp was set back from. But she didn't want to look stupid.

Ken nodded. He took her hand, and she pulled it back.

We live at 123 Smith Street, Freddie told the nurse.

Is that here in Coshocton?

Oh yes. Not far from here, in fact.

The nurse told Freddie she could go in and be with her mother and sister, if she wanted to. The doctor was bending over Holly, listening to her breathe with a black thing that came out of his ears.

"You mean a stethoscope," Ken said.

"I guess."

The doctor said Holly probably had polio. Freddie had never heard of it before, but Nora certainly had. She paced about the small room. She asked if there was a telephone she might use, then changed her mind. She didn't want to needlessly alarm anyone. The doctor asked if either Nora or Freddie had had the vaccine. Neither had. He made them each eat a sugar cube with a pink dot on it, and said they might already have been infected, which would render the vaccine useless. Then he said he would have to contact the Health Department.

Oh, no you don't, Nora said. He insisted. Nora took a wad of cash out of her pocket, put it on the desk in the examining room, and said she was giving her personal guarantee that everyone in the camp would be examined and vaccinated, but he needed to keep this just between them.

Will she be all right? Freddie asked.

When the fever breaks, if there is no paralysis, then yes, the doctor said.

What's paralysis?

When you can't move something. Legs, arms. See what I mean?

The doctor gave Freddie a lollipop. He gave Nora a prescription for an elixir to bring down Holly's fever.

With Holly again in the backseat, but with Freddie now up front, Nora realized that taking them back to the camp would be impossible, so she found a motel room with a kitchen, bought a lot of food, left a few dollars with Freddie, and told her to stay put until Holly was better.

I'll be back in five days, Nora said.

When's my mother coming home? Freddie asked. Nora didn't know. Probably not for another week or two.

The sunny day Freddie and Ken had been enjoying gave way to a bank of thunderclouds. The air cooled quickly, and Ken offered to drive Freddie home. On the way he asked if everything had turned out all right.

"Sure. She recovered just fine. I don't think she even had polio. That doctor was probably just trying to scare us," she said.

In truth Holly had lost some sensation in one leg—her right—though she was able to use it reasonably well. She limped slightly. When people asked why, she said she'd fallen off a horse. Other times she said it was a skiing accident, a car crash, and once, when she was tipsy, a run-in with the law.

Had to jump out a window!

Ken asked if Freddie's mother ever learned the truth about Holly's illness.

"No. Nora made us promise not to tell."

Lorraine had seen the limp, though. Everyone did. *Stop trying to get attention*, Lorraine hissed, to which poor Holly would say, *I can't help it, I can't help it!* Holly would sometimes slap her bad leg.

"And no one else at your camp got sick?" Ken asked.

"No."

❧

When they arrived at Freddie's home, and she got out of the car, she assumed she'd never see Ken again after sharing a story like that. But he was back the next day. From then on he "stuck to her like glue," Holly said. In fact, it was Ken's devotion to Freddie that made Holly restless and hungry for a life and love of her own. She was sure she wouldn't find it there, in Sioux Falls, so she moved away to Minneapolis. She knew how to type and take shorthand. The first job she got was in the same accounting firm where Jack worked, the one he now owned. Freddie went straight there from the airport. She still didn't know the name of the hospital, and Jack wasn't answering his cell phone. She assumed— hoped—that Holly's condition hadn't worsened, since he hadn't called her again. The receptionist looked at Freddie coldly. She'd been crying. Her sorrow couldn't be about Holly, Freddie was certain. Probably Jack had said he couldn't be on tap as much just then, because his wife was ill. Freddie made her look up the directions on her computer and print them off. She didn't know Minneapolis very well, and didn't want to get lost. An hour and twenty minutes later, after taking the wrong exit despite the paper taped to her dashboard, finally figuring out how to enter the huge parking garage, then forgetting what floor she parked on and going back to double-check, she was at the foot of Holly's bed, watching her sleep.

Thirty-One

1961

The year after Holly (Hope) got sick, another poor, desperate woman wandered into the camp. She was fed, given a Bible and a place to sleep. Freddie—Faith—performed those chores, and the woman soon became fond of her. One day, she asked Faith where her father was. Faith said what Lorraine told her, that her father died in the war. The woman, Amanda Littleton, didn't press Faith for more information. She didn't want to be a nuisance.

But then something changed inside Amanda Littleton. The despair that led her to follow Lorraine's fiery words went away. In its place came a quiet rage. Amanda Littleton took a deep dislike to Lorraine for many reasons. She knew she was sleeping with Joseph Swinn, which struck her as highly immoral for two people who claimed to have a direct line to God. Then there was the way both of them, Lorraine in particular, wheedled money from people who could ill afford to give it away. Lastly, there was Lorraine's treatment of Faith.

Amanda Littleton devised a plan to steal Faith away. She would feign a toothache, and beg that Faith be allowed to go with her to the dentist in town. From there, it was simple. They would go to Chicago, where Faith said her grandparents lived.

When Amanda Littleton revealed the true reason for their departure from the camp, Faith would have none of it. She cried and carried on, and pulled herself free from Amanda Littleton's surprisingly strong grasp. She ran through the streets of Coshocton, weeping and hysterical, until someone brought her into a drugstore and helped her wash her face. She said she belonged to Joseph Swinn. Most people knew of Joseph Swinn's camp and his changing group of followers. They were frowned upon. Faith and Hope were the only children living there, and their presence hadn't really been known before Faith came lurching down the sidewalk screaming for her mother. She was asked if the camp had a telephone. She said it did, in the kitchen, where Nora and Magda used it to order groceries and other necessities. Then she was asked if she wanted to call home. Faith had no idea how to. *You don't know how to use a telephone?* Two police officers and a social worker drove Faith to the camp to interview both Lorraine and Joseph Swinn in Joseph Swinn's office—a small section behind a curtain at the back of his own tent. Faith told the social worker she had to go to the outhouse, then listened unobserved through the dingy gray canvas.

Lorraine described Faith as disturbed and simpleminded, unable to keep up in school. Of Hope she said nothing. Nora had taken Hope off the property, Faith later learned, so that if the authorities decided to take custody of her, they couldn't take Hope, too. As Lorraine talked, with the ring of deep compassion and grief that a struggling mother feels, Faith wanted to pull the whole tent down on everyone inside. She wasn't disturbed and she wasn't simpleminded. Though she was well acquainted with her mother's cruelty—the incident with the kitten Marigold never forgotten—that was the first time she realized her mother was also a liar.

Whatever Lorraine said satisfied the police and the social worker, though she was warned that Faith must attend school, and that her enrollment must be verified. That same night, Lorraine and Joseph Swinn didn't preach, but sat alone and spoke in voices that were often raised. It was decided that Lorraine should leave camp with both children and once more strike out on her own. Unlike the time before, Lorraine was leaving under favorable circumstances. The first time, she ran off because of something she discovered about Joseph Swinn. Faith remembered her crying that the Devil can keep the truth hidden only so long before the angels pull it into the light. What this truth was, Faith didn't know, but later she suspected it was something ordinary, such as his involvement with any of the women who came through the camp. Now Lorraine would go and offer spiritual comfort to young women who found themselves victims of misfortune, or so the story went to the congregation after prayers the following morning.

Into Your hands I place our dear sister, whose works will carry Your word to the end of Your kingdom!

Lorraine said she needed to put Ohio behind her, so they headed west. Lorraine's zeal faded as the miles passed. The old Chevrolet Joseph Swinn had lent her—by then the camp had a number of vehicles—became too much for her to manage through her bitter tears, so she pulled over, ordered Faith behind the wheel, and got into the backseat with Hope, where she fell fast asleep. Faith knew how to drive. One of the men at the camp, Cedrick, the mechanic and carpenter, had taught her. The thing was not to alert the police, so she had to drive well, preferably at night, when it would be that much harder to guess her young age from just a passing glance. They ate the food Lorraine had packed, which by then was getting stale and hard. When they got thirsty, they went to a service station and drank from the hose used to top off radiator tanks. Even after Lorraine woke up, Faith went on driving. She prayed.

Deliver us, oh Lord. Guide my weak hand. Fill my hollow heart.

Her own words. Never her mother's, nor Joseph Swinn's. Nor the Bible's, not that she could say for sure, since she'd never read a single verse. She couldn't read. Lorraine refused to let her learn.

Everything you will ever know, you will know from me.

The trees thinned, the sky widened. Not at all like Ohio, with its close rivers and streams, all those thick, drifting clouds. Here there was no place to hide. One had to stand, unabashed, in the world that He had made.

Exhausted, Faith pulled the huge car to the shoulder and turned off the engine. Hope had been awake for hours, combing the hair of her rag doll. Lorraine was up, too, staring into the empty darkness before her. Lorraine instructed her to make for the lights in the distance. That's how they came to Sioux Falls.

Once there, Lorraine pulled even further away. Money came from Joseph Swinn, so no job was required, but the need to preach and heal made her restless. Faith and Hope were often alone. Faith found the elementary school, and started showing up every day. They accepted her easily. When it was pointed out that her reading skill was far below grade level—nonexistent, in fact—Faith said she'd suffered a long and difficult illness in her younger years that kept her from the classroom. She marveled at her ability to lie. Lorraine had taught her well.

Thirty-Two

The girls shared a sagging double bed in a small room at the back of the house. Lorraine had the room next door. When sleep wouldn't come, she sat in the kitchen, head in her hands, at a wooden table with three good legs and a stack of bricks where the fourth had been.

Her life was a lot like that table, she thought. Without Joseph Swinn, the three of them had nothing to keep them steady and strong. They wobbled. They lacked integrity. In time they would crumble and fall.

Her faith in God must become that missing leg, and she prayed daily for strength. So far, it hadn't come. She was thirty-nine years old. She had been with Joseph Swinn for twenty-two of those years, and now she was alone. He sent money every week. It arrived in a plain white envelope, wrapped in a blank piece of paper. The paper contained no note, nothing personal to prove that his hand had ever held it. Her address was in Nora's writing. The cash was surely from the metal box under Nora's bed to which she had the only key.

Nora was an odd case. Many times Lorraine found herself wondering how God had brought her to Joseph Swinn. Nora didn't have a faithful bone in her body, yet she remained with the group year after year. Joseph Swinn once told Lorraine that Nora was one of those necessary souls that God steers towards a higher end. "Shuttered," was the word he used, because Nora was like a shuttered window that didn't allow the light of God to shine through. Yet by virtue of her own experience, which was purely of this world, she was an instrument of doing good. Her family had shown her coldness and withheld its love from her. She had sought a community, a place to belong. She needed independence, yet wanted to be needed. That she was wealthy solved this particular problem for her. Her father made a fortune in real estate during the Depression, buying foreclosed homes for very little money, holding on to them, then selling them at just above market value to people who couldn't get a mortgage from a regular bank. Every now and then the bare-bones life she led with Swinn got to be too much, and she took herself on a vacation. Europe. Palm Springs. Miami. She stayed in five-star hotels and bought expensive clothes, which she later gave away to the many women who came through the camp, donated to a church, or sold through a secondhand store, turning the money over to Joseph Swinn.

Lorraine gradually came to accept Nora, though she never liked her. Nora was too far on the outside. She couldn't be brought in.

One evening, a handful of ragged people made their way to the camp to hear Joseph Swinn preach. He said they were God's creation, and thus sacred, and that whatever torment they endured from Him was a building block of glory and salvation. He told them not to fear.

He died for your sins. Now you must live for faith, and only for faith!

Their plain faces were graced by the electric light Nora's money bought. The light was a subject of considerable conversation between Nora and Joseph Swinn. He wanted it to be simple, like one you'd find hanging in a country school. Nora said it must be fancy, with carved glass, so that his followers could bow their heads and pray, then open their eyes to something wondrous. A suggestion of Heaven, and the world to come, and all the while standing firmly on the rough wooden planking of Joseph Swinn's tent. For that's how she perceived faith. Something better that lay ahead, not necessarily in the future, or after one died, but something that came about from a simple change of heart.

During Joseph Swinn's sermon that evening, Nora stood by the open canvas and drank from a flask. She was brazen. Then, as listeners were leaving, Nora pressed a fifty-cent piece into each grimy palm.

When they were alone, Lorraine asked, *Why do you even stay?*

Nora said, *Same as you. 'Cause I believe.*

You do not believe.

I believe in Swinn. He may be a weak, needy, son of a bitch, but his motives are genuine.

Lorraine was angry, but she felt the truth of Nora's words. Recalling them now, as her girls slept, Lorraine knew that Joseph Swinn was strong because he had no doubt in his heart.

Lorraine has nothing but doubt. She could not speak to God without using Swinn's voice. God took her away from Swinn so she could find her own voice.

At first light one morning she bathed and dressed. The suit she wore was one of Nora's. It was too tight across the shoulders. The hem had been lowered until there was almost nothing left of it, so that in places the tacking Lorraine had sewn herself came loose, and threads hung down like the frail tendrils of an underwater plant.

She made for the address Joseph Swinn had written out for her. She stopped at one service station, then another several blocks away, to ask directions. At a third a young man in a filthy jumpsuit suggested that she buy a city map.

"It's only a quarter. Handy thing to have in your glove box," he said.

Lorraine shook her head, rolled up her window, and drove away. When she reached her destination, she turned off the car's motor and sat looking at the small, plain house on an equally plain tree-lined street. She checked the address in Joseph Swinn's letter against the house numbers painted on the curb. She left the car and went up the walk. Her first knock was unanswered. She knocked again. From inside the house there was the sound of a door closing, followed by the approach of slow, steady footsteps. The man who opened the door to her was a good six inches shorter than she. Though his face was youthful, he had white hair that he must have just combed, because the grooves left by the teeth were firm and straight. His red bow tie was crooked. The buttons down the front of his plain shirt were unevenly spaced, as if the person who'd sewn them on wasn't used to handling a needle and thread.

"Yes?" the man said. Lorraine handed him the letter. The man removed a pair of gold-rimmed eyeglasses from the breast pocket of his shirt. He unfolded the letter, and read the short paragraph, which introduced Lorraine and referred to her a "child with true calling." The man was Pastor Banner, and he preached at the Baptist Church on Scarsdale Road, four miles from the south edge of Sioux Falls.

Pastor Banner invited Lorraine to step inside. As she settled herself on the bumpy, worn couch in his living room, he sized her up. She took few pains with her appearance. Her white gloves were soiled. So were her white high-heeled shoes. There was a long run in one stocking. Her purse strap was broken. Her face was unusual, he thought. The cheekbones were prominent and high. A Middle Eastern face. She could have been Jewish, but that struck him as unlikely. A Jew becoming a Baptist? But then, who knew?

"And how is Joseph fairing?" Pastor Banner asked.

"The Lord keeps him quite well."

"He is a man of great gifts."

Pastor Banner knew Swinn from years before, when they had gone south to minister to flood victims. Swinn had had a church of his own in Lexington and gave it up to live on a scrappy piece of ground in the woods. A misplaced sense of humility, perhaps. Or needing a kind of loyalty that the outside world couldn't provide. Maybe he found that if you isolate people, their devotion to you becomes total.

"It says here that you are a widow," Pastor Banner said.

"Yes."

"And your husband, he—"

"Died in the war."

"You have two daughters."

"Yes."

"And where are they now?"

"At home."

"Alone?"

"Faith is eleven."

"I see."

Lorraine found the room uncomfortably warm. She removed a dingy handkerchief from her purse and patted her forehead.

"You wish for me to find a place for you in my church," Pastor Banner said.

"In your pulpit, sir."

"Ah."

"I have brought many into the sight of God."

"Joseph seems to think that your power to heal is strong."

"Yes."

"Most of my congregation are already firm believers. They don't need to be persuaded as to God's glory. But the world still provides them with many trials. The death of a loved one, for instance, can test even the most faithful. Could you help a person keep God in his heart when he's in peril of losing Him?"

Lorraine balled up her handkerchief. She was perspiring heavily.

"Of course I would do my best," she said.

Pastor Banner smiled. He reminded her of an elf she'd once seen in a children's book. The elf jumped through a window into a little girl's kitchen and helped himself to the freshly made oatmeal on the stove. Recalling that made Lorraine hungry. She'd had no breakfast, or dinner the evening before. The girls had cereal for both meals.

"Where are you from? Originally, I mean," Pastor Banner said.

"Chicago."

"And your parents?"

"They are godless."

Again the elfin smile.

"Oh, I should think so, really. In my experience most people believe in God, to some extent or another, but can't find a clear path to Him, or lose it through one thing or another."

"But my daughters are committed to the ways of the Lord. I've seen to that," Lorraine said.

I bet you have, Pastor Banner thought. He wasn't a cynical man. He didn't take a dim view of human nature. But he could recognize the capacity for cruelty. Lorraine had it, and didn't know. She would say she was vigilant, zealous, and true.

"I would very much love to make their acquaintance. When it's convenient, of course," he said.

Lorraine stood. So did the pastor. Just as she was about to walk through the front door, she stopped and asked if she could trouble him for something to eat. She thought her girls were getting tired of cereal. The pastor was at a loss. He said he had a colored woman who came in to make his meals at dinnertime. He was on his own, otherwise. He normally took himself into town for a bite at one of the coffee shops. He went into the kitchen and returned with a half-empty box of chocolate mint cookies. He'd bought them from the Girl Scouts two months before, and thought they mightn't be too stale. Lorraine thanked him. She went slowly back down his front walk and got into her car. She pulled out into the street without looking for other traffic. Pastor Banner watched until she was out of sight, and wondered what he'd gotten himself into.

Thirty-Three
1961

Lorraine's letters home were spare, flat, and dry.

Our new home in Sioux Falls is quite pleasant. Faith and Hope are happy here.

The squalor they lived in was easily imagined by both Anna and Olaf, who'd taken a reluctant interest in their daughter's correspondence. As to the happiness of their granddaughters, their interpretation differed. Olaf assumed that children had within them a natural and rather blind ability to take pleasure from life. Anna was certain that the girls were miserable. She thought of them often. They were one good day's drive away, not much further than they had been before when they lived in Coshocton, yet she didn't consider visiting them. She thought it best to leave things as they were. She was afraid that should they become a part of her life, that their inevitable withdrawal from it, at Lorraine's hysterical and misguided behest, would be too painful.

Please give them our love, Anna replied. She wanted to make a gift to the girls, but knew perfectly well that Lorraine would send that money right off to Joseph Swinn, or to whoever was now her taskmaster.

Anna was seventy-one. Time had not been kind. Her slenderness had long given way to a gradual thickness, which began in her waist, and was now pervasive. Even her small, delicate feet, once her prize, were swollen and fat. Getting up the stairs was a chore. Her chest tightened after the third step. Death, which had resided in the deepest, darkest part of her, was working its way out.

She wasn't afraid, only tired. Olaf begged her to follow her doctor's instruction and avoid all consumption of salt and alcohol. Alcohol was one thing, salt another. Nothing had any flavor without it, she found. Rochl was still with them, and prepared all their meals. Olaf told her in private not to add salt to anything, so that when Anna heaped it on at table, she might do herself that much less harm.

The boardinghouse was now occupied primarily by young women, college girls who didn't mind the bus ride to Northwestern University. Anna thought she might as well be running a sorority, given the noise and chatter that went on day and night. She reflected that once she would have been worried about Olaf's wandering eye in such a situation, but at sixty-six, he looked, and behaved, as a kind uncle whose romantic interests, if there were any, stayed hidden.

❦

Olaf saw his future as a black ocean that would drown him the moment Anna died. His thoughts turned to Aalia. They had corresponded only once since she left Chicago years before, and he wrote again to the address on the envelope he kept hidden in a book of Swedish folktales.

His letter to Aalia wasn't returned, nor was it answered. He felt like a fool, though he'd been neutral in his words, asking how she was, giving small, unimportant details of his life. He had made it a point not to mention Anna in the hopes that Aalia might be encouraged to respond, thinking that perhaps they had separated. He realized that he had also meant to suggest that possibly Anna had died. The idea of Aalia taking sympathy on him as a widower had come and gone from his mind, yet stayed long enough to make him ashamed of what he said, and didn't say, in the letter.

What had Aalia thought of hearing from him? Maybe she threw the letter away without ever opening it. Maybe someone she lived with, a husband most likely, who knew his name because she'd been candid just before their wedding day, wanting to get her past off her chest, got to it before she did and disposed of it.

With Aalia most definitely gone from his life, and Anna's continuing decline, Olaf despaired. He had long thought of himself as a fundamentally lonely man. He had no friends. He had no siblings. Anna had

191

been his one companion. His few business ventures hadn't lasted, and for many years he'd spent his time reading and tinkering around the house.

He turned then to his daughter, at least to the version his imagination supplied, which was different from what Anna perceived whenever she thought of her. Where Anna found her demented and remote, Olaf gave her a depth of character that would respond with great affection to his overtures.

He came right to the point.

Your mother is unwell, and desires to see you very much.

Lorraine replied with *I will pray for her.*

To which Olaf was further moved to write, *She yearns for the sight of her granddaughters.*

The Lord will bring them to her in prayer, Lorraine answered, that time on the back of a postcard with a shiny photograph of Sioux Falls on the front.

Another time Lorraine responded on stationery embossed with the name of a Baptist church. *Pastor Richard Banner* appeared in smaller letters just below. Olaf was glad that Lorraine had a job, and assumed that it was perhaps secretarial in nature, since she clearly had access to the pastor's private office.

ᴄ⁊ɔ

Lorraine's job was, in fact, to write letters of recommendation for the members of the congregation who were looking for work, or a room to rent, once even for a man who wanted to buy a car to visit his mother out of state. She was no good at it. Pastor Banner had to rewrite every one, because Lorraine couldn't refrain from religious hyperbole.

This man holds Christ firmly in his heart scared off the potential landlord who feared a proselytizer annoying her other tenants. Pastor Banner penned another, tamer version, which said, *In our private talks it is clear that this man strives, above all else, to be responsible.* Lorraine didn't grasp that most people viewed religion as a necessary pastime that should be experienced, like most things in life, in moderation. Pastor Banner had given her one chance to preach a Sunday sermon, and she ranted so long about fire and brimstone that some of the congregation actually walked out. He wrote to Joseph Swinn, suggesting that Lorraine would be happiest back with him, or at least on the tent circuit. But tent preaching had had its day. They both knew that. Joseph Swinn hoped to build a permanent camp that would provide a Bible school and prayer vigils to the needy and bereft. He had no place for Lorraine, however. *God has put her into your capable hands*, he wrote to Banner. *You must keep a gentle yet firm hold of her.*

Pastor Banner prayed on the matter long and hard. Lorraine wanted to bring people to Jesus, and that's what she must do. He contacted a number of gospel missions across the state, and in Iowa and Kansas, as well, and while the men of God who ran them weren't always Baptist, he further prayed that she would find acceptance as a true Christian. Some expressed concern that a woman on her own might shrink from the company of desperate, sometimes loathsome, men. Pastor Banner said she was used to meager surroundings, and the distasteful ways of God's miserable creatures.

The problem was her daughters. They could hardly go with her, and stay enrolled in school, so Pastor Banner offered to have them move in with him. He told Lorraine it was in no way inappropriate, given that he was both old and a man of the church. Lorraine said that she had already made arrangements. What those arrangements were, she didn't specify.

They amounted to leaving the girls entirely on their own, for two or three weeks at time, with cash in an envelope taped to the refrigerator. It was Faith's job to make sure there was enough to eat, and since she barely knew how to cook, that amounted to a lot of frozen dinners and more cereal. She also had to make sure that both she and Hope got to school every day—this mandate was Faith's own, and not Lorraine's. Lorraine's lack of interest in her daughters' education had never changed.

They really didn't mind being alone. Their mother's absence created a necessary sense of peace. They each discovered that without Lorraine they were more disciplined and resolute. Dishes were done promptly. Homework always turned in. Clothes were washed at a Laundromat five blocks away. They hauled the striped laundry bag in a red wagon they found abandoned in the garage out back. There was no television in the house. No radio, either. No telephone meant that Lorraine couldn't call and check up on them.

They played often in the dry stubbly grass next to the house, moving plastic dolls they'd acquired over time in a long, drawn-out game they called "Nomad." They took turns being the leader. The leader decided how to navigate the terrain ahead, and where they would next set up camp. An old shoebox served as their tent. If a long distance was to be traveled, the red wagon was used to transport the dolls and their gear, which consisted of several tiny plastic cups and bowls. The girls loved letting their minds roam in the safe confines of their overgrown side yard, which is where Olaf found them the day he took the train out from Chicago.

❦

He told Anna he was going to Pittsburgh to meet a man who might want to invest in another furniture business. He had been in correspondence with this man, which lent some truth to the lie, or so he hoped. But Anna asked no questions. She spent more and more time resting, so she could elevate her chronically swollen feet. Watching her, he was swallowed once again by the pending grief of loss. As he looked ahead in this edgy, urgent frame of mind, the idea of his granddaughters came to him one afternoon, as he sat alone in Anna's study, sipping a large glass of sherry, a habit he'd recently acquired. Their one visit to them a few years before wasn't enough. It was necessary that he know them, and they he.

To hell with Lorraine, he thought. He could never re-establish contact with her. He recalled her wild, wandering eye. The peculiar brightness in her gaze. The sudden, private smiles followed by a deep breath and closed eyes. She never needed him, nor Anna. Of course he'd thought of her almost every day since she left home. And after many, many days had passed he came to tell himself that it wasn't possible to miss someone who was never really there.

The train took him back to 1918, the last trip to Calais to catch the boat to England, and then home. On that day, his future was a blank. The knees of his uniform were worn smooth. His left boot lacked a heel. His right hand shook without warning, which made lighting the occasional cigarette a challenge. Olaf extended his right hand now, wondering if the idea of seeing his grandchildren would cause it to tremble. The hand was steady. Nothing was the same for him as it had been then, except that the future was just as hard to see.

At the station he got into a taxicab and gave the driver Lorraine's address. He made note of the route. He suspected he'd have to find his way back on foot, at least as far as a main street where another taxi could be secured. He was sure Lorraine wouldn't offer to drive him. He was also sure she would have no telephone for him to make the call himself. Then he felt ashamed for assuming the worst about his daughter's state of affairs. He ought to keep an open mind.

The girls didn't notice him standing with his small suitcase on the concrete path a few feet from where they knelt. When they turned at the sound of his voice in greeting, Hope didn't know him at all. Faith remembered his face, with its deep blue eyes.

"You're her father," she said.

"Yes."

"She's not here."

In the kitchen, Faith mixed a pitcher of orange juice. Olaf sat at the wobbly table, making a mental note to repair it before he left, and marveled at her efficiency. Hope sat there, too, holding a small plastic doll with a missing arm and no eyes. The doll saddened Olaf more than the dreadful house, because Hope seemed to love it so from the way she stroked its tangled, plastic hair from time to time.

The girls had little to say, which forced him to ask questions. They answered without hesitation. Their mother was gone for another ten days. They didn't hear from her during her trips. No, they didn't know which mission she was visiting then. When Olaf asked if there was anyone at all in the whole town of Sioux Falls who could be called upon in an emergency, they looked confused.

Then Faith said, "Pastor Banner."

Olaf didn't inquire further. The picture was clear. He was torn. He was observing a carefully balanced, precarious existence that would tip and fall if he were to interfere. He could demand that they return to Chicago with him, and they would no doubt refuse. Was he up to forcing them? He had grounds. Lorraine had abandoned them and would continue to do so indefinitely. He didn't know if she would come after them or not. He thought she very well might take their departure as another one of God's mysterious tests of faith. That meant he'd be responsible for two young girls who, if nothing else, had learned how to sustain themselves, and would probably have a very hard time adjusting to yet another new life. Their calm, smooth faces gave a story of ease and acceptance, but there was something in their eyes, Faith's more so than Hope's, that said they'd been through too much and might not handle another crisis. Faith looked at everything, as if to glance away even for a moment would mean disaster. He studied how precisely she placed the glass in front of him. She stood absolutely still as he brought it to his lips, and when he didn't return it to the exact spot where she'd originally put it, her face grew tense. After a moment she reached across the table and moved it the tiniest distance.

The girls said they liked school. They said they were doing well there. Yes, they were both quite healthy. Olaf had instantly noticed and didn't remark upon Hope's obvious limp. When Faith rubbed her jaw and Olaf asked her why, she said she had a toothache. He wanted to know when she had last seen a dentist. The girls looked at each other. They clearly had no idea what a dentist was.

"A doctor who takes care of teeth," Olaf said. Again they exchanged glances. Olaf formed a plan, which he executed the moment he returned home. He telephoned Pastor Banner long distance, identified himself, and gave the details of his brief visit to Lorraine's children. He said he knew the pastor would understand that no direct involvement was possible, given the sheltered and delicate lives the girls were living. Olaf would send money every month to Pastor Banner, which he was to apply to the girls' welfare. When Lorraine was away, he would make sure that they both saw a dentist, had new clothes, even saw a movie once in a while. Lorraine would probably not ask any questions, and if she did, the pastor could say the girls had been noticed by some kind women at church. The pastor said the girls didn't attend his church, or any church, as far as he knew. Olaf said that in that case, the pastor would have to use his imagination as to the tale he'd tell Lorraine. The pastor agreed. Olaf closed by saying that if the pastor had any notion of using the money for himself, Olaf would deal with him personally.

"I've done it before, you know," Olaf said. The memory of the restaurant going up in flames pleased him for a moment.

The pastor huffed. He was a man of God, not one to take advantage of a Christian kindness.

Before leaving Faith and Hope's little house Olaf gave them a hundred dollars, which he instructed them not to show or mention to their mother, and also his address and telephone number on a piece of ruled school paper Faith provided. He assumed they would forget him soon, so he slapped down a photograph he'd carried in his wallet, taken not long ago against the side of the boardinghouse by Rochl.

It's a nice day, he'd said. *Capture me for posterity.*

Hope lifted the picture, and tucked it in the pocket of her cotton dress.

❧

Fifty-one years later, Freddie found that picture in the same alabaster box that contained the five-dollar bill Anna sent to Lorraine, which Lorraine, for some reason, elected not to give to Joseph Swinn. The box was on the counter in Holly's master bathroom. It had a greenish tint, and was decorated with etched swirls in red and gold. The metal hinges holding the lid were blue with age. One was broken. The lid needed to be lifted carefully, so that it didn't snap off the base entirely. Also in the box were letters and photographs Freddie had never seen before, a luscious strand of red and white beads, and a cameo broach. Their origin was unknown, and just then, as Freddie was attempting to reintroduce order to Holly's large house, which, by all evidence, hadn't been vacuumed, dusted, or mopped in some time, she put the matter from her mind.

Freddie was on her second day in Minneapolis. Holly was due home from the hospital that afternoon. Freddie and Jack had been told to expect a time of rehabilitative therapy. Holly might need a walker to get around for the time being, and given that her house had two sets of stairs, this presented a problem. Freddie told Jack to arrange for two walkers to come home with her, one for each floor. She didn't know if he took in her words. He had a vague look to him, as if his hearing had gone bad and every voice addressing him was a mumble of meaningless sound.

Yet when Holly arrived, she was able to make her way alone, holding on hard to Jack's arm. Freddie stood in the open doorway and watched her progress. The leg weakened by the stroke was the same leg afflicted by polio. *Maybe that's a blessing*, Freddie thought. *Holly's used to making up for that leg, isn't she?* Holly's expression was fierce as she came up the walk.

"Know what I want? A cigarette!" Holly called.

The doctor had strongly advised against Holly smoking. He said that she should quit by whatever means necessary. There were patches he could prescribe. Some patients tried hypnosis. She could join a support group. Freddie recalled that doctor's face, young and earnest, not unlike the doctor who offered her his apology when Ken was close to the end. He, too, suggested that Freddie join a support group. Grievers Unite, or something equally stupid. Living was the cure for grief. Staring back at death. And while a cigarette now made no sense, given how Holly ended up where she was, it was still somehow life affirming, wasn't it? Because Holly wanted it, and to desire anything was to remember that you were alive.

"Coming right up!" Freddie called back. The objection she expected from Jack wasn't voiced. His face showed more strain than Holly's did. The underarms of his sport shirt were damp.

Jack got Holly inside and installed her on the sofa in their large, unfriendly living room. The fireplace had logs that had never been lit. The bookshelves had no photographs of family members. Everything was new and untouched. Freddie didn't see why he'd put her there, when the kitchen or family room was so much cozier. Then she understood that he needed her to be someplace he wasn't used to seeing her, as if the small changes in her—and thank God they'd been small—would be less noticeable there. Her speech was still slurred, but barely. Her right arm functioned pretty well, though she didn't seem able to lift it above her head. Yet that was the hand she used to hold the cigarette Freddie gave her from a pack she found on the kitchen counter. She used her left hand to guide the other closer to her lips.

"An invalid," Holly said. The pleasure she took from blowing out her smoke over Freddie's head was almost obscene. Jack was in his den, pouring himself a drink. He didn't offer one to Freddie. From behind the half-closed door, his voice on the telephone could be heard. The girlfriend, maybe. Did Holly know about her? Holly didn't miss much, though she pretended to.

They discussed logistics. Holly had been told not to drive for at least a month. At that point, the strength on her right side would be reevaluated. Jack offered to cut back his hours and help out. Freddie said not to bother. She would stay up to two weeks. After that, the hospital could put them in touch with someone who could visit on an hourly basis to pick up the slack.

"I don't want any fucking strangers in my house, messing with my things," Holly said. It wasn't like her to swear. Maybe the stroke had set free an alter ego, or a deeper, truer self. Maybe Lorraine's visit was to blame.

Freddie made tea, though neither of them cared for it much. The box in the cabinet was ancient. Freddie opened it with her teeth and pulled out two shriveled bags. A note on the freezer said there was food inside. The note was from Margaret. She was the neighbor across the way. She'd come by yesterday, apparently. Freddie was out then, picking up Jack's dry cleaning. When she mentioned Margaret's name to Jack, he looked blank. Then he said they'd asked her to watch the house once, when they went out of town. She must have known that the spare key was still kept under a flowerpot on the porch. She'd have seen the ambulance come and go, and assume an illness had taken place. Jack and Holly kept very much to themselves. They didn't socialize with the neighbors, though they'd lived on that cul-de-sac for almost thirty years. Jack had friends through work. And Holly? Freddie didn't know who her friends were.

"Book club," Holly said when Freddie asked her about Margaret. Their teacups sat steaming on the coffee table, untouched.

"Thought you gave that up."

"Went back. They begged me."

"Really, why?"

"I was the biggest crab. Never liked anything. The crap they chose sucked. You know, smarmy bodice rippers. That sort of thing."

"And they couldn't get enough of your sharp tongue."

"Found me entertaining, I guess."

Holly lifted her teacup unassisted. Her hand shook a little. She lowered the cup to the saucer, then lifted it again. The shaking was the same.

"Practice makes perfect," she said. The physical therapist at the hospital told her she'd have to retrain her muscles—jog their memory, as it were.

Jack emerged from his study. He looked less worn, almost cheerful. He wanted to know if Freddie could hold down the fort so he could run down to his office and check on things there. Freddie said there'd be no problem. She told Holly she'd walk her into the kitchen so she could sit while Freddie made them all something to eat. Jack said not to count on him, that he'd grab something downtown.

Someone, you mean.

Way to go, hon.

Holly pretended to be put off, but brightened as soon as he was gone. She was heavy on Freddie's arm as they went. The last few feet she managed on her own just fine.

"I know how to handle this bum leg," she said, happy in her chair. "Jack forgets that."

Freddie opened the wide door of Holly's sub-zero refrigerator. She remembered the food in the freezer. She asked how Holly would feel about scrambled eggs instead. Eggs were fine, she said. Freddie dug through several drawers until she found a corkscrew to open the bottle of French wine on the counter. She wondered why it was there. Jack drank hard liquor and Holly seldom drank at all. Another neighbor might have brought it, though a bottle of wine seemed like a strange thing to give at a time like that.

"Maybe she left it for me. Maybe she knows I've taken up the habit," Freddie said.

"Who?"

"Mother."

"What are you talking about?"

"You said she was here. Don't you remember?"

"No."

Freddie poured some wine into a crystal glass she found in the china cabinet. She shook the glass a little bit.

"You're supposed to let it breathe," she said.

"Uh-huh."

"I'm not crazy, you know. When you called that night, you said she'd been here."

"Did I? I don't remember."

"You did."

"*You* must have thought *I* was crazy."

Freddie wondered if Holly's imagination had been brought to life by the letters in the box. There were so many, far more than Freddie had gotten after Lorraine died. Why the unequal distribution?

Freddie brought the box downstairs. She removed its contents, and spread them over the table.

"Why didn't you tell me you had these?" Freddie asked.

Holly shrugged. The light outside was sickly bright—the start of a heavy, vicious snow.

"Did they come from Swinn or from her?" Freddie asked.

"Swinn."

"After she died?"

"Yes."

"He didn't know where you lived. I had to send you his letter, remember?"

Swinn wrote each of them. Holly's letter was sent care of Freddie. Then Freddie got the packet she and Holly reviewed every year in Sioux Falls. At the time Holly said she didn't want to have anything from it, and that it should all stay with Freddie for safekeeping.

"I wrote him back," Holly said.

"Why?"

"It seemed like the right thing to do."

"Then what happened?"

"He wrote to say had he more things of hers, and asked if I wanted them."

"And you didn't think I'd be interested in any of it?"

"I knew how you felt about her," Holly said.

"You didn't like her any more than I did."

"Look, I thought it would upset you to hear from him again, or to see anything that reminded you of that life, so I just didn't say anything. It took a long time for him to send the box, a few months, in fact, and by then I wasn't interested anymore. I didn't even open it until very recently."

"When, exactly?"

"The night I got sick."

Freddie's head hurt, and her neck was sore. She examined Olaf's photograph.

"Do you remember him?" she asked.

"A little."

When Olaf gave up writing to Lorraine, he wrote only to the girls, care of Pastor Banner. *No rain for over a month now*, Freddie remembered one letter saying. And, *Your grandmother is faring poorly*. They kept them hidden behind a loose board in their shared bedroom so Lorraine wouldn't find them. They divided up Olaf's letters, which were always addressed to the both of them, after each established her own household. Freddie still had hers somewhere. She never added them to the envelope from Swinn. It didn't feel right somehow.

She pushed the letters aside, and focused on the photographs.

As a child Lorraine was sullen, never smiling. Her clothes were tidy. Her hair wasn't. Long, as Freddie remembered, wild and kinked. *Mommy, it's so beautiful* . . . and then a harsh hand pushing hers away. *This is the Lord's trial upon me.* . . . Lorraine brushing it out hard, exorcising its sin, and then praying over it because her eviction wasn't enough. *I am unworthy. I am unworthy. I am but a whore who seeks your redemption.* . . . And Faith there on the cot in the candlelight while Hope slept soundly, not comprehending the river their mother sailed down.

Freddie felt that loneliness still, and even more so, there in her sister's home.

Hang in there, hon.

I miss you, Ken!

Shut your eyes and go to sleep, then. I'll be along soon.

There weren't any more photographs after Lorraine reached the age of about sixteen or so, which would have coincided more or less with the time she ran off to Joseph Swinn. In another group, banded together, were a few of Swinn himself. Tall, broad-chested, with a bulbous nose and a shiny forehead. The sudden memory of his wet hand on her face. And the way he smelled. Like sour earth.

Holly had grown pale.

"You better get some rest, now," Freddie said.

"I could use another smoke."

"It can wait."

Holly nodded. Freddie put the photographs and letters back in the box. The box was beautiful.

"Was that hers?" Freddie asked.

"Anna's?"

"Yes."

"I'm surprised Mother didn't hock it."

Again Freddie thought of Olaf sending Anna's things to Lorraine, and of Lorraine hiding them away for so long.

"I wonder when he died. Olaf, I mean," Freddie said.

"Who knows?"

"Exactly. Swinn must not have been around to hand out the news."

Holly got up without Freddie's help, but needed an arm to manage the stairs up to bed.

Thirty-Four
1964

The telegram announcing the death of Lorraine's mother came to Pastor Banner. He didn't for a moment question why. For three years money and letters had arrived there from Olaf Lund.

Pastor Banner knew that the proper—and Christian—thing to do was to take the telegram to Lorraine himself. He didn't know if she was there, in town, or visiting a mission. She kept her own schedule. The scant news he did receive from her was often roundabout. Someone who had known her from Joseph Swinn's camp wrote once to express his admiration for her zeal. A member of Banner's own congregation had heard that she had practically overhauled the kitchen at the Des Moines, Iowa, mission single-handedly. There was no doubt that everything she did was energetic and heartfelt. Except where her own children were concerned.

Those poor girls! Such unfortunate creatures. He had come to know them a little. Faith, now fourteen, was tall for her age and awkward. She dressed as if from an earlier generation. Her hemlines were always at mid-calf, while the girls nowadays showed their knees freely. Her hair wasn't bobbed and clipped in the current style, but long and loose, and clearly difficult to manage. She seldom spoke. She didn't make eye contact. Her strength and intelligence seemed to lie in her hands, which were large and raw-looking, as if she washed everything in strong soap. Hope was more sociable, but also shy, probably because of that limp of hers. Lorraine was unaware of her daughters' shortcomings, or their virtues either, for that matter.

Pastor Banner drove to Lorraine's house. He knew the way well. He went by there often, just to cast an eye about, as Olaf Lund had implored him to do. The girls kept everything tidy. Even the grass was cut. He had to think that it was Faith who did the mowing, given that she was clearly the stronger of the two. That morning Pastor Banner discovered an empty cardboard box in the front yard. A woman's pink sweater lay across a bush. The milk bottles hadn't been brought in. As he went up the stairs, he encountered a single slipper, soiled and torn.

Faith opened the door before he had a chance to knock. She was wearing a pair of denim coveralls. Her cheek was smudged. Her unruly hair was bound with a red handkerchief. A strong smell of perfume assaulted him upon crossing the threshold. The window in the tiny front room was bare. The curtain rod lay broken on the floor, ripped from the plaster, leaving two large, ragged holes. Hope sat on the couch in a wrinkled green dress, an open book in her lap. She looked at the air in front of her, and not at the page. At the kitchen table with its one mismatched leg—square shaped, while the other three were round—sat Lorraine. One look at her said she was drunk. She leaned heavily on her elbows, which made her shoulder blades prominent through the back of her blouse.

His first thought was that she'd heard the news already. Perhaps Olaf had sent two telegrams, one directly to her. He looked at Faith. Her face was blank.

He sat opposite Lorraine.

"Calm yourself, my child," he said.

Lorraine had been weeping, and from the look of her, had only left off a few moments before his arrival. Her wrists were bruised. So were her upper arms. She shook her head, and wiped her nose on the back of her hand. Pastor Banner produced a white linen handkerchief, which Lorraine refused. The bottle she drank from—the cheapest brand of whiskey, or so the pastor assumed, himself not a drinking man—was empty and on its side at her feet. Lorraine folded her arms and buried her red, tearstained face in them. Then she snored.

"Heavens," the pastor said.

Faith got under one of Lorraine's arms, and indicated that the pastor should take her other side. Lorraine was a good-sized woman, and wrestling her first to her feet, and then down the dark, narrow hallway to her room was hard. The Pastor was shocked to see that Lorraine's bed consisted only of a bare mattress on the floor. Also on the floor was a small lamp with no shade. A battered suitcase lay open by the lamp. The contents were random and disorganized, as if someone had been looking hard for something, and made bitter by not finding it.

They left her on the mattress and closed the door. They returned to the kitchen. Hope was now at the table, but without her book. The pastor sat down. Faith filled a small, dented kettle with water, put it on the stove, and lit the burner beneath it. She took the still-burning match to the sink, turned on the water, and doused it in the thin stream. She sent the match down the drain. She joined the others.

"Do either of you have any idea what ails that poor woman?" the pastor asked.

"She's an inebriate," Hope said. She knew the word well. Her mother used it often when describing some poor congregant.

"Not habitually, though, I'm sure of that."

Hope shrugged.

"She started yesterday, after she got home. Things didn't go too well down in Joplin, or so she said," Faith said.

The pastor thought he might be able to make a long-distance call that would shed light on the matter. He'd have to couch his words carefully. He could say that Lorraine was ill, and concerned that she might not be able to return to her duties there for some time. That would lead to a discussion of her success in ministering to the wretched men who came through the door.

"She says he turned her down," Faith added.

"Who did?"

"Don't know."

They all thought a job, or some sort of assignment, had been at stake. Each was well acquainted with Lorraine's passion, her need to be useful, to have her labor accepted, though not necessarily praised. She wasn't vain. She didn't suffer from a big ego. She was a truly humble person, and it was that humbleness that now made her suffer in ways they would never know.

☙

She had thrown herself at a man and begged him to love her. It wasn't so much a brazen act, as one of humility. She had actually gotten to the floor and kissed his dusty boots. This man went by the name of Leonard King. She met him at the Joplin mission. He wasn't someone who'd come in need of help, but an employee, a kitchen worker and general handyman around the place. He slept in a basement room. Lorraine did, too. On the floor above them, men with nowhere else to go tossed and turned on narrow cots that she and Leonard set up every evening after dinner had been cleared, the dishes washed, and the wooden tables and chairs moved aside, against the walls.

Like a dance, Leonard said one evening, as the men who needed a bed for the night formed a line outside the temporarily locked door. Lorraine didn't know what he meant.

Where I'm from, when folks want to have a dance, they move all their furniture out onto the lawn, he said.

And where are you from?

Some little town you never heard of in the Texas panhandle.

He was nothing like Joseph Swinn. Whereas Swinn was calm and cool—except when seized by the Spirit—Leonard King was given to loudly expressed passions, though seldom of anger. Listening to a baseball game on the radio might make him cheer wildly. Once he banged two pots together in joyous celebration of a Yankees victory. He laughed a lot, usually over something he read. He had a small volume of James Thurber he kept in his back pocket, and took out when work was slow. One evening, the sunset lit the sky with bands of purple and gold. Leonard King gazed through the grimy window of the kitchen and said that no one needed any further proof of God's existence than the sudden, extraordinary beauty of nature. He liked to think that God's best work was the world itself, and not so much the stupid human creatures that were working awfully hard to wreck it.

He knew his Bible as well as Lorraine did, yet he didn't bow his head when Lorraine said Grace before each meal. Other men kept their heads up, too, but Lorraine assumed that they were godless souls. Why Leonard King didn't pray, she couldn't guess. One day she asked him.

Praying's kinda private, doncha think?

Sometimes his country accent was stronger than usual. The deeper drawl went with a certain stance—folded arms, leaning more on his right leg—as if offering a challenge to the person he was talking to. To Lorraine that challenge wasn't one of faith but of something even deeper within her—lust. She had never really felt it before. Joseph Swinn had commanded her respect and devotion. She gave herself to him out of a sense of duty. He needed to lie with her. He was an admitted sinner who yearned for the pleasures of the flesh. That she didn't enjoy sex with him made the act cleaner somehow. Both of them were absolved in the eyes of God.

The power that Leonard King had over her was something else entirely. She wanted him the way she'd never wanted God. She wanted to consume him and let him reside in the hollow of her bones. The desire to put her hand on his arm made her shake and stammer. Her face grew hot each time he looked her way. In her saner moments, she reviewed the fact that he was not a particularly handsome man. He was, however, masculine, and thoroughly so. He was almost rough. She suspected him capable of dangerous acts. He was a man who would take what he wanted without hesitation. She prayed all the time that he would come to want her.

Ѥ

He didn't. He couldn't say he wasn't flattered by Lorraine's obvious interest. He'd seen the same look in women's eyes many times before. In his youth—he was then just past forty—he'd taken liberal advantage of it. He enjoyed the chase—watching a woman resist on moral grounds and then making her give in. He got more than one woman pregnant. One he found an abortionist for. The other left town, and he didn't hear from her again. He wondered if she'd borne his child, and what that person was like. He didn't allow himself to think of it often. He found it surprisingly painful.

When Lorraine declared herself to him, he was patient. She sat on the end of his bed where he been asleep until her persistent knocking roused him. He wore a T-shirt and boxer shorts. Lorraine was in her nightgown. She'd neglected to put on a robe. She said she had a sinner's heart and that she despised herself for it.

I've lost everything important in this world, she said. Leonard King knew she had children, and wondered if their father had reclaimed them.

I cannot lose you, too. She was desperate, he could see. He'd seen her scold men for not believing, and bully them into accepting the word of God. She never praised them, never rewarded their piety with kind words. Even the drunks who'd been persuaded to abandon the bottle received nothing from her. She was the hardest woman he'd ever seen, and there she was, ready to strip herself naked and lunge at him.

He himself should have been ready to lunge. He was a man, after all, with a man's needs. He'd have no problem facing her in the morning. He'd feel no guilt whatsoever. But he didn't want to start something he'd have to quickly finish.

Lorraine threw herself down and wept. He told her to stop. He even extended a hand to help her up. Her unrelenting grip was painful. He worked himself free. He grabbed her hard. He wouldn't release her until she calmed a bit. He gave her a handkerchief to wipe her face with. She didn't take it. Then she left him alone.

The next morning, Lorraine came into the kitchen with her suitcase packed, carrying a note for the man overseeing the mission. She charged Leonard King with delivering it. Then she dropped on all fours, and kissed first one boot, then the other. Leonard King was so shocked he stood absolutely still. For a moment, after she turned and walked away, he thought to go after her, but he knew that to do so would signal his acceptance.

❧

After getting Lorraine to bed, Pastor Banner gave Faith and Hope the news he'd come to share. They seemed unmoved. Their composure was no surprise. They no doubt had learned to conceal their feelings from strangers. He asked them if they wished to pray for the soul of their late grandmother. They shook their heads. He told them to take care of their mother, and to come to him at once if the situation got out of hand. They promised to. After he left, Hope went back to her book, and Faith sat on the back stairs and cried.

Thirty-Five
1968

Christ is a fisher of men, my mother a healer of souls, and I a counter of pennies. Faith thought herself witty. The phrase made her smile. She worked hard at the grocery store, ringing up orders. Old Mr. Jameson paid her under the table, which he normally didn't do, but he liked her, perhaps took pity on her. Faith was eighteen, out of school, and willing to come in every morning at five o'clock. She had no social security card. Hence the unorthodox payment method.

She was careful with money. Olaf hadn't sent any since Anna died, but she and Hope both had set certain sums aside. Faith thought often of Olaf and the home in Chicago where her mother grew up. She wanted to see it, she decided. She wanted that connection. Going out into the world, even the small world of Mr. Jameson's family grocery store, made her realize how isolated and lonely she was.

That grim sense was made worse by Lorraine's increased presence. For the last few years, since the crisis over Leonard King, she'd stayed closer to home. She had tried a number of ventures, the most recent of which was teaching Sunday school to troubled teens. Pastor Banner knew that the young people ignored her most of the time, but in those moments when she was fired up, she commanded their attention, if not the caliber of their future deeds. One young man took quite a shine to her, in fact. He was motherless. He invited himself to Faith's home on Sunday afternoons, hoping for a hot meal and a friendly face. He received neither, yet he persisted. Faith realized that the man—Louis—was actually interested in her. Lorraine was totally unaware of his inclinations. When he was in the home, she retired to her small bedroom, still sparsely furnished, to read the Bible and pray.

It was to Louis that Faith revealed her desire to visit Chicago. She felt silly for saying so, then realized she had no one else to tell.

Faith wanted to buy a cheap used car. She hadn't driven for years, not since the flight from Joseph Swinn's camp, yet she was certain it would all come back to her as soon as she was behind the wheel. Louis asked her how long she had had a driver's license. She had no license. It hadn't occurred to her that she would need one. Rather than tell Louis that, she said she'd gotten hers when she was sixteen. Louis then asked if he could kiss her. Faith told him to go home and ponder his sins.

She looked up the address of the Department of Licensing, and went there one afternoon. She was told she needed to produce a birth certificate. She had no idea if she had one or where it was. She briefly considered asking Lorraine about it, and knew it would be pointless. Lorraine had that look to her again, the one that said she needed to move. She told the girls that Joseph Swinn had asked after her recently, though neither remembered seeing a letter. They both thought it possible that Lorraine had decided, after a long and difficult prayer session, that Swinn was reaching out to her. The proof was that he was once more firmly in her thoughts.

One morning she snuck out before dawn. She left no note, nor any money. She'd said a few days before that Faith was earning plenty to buy groceries and pay the electric, water, sewer, and garbage bills. Faith said she didn't want to spend her own money on those things. Her remark was followed by a sudden, powerful slap that made her reel and stagger against the kitchen counter.

This is all up to you now.

When the hell hasn't it been?

Faith was certain that Lorraine hadn't heard her. She'd have hit her again, if she had.

The usual peace that descended after Lorraine's departure was marred by the bruise on Faith's face—and not knowing where to find her birth certificate. Lorraine's barren room yielded nothing.

"Try the attic," Hope said.

Faith didn't know they had an attic. Hope pointed to the door in the hall ceiling.

"What did you think that was for?" she asked Faith.

"I thought it was . . . I don't know." Faith had never thought about it before. She couldn't say she'd even noticed it at all.

"Just get a chair from the kitchen and pull the handle down. There are stairs inside," Hope said.

"How do you know that?"

"How do you think? From watching her."

Faith walked down the hall.

"You'll need a flashlight," Hope said.

"Where is it?"

"In the kitchen drawer, where it always is."

Faith expected the attic to be bigger than it was, something that ran the length of the house. What she entered was more like a crawl space, where standing was possible only if she hunched forward. The air was close. She thought there might be rats in there, though she reasoned if that were so, she'd have heard them scurrying overhead. She discovered a rocking chair and a lamp she'd never seen before. Also some stuffed animals that were quite old, given how worn they were. There was a cardboard box that held photographs Faith didn't take time to look through. Next to it sat an ordinary shoebox, which surprised her, since their shoes had always come from the church charity bins. She took the shoebox with her down the rickety stairs and into the kitchen.

Inside were poems, written in pencil on lined school paper. It took a moment for Faith to realize that these were by Lorraine, as a child. *In spring, birds sing, and bees sting.* And *The dog has the eyes of God, that is clear to see.*

Other papers appeared to be lists Lorraine had made—items to be purchased for Swinn's camp and later for some of the missions she visited.

Light bulbs, toothpicks, cheap flatware, better quality toilet paper.

How odd it was to entertain the thought of her mother considering such mundane matters!

The birth certificate was toward the bottom, and as she lifted it out of the box and spread it open on the table, she prepared to see her father's name in print for the first time.

He was no stranger. Lorraine had spoken of him several times. He came through the camp not long after Lorraine joined. Then he was called away, back to his home farm down south to help his struggling parents. He returned when he could. After a long while, realizing that they were meant only for each other, they were secretly married in Cleveland. Lorraine kept her maiden name, to avoid detection. Faith's father engaged in a similar act of subterfuge by shortening his last name from Fullerton to Full. *Howard Fullerton was a fine man*, Lorraine said on many occasions, with her bottle of whiskey close at hand. Lorraine never explained why their marriage couldn't be known, and Faith developed a romantic notion that her father was an important person, perhaps even a spy. Lorraine alluded to his military involvement. She said he died in the war. The year she gave, 1950, didn't sound quite right to Faith, but she wasn't much of a history student. Hope, who was better at these things, pressed the point one day, and Lorraine said that he'd been taken prisoner, and was never released. This supported Faith's idea of high-level espionage. It thrilled her to imagine her father, holding onto his secrets even under torture.

Name of Father: Joseph Prosser Swinn. Several random documents below, there was Hope's birth certificate, bearing the same name.

"What's the matter?" Hope asked. Faith handed her both birth certificates. Hope examined them carefully, and gave them back.

"So what?" she said.

"What do you mean, 'so what'? My father—our father—that, that . . ."

"Self-righteous fathead?"

Hope brought Faith a glass of water.

"How can you be so calm about this?" Faith asked.

"One, because there's nothing I can do about it, and two, I mostly figured it out before."

Hope sat. Her face was clear.

"And you didn't think you should tell me?" Faith asked.

"I thought you already knew. It was so obvious."

All that stuff about Howard Fullerton, what about that? Hope reminded her that Lorraine was a practiced liar. Hope learned not to take anything she said seriously. Faith wished she'd done the same. She knew that Hope was right—there was nothing to be done. A fact was a fact, after all.

She buried it away, and carried it through the years. The moment of discovery would return suddenly. Someone might say *My father did this* or *My father said that*, and she would remember. A man that resembled Swinn might cross her path. And then there was the terrible thought of her half-brothers or half-sisters—Swinn's children with his wife. They never came to the camp, but were spoken of by Swinn when he wanted to remind people that he knew the sorrows and joys of fatherhood firsthand.

"Sometimes I still think we should have looked for them. It's too late now. They're probably all dead," Freddie said. They were walking slowly around Holly's cul-de-sac. Her daily regimen required it, morning and afternoon. She finished her cigarette, dropped it to the pavement, and ground it down with her shoe.

"Looked for whom?" Holly asked. Freddie filled her in.

"How would we have explained that to Jack and Ken?"

Both men were told that Howard Fullerton was their father. Freddie and Holly agreed to keep their stories the same. *Such a terrible tragedy! No, there aren't any photographs—he was careful about that sort of thing, given his work, you know.*

"Did you ever tell Jack the truth?" Freddie asked.

"No."

The air was brisk. Snow was on the way. Holly wore a lovely purple scarf Jack had recently bought her from a hand-knit shop downtown. The purchase was to ease his sense of guilt.

He's cheating on me again, you know, she'd said only that morning. Freddie pretended she didn't know, but she couldn't feign shock, either. She hoped Holly interpreted her lack of response as quiet wisdom, as if to say that she was willing to hear the whole story if Holly chose to tell it. She was grateful that Holly didn't. She was also glad that Jack was away on business again. His presence was irksome.

"Did you ever tell Ken?" Holly asked.

"No."

"Do you wish you had?"

"Oh, I don't know. I didn't like keeping it from him, but as time went on, I didn't see what difference the truth would make, except as something I'd withheld. He wouldn't have liked that."

Though he had plenty of secrets himself. The pretty police dispatcher he didn't think Freddie knew about. She couldn't believe how stupid he must have thought she was, not to have understood the glances that passed between them at the precinct Christmas party. And the money he lost more than once at the goddamned racetrack, betting on dogs, no less. Couldn't even step up to horses.

Freddie didn't want to think ill of him now, at this late date. Ken was who he was. Just as Lorraine was who she was.

You're not putting us in the same camp, are you, hon? I mean, I know I had my faults, but that one . . . well, you know . . .

Don't worry, I do. Better than anyone.

Holly said she'd had enough. It was time to get inside, build a fire, and be cheerful. She looked at Freddie, who wore an amused, private expression.

"What's so funny?" Holly asked.

Freddie shook her head. She wasn't up to explaining her private conversations with a dead man.

Thirty-Six

1987

Faith's rejection hit Lorraine hard, though in her honest moments, she knew it was fair judgment. She saw mothers in the camp, in the missions, in Pastor Banner's church. They weren't like her. Their hands were gentle, their voices kind. Not always, of course. There was the usual share of stern warnings and tight grips on small, thin arms. She seldom questioned her harsher approach, and when she did, she told herself it was God's will that she be tough on her children so that they would fully learn His ways.

Doubt grew. She was tired as she had never been before. All her life she had been full of energy. Now, any task she attempted required great effort. She was unfocused, given to overwhelming sorrow at random moments. Memories, dismissed for many years, returned. Her mother playing cards with residents of the boardinghouse. Her father chopping wood in the backyard, though he could easily afford to pay a man to do it for him. Watching snow fall behind the frosted windows of her bedroom. Touching her Christmas stocking, guessing at what it contained.

The past pulled too hard. She couldn't resist. She lined up her shoeboxes on her bed and went through them all. Letters, photographs, a hair ribbon from her childhood, a silver coin, a watch fob, a broken strand of pearls. Also the things of Anna's that Olaf sent along after Anna died. Which of her daughters should receive what, when the time came? She considered them both. Hope had given her less trouble, but was also less reliable. Lorraine had always understood that about her. Hope was disconnected on some level. Not fully involved. Faith had her feet on the ground. That's why she married a police officer, Lorraine was sure. She knew very little of Hope's husband, only that he was ambitious, a young moneymaker.

Lorraine was dying. She didn't know how, or why, only that she was being consumed by the dark. Nothing could dispel it, not even Joseph Swinn.

He had troubles of his own, although the camp was well established, with permanent buildings, a fine Bible study program, a youth group, and senior outreach events. His wife had asked for a divorce. He refused, on the grounds of his faith. She divorced him anyway. He hadn't seen his children for a very long time. He was seventy-eight, slow in his movements, careful with his words. The fire in him had gone out.

When Lorraine came to him with her sense of doom, he instructed her to pray. Then they sat at the same wooden table where they had whiskey so many years before. The table was now in a small building Joseph Swinn used for an office. On one wall was a cot where he often napped. His actual quarters were at the other end of the camp in a small bungalow. Lorraine slept in the bungalow next to it. As always, it was simply furnished. Of late she'd added two small, framed photographs of her daughters taken at school as part of a routine affair that happened every year.

It's only a dollar thirty-five cents, Faith said. Excitement made her voice high. How she combed her hair for that day, and dressed Hope nicely, too. Lorraine never gave them gifts, but she let Faith have the money, because of the light in her eyes.

"I failed them as a mother, and now it's too late," Lorraine said.

Joseph Swinn considered pouring them both a drink. He consulted his pocket watch. Its glass face had cracked long ago. It was early afternoon. That was one reason not to pour them both a drink. That and Lorraine had struggled with her own weakness for some time. The last several episodes of excess had kept her in bed for two days each.

"I should have helped you. I should have told them who I was," he said.

"You know you couldn't. What would people have said? What would have happened to your reputation as a man of God?"

"Even men of God sin. And sometimes the truth is the best weapon against that sin."

Joseph Swinn thought again about the whiskey under the pillow on the cot. Surely it might ease his mounting distress.

"I should never have taken you away from your family," he said.

"Don't be silly. You've been more of a family to me than they ever were."

Anna pressing a cool washcloth to her fevered forehead. Olaf humming a folk song from his own childhood. They were strict at times, to be sure. But they had also been loving. And she had turned away from that love, and thought them lacking because they didn't believe as she believed in the value of one's immortal soul above all else.

As if to settle the question of whether it was too early in the day for a drink, Lorraine stood wearily and fetched the whiskey from the cot. She didn't know where glasses were kept, and resigned herself to swigging right from the bottle. They had done so before, she and Joseph Swinn. She found it even more intimate than being in bed together.

"You know, I used to think that people were all one thing, or all another," she said. She offered the bottle to Joseph Swinn first. He drank.

"My mother used to say that everyone is like a patchwork quilt. A little piece of this sewn to a little piece of that," he said.

"If someone didn't freely profess a love of the Lord, and a complete willingness to do His work, then they were . . ."

" . . . by default . . ."

". . . yes, by default . . . immoral sinners." Here Lorraine drank a little more. Liquor didn't soothe her as it once had, more proof of her descent.

"I assumed this of my own children. But there is goodness in them, too," she said.

"If you feel you have wronged them, tell them so."

"They won't forgive me."

"But at least you will be heard. You will have acknowledged your own past. You will do the right thing, in the eyes of God."

"I don't care."

And it was true, she realized. Whatever it was that was causing her to sink away from the world had also turned her away from God. She had done bad things in the name of good and wished she hadn't. There was no going back, though. She was both lost and condemned.

"When I'm gone, tell them I cared. In spite of everything," she said.

Joseph Swinn put his hand on top of hers and told her she looked pretty healthy to him. He lied. He saw how pale she was, how dark the skin beneath her eyes. In another month's time, when the pain she'd suffered in her knee finally drove her to the doctor where she learned she had bone cancer, he still maintained that she would outlive him. She didn't object to his failed attempt at comfort. For the first time in all of their years together they spoke not of God but of life and what must be done once she had left it.

Hence the letters he wrote, one to Faith, one to Hope, who by then were long used to being Freddie and Holly.

In spite of her immense suffering, her faith remained unshaken.

Freddie hadn't kept her letter. Holly had kept hers, and on the ninth day of Freddie's visit, she wanted to look at it again, only she couldn't find it. She went through drawers and cabinets, because she couldn't recall where for the life of her she'd put it all those years ago. She even took everything out of her dresser and threw it on her enormous bed. Freddie felt duty bound to fold all the articles of clothing again for her. As she finished that, she could hear Holly in the guest room she was staying in, going through the nightstands. Freddie asked why it mattered so much. Holly said she didn't know—it just seemed important all of a sudden. To distract her, Freddie made another pot of tea. She made at least one a day, for the sake of ritual, though little of it was ever consumed. Holly gave up and joined her in the kitchen.

The snow fell hard, and Freddie said she'd made plans to go home early the following week. She felt guilty about being away from the shelter, and God only knew what Beth had done to the house in her absence. Freddie called every day, and Beth always said things were absolutely fine, which worried Freddie more than a little.

"I'm sorry you're going, but your timing's good," Holly said.

"How so?"

"I need to be on my own for a while."

Jack was off on another trip. He was seeing about opening a branch of his firm downstate, or so he said. Freddie didn't like the idea of Holly being alone, but there was no talking her around.

Holly ground out her cigarette in the crystal ashtray in front of her.

Her face took on a strange expression, as if she were listening to something far away. She said it made perfect sense now. Lorraine had taken the letter away with her, which is why she'd been there in the first place, the night of her stroke.

They hadn't talked about that incident since the day Holly came home from the hospital.

"Why would she want it now, after all this time?" Freddie asked. Better to indulge her, she thought.

"Because it was a lie. She lost her faith."

"Swinn didn't think so."

"He was wrong."

Freddie glanced out Holly's kitchen window. The snow had stopped. Holly wanted to believe that her stroke was connected to Lorraine's visit, when her own life choices were to blame. She always had a tendency to insulate herself from painful truths. As a child, the stories she told herself, such as why an injured bird couldn't be saved (because he was really an eagle and unable to bear captivity), or the reason her hands stayed chapped all winter (the elements hated their beauty), Lorraine called her "little follies."

Freddie put the tea things in the sink. She switched on the back porch light, then the front porch light, which was a good distance away.

"Let's go to bed and forget about your missing letter," she said when she returned.

"A final smoke, then we'll go."

"That can wait."

"Oh, all right."

Up they went together, slowly and in silence.

Part Four

Thirty-Seven

2012

Beth knew Nate was thinking about his wife. She'd come to see him that morning while Beth was out. Beth didn't know what they talked about, but if she had to guess, the wife made some last-ditch effort to get him back. The set of Nate's jaw said he was considering her request seriously. Beth wanted to kick his teeth in.

They had the house to themselves. Freddie was still at Holly's. It was Nate's day off. They'd had sex twice since lunch. Nate sat in the living room, shirtless, in a pair of new blue jeans. Beth wore a silk bathrobe. Now that the glow was gone, she pushed the point.

"So, what happened, exactly?" she asked.

"She asked if I wanted to see her hair."

"Her hair?"

"Yup."

Elaine—Bahira—said she'd been hasty in her understanding of Islam. Her husband was the one man who could view her hair, and the rest of her body, which was also draped and hidden away.

"Sounds like she was asking if you wanted her to take her clothes off," Beth said.

"More or less."

Beth pulled the belt of her robe tighter across her waist. She never asked a man if she could take off her clothes. She figured they wanted her to, so if she felt like it, she did.

"What did you say?" Beth asked.

"I didn't say anything."

"And then?"

Elaine apologized for what she'd put him through. She'd been made to see that she had neglected her duty as his wife. The law was clear—she had not divorced at the time of her conversion. She was still married, and subject to his will.

"Wow," Beth said.

"The thing is, she seemed to believe it. I mean, this woman never took orders from anyone. Now she's all submissive."

"Or pretending to be."

Beth stood up. She lit a cigarette, ignoring her mother's rule about no smoking in the house.

She looked at Nate. He was going bald. The stubble on his chin was white. He was eleven years older than she was. He made little money, wasn't as good in bed as Father Mark had been, and didn't have much to say for himself, but he made her feel safe, as if she didn't need to try to impress him because he saw her for who she was—someone who'd screwed a few things up and was doing better now.

Beth went into the kitchen and put last night's dishes in the sink. With Freddie away, she gave making a real dinner her best shot. The results were macaroni and cheese from a box, prewashed salad greens from a bag with bottled dressing, followed by ice cream. Back in Vegas she took food from the strip club all the time. The kitchen was always hopping. You wouldn't think that men who came to see naked girls would get hungry, but they did without fail. The menu was limited but reliable. The servers, all fat, middle-aged women with thin, frosted hair, had done their time, in life, in the joint, or right there in Jerry's dive. They told Beth to help herself. They all did, whether Jerry was looking or not. One was his sister, so it was said; another two were aunts. A whole family transported out from Arkansas to help the wonder boy make his fortune. Beth indulged. The cooler had French ham, roast beef, turkey, and several kinds of sliced cheese. Cheddar was Lawrence's favorite. She also took the French fries that came back on the heavy white oval plates, dropped them in the paper sacks used for the occasional carry-out lunch (*Hey, I'm just here for a quick pussy view, but I'm on the job, you know?*), then reheated them in her microwave. She learned that if you wrapped them in a damp paper towel, they came out pretty well. She helped herself to hamburger patties and barbecued chicken wings. Even the occasional bottle of champagne when the bartender wasn't looking. Jerry never minded. Then he started minding. There were words, some ugly.

Nate came and put his arms around her from behind.

"Look. If you're trying to tell me you're going back to her, you should just say so," she said. She was surprised that her tone was so even. Her heart beat hard, and the thought of losing him sent a sharp ache down both of her arms and into her hands.

"That's not what I'm saying," he said.

"Is it what you're feeling?"

"I'd be lying if I said it never once crossed my mind."

She broke away and faced him.

"Go back to her, then," she said.

She slammed the bedroom door behind her. He knocked softly. She didn't answer. After a moment she came out.

"I'm sorry. I'm acting like a big baby. It's your life. You need to live it," she said.

"Come on, get dressed. Help me clean out those gutters."

Nate had offered to do that for Freddie. He figured without a man around, it was the sort of thing she could use. Freddie hadn't thought about them at all, then realized it had been at least two years since anyone had given them a look. Ken died a year ago. The year before that he was too sick to do much of anything. Nate sympathized. The whole thing sounded rotten as hell.

Nate pulled on his T-shirt and track shoes. Beth got into a denim jumpsuit and cowboy boots, things she hadn't worn since coming to South Dakota. She needed a quick taste of her old life, she thought. Just to remind herself how tough and hard she could be, in case Nate made up her mind against her.

They went outside. In the garage was an extension ladder hanging from a pair of sturdy hooks on the back wall. More tools were installed on either side. There were pruners and clippers, neatly coiled extension cords, a weed-whacker, a chain saw, a reciprocating saw, and wrenches in line from small to large, not one out of place. Nate liked a man who kept his tools that way. A man who respected tools was worthy of respect himself.

Nate carried the ladder out of the garage and set it up on the south side of the house, next to the back door. Beth stood nearby, not helping him, just watching the prairie dogs scamper in and out of their holes. She smoked.

"What was he like, your dad?" Nate asked. He was up the ladder, peering into the gutter.

"A hard-ass."

"Cops usually are."

"On the job, sure. They don't have to be that way at home."

"Strict?"

"Mean."

"He was probably scared."

"Of what?"

"The trouble a gorgeous daughter can get into."

Nate could see the whole length of the gutter. He climbed down. He saw no reason to check the one in front. He was disappointed. He needed to work on something for a while and keep his hands busy.

"Looks okay to me," he said.

"Glory be." Beth ground out her cigarette. Nate regarded the house as a whole. It was in good shape. The roof was only a couple of years old. The paint newer than that. Only the chimney leaned a bit. A thick gray crack ran at an angle across the upper third.

Nate put the ladder back in the garage. His need to move grew. He couldn't stay there right now. He didn't know how to say so.

They went inside.

"Do you want to go to the falls?" he asked.

Beth reckoned the time until she had to get Lawrence. Two more hours.

"Or, we could get a quick drink," he said.

"What, now?"

"Just a thought."

"Tell you what. Let's just cruise around."

They got into his truck. The air freshener hanging from the rearview mirror was in the shape of an evergreen tree. He drove down her street, then took a series of turns, heading nowhere in particular. The slowly passing world calmed him down. Sometimes there was nothing worse than feeling stuck in one place.

That's why his wife had left him. Because she felt stuck. The religious conversion was a way out. Now she was sorry, and he didn't believe it. Contrition didn't become her. That morning, she had begged him to understand her situation—that she was called by Allah to be a good Muslim wife. Her voice had been ragged. It used to be firm and full of scorn. Then she'd begged him to come and meet the imam at the mosque. They would be counseled together.

Not gonna happen, he'd said. She didn't press. She knew there was no going back. She'd cried. He'd taken it as a ruse.

He never really trusted her, he realized. Not even in the beginning. Maybe he knew deep down that while she might have loved him, she never needed him. Even her wanting forgiveness and to be his wife again had nothing to do with him. It was all about her, and that religion she'd swallowed. Beth's need of him was healthy, as if he completed her, and made her whole. What he had to figure out was how to keep Beth from feeling trapped. Beth was like Elaine in that she needed a sense of motion—progress even. Elaine had been impossible to keep happy. Beth seemed like less work, maybe because she valued happiness. Elaine hadn't, until the lack of it drove her nuts.

❧

Beth sat beside him, silent. She looked at the bare trees. Against the sky, their branches reminded her of lace.

They turned another corner.

"Wait, go back," Beth said.

"Why?"

"Just back up."

Beth told him when to stop. They were in front of a tiny house, with a leaning For Rent sign tacked to a wooden stake in the grassless yard. It was old, and poorly kept. There were two windows, one on either side of a short flight of sagging stairs. One of the windows had shutters. The other didn't. A box that might once have held blooming flowers beneath the shuttered window was full of dead, brown plants. A brand-new SUV sat in the driveway.

"You're not thinking of moving in there, are you?" Nate asked.

Beth got out of the truck and looked at the house. Nate turned off the engine. He got out, too.

"My mother used to live here," Beth said.

"I'd say she's moved up in the world."

"At least, I think it's the same place. She took me by here once, years ago. But I remember that tree, I think." The cottonwood was huge. Its roots lifted the sidewalk.

On the day in question Ken got mad at Freddie. Beth heard them arguing in the kitchen. She was in middle school, and her mother had a job her father didn't want her to have. A lot of Beth's friends had mothers who worked. Freddie worked in a grocery store, something she'd done before, apparently, or so she said as she and Beth drove aimlessly around the neighborhood, waiting for Ken to cool off.

They came to this house, got out, and stood, just as Beth and Nate were doing then. Beth was bored at that point. The novelty of being plucked from her routine had worn off. She asked if they could go home yet. Freddie said to give it a little longer.

He's a jerk, Beth said.

At least you have a father.

Beth didn't know a lot about how her mother grew up. She let things come out slowly, at odd moments, like that afternoon, when Ken said that getting a job meant she was neglecting her duty as a wife and mother.

I'll tell you what a mother who neglects her duty really does, Beth. She takes off, leaves you alone, forbids you to go to school.

"She was talking about herself," Beth told Nate.

"She didn't go to school?"

"Not until she was like eleven or twelve."

They walked down the driveway, past the SUV. There was a metal pole pounded into the hard earth. The pole had a string secured through a metal loop about a foot from the top. A ball must have been attached at the other end. Children would have stood there, batting the ball back and forth.

Beth looked delighted. She gave a wide, winning smile. Nate smiled back.

"We had one of these on the playground at school," Beth said.

"Was it ball-less?"

"Ha-ha."

Beth looked at the pole. Her hands were on her hips.

"One day I grabbed that fucking thing, launched myself off the ground. I wanted to swing around it like a monkey at the zoo, but of course I ended up right on my ass," Beth said.

"No lasting damage, from what I can see."

She jumped for the pole, grabbed it hard, then swung her legs up over her head and slowly rotated. She came back upright, hooked one leg around the pole, and spun around. The friction between her palm and the pole made a screech. She hopped back to earth.

A man was at the back door, watching them through the small dirty window.

Beth grabbed Nate's hand, and they ran down the driveway back to his truck. They got in. They were still laughing a minute later, as the house faded in the rearview mirror.

"Bet your wife can't do *that*. You keep that in mind when you take her back. There you'll be, some dull, homey evening while she knits by the fire—"

"Knits?"

"—and you'll remember me on that pole. And you'll be sorry!"

"No. I won't."

The color rose in her cheeks as she prepared to attack him for the insult, not to mention her hurt feelings, but he told her to stay quiet because he wasn't letting Elaine come back, now or ever.

They came to a stop sign. Nate turned towards the falls. His divorce would be final in another two weeks. He wanted Beth to understand that the last thing he wanted to do was rush into getting married again, assuming she was even thinking along those lines, which given what he knew about her, seemed unlikely as hell. Even so, if she could see her way clear to making some sort of life with him, he'd be grateful. No, not grateful exactly, that wasn't the word he wanted, it didn't sum up what he was trying to say at all—

"Honored?" Beth asked.

"Honored works."

Thirty-Eight

Three days later, after Elaine had recovered from her temporary despair, she asked to bring the divorce papers there to the house. It was Saturday.

"How did she get them so fast?" Beth asked.

"Had them for a while, apparently."

"Stalling for time."

Beth went on plucking her eyebrows. It hurt like hell. She swore with every yank. Nate was unhappy, too. He didn't want Elaine there, either. He told her to come around 4 p.m.

The phone rang. Beth answered in the kitchen. It was Freddie, making her daily call.

"You're early," Beth said. It was just shy of noon.

"Holly's taking a nap."

"She doing okay?"

"I think so."

Nate took a beer out of the refrigerator. Beth gestured for him to put it back. He didn't.

"How are things there?" Freddie asked.

"Fine. Same. Only, well, I do have a bit of news."

"You got a job!"

"No, sorry."

"What, then?"

"Nate and I are getting pretty serious."

Nate appeared in the doorway. He gave a thumbs-up. Beth ignored him.

"So, is the wife out of the picture?" Freddie asked.

"They're signing the papers today."

"Oh, that's wonderful."

Freddie asked after Pudgy. Then she wanted to talk to Lawrence. He was at a friend's, spending the night. *And thank God for that*, Beth thought.

They finished and said good-bye. Beth couldn't sit still. She tidied up the kitchen. Then she went to work on the dining room and living room. She wasn't about to have Elaine think that she couldn't make a nice home for someone. She stopped short, in the middle of fluffing up one of Freddie's inane frilled sofa pillows. *What the hell's wrong with me?*

Your inner domestic goddess is coming out, that's all. That's what Father Mark would say. Beth had had only one postcard from him, several months ago. He was in Florida then, for some reason, taking in the deco architecture in Miami.

The last chore Beth took on was to clean the bathroom. She left Nate's disposable razor in a prominent place, right on the counter, next to his can of shaving cream. Nate wandered in, and said he had to use the toilet. He gave her a warm, beery kiss.

"Don't you worry about old Elaine. I'll get the papers; she'll be on her way," he said.

"Better be."

As Beth thought might happen, Elaine was late. She arrived in an ancient Volkswagen Bug that sputtered and rocked a few moments after she turned off the engine. As she got out, the hem of her long black dress got caught in the door. Her face twisted in frustration.

Shortly after, as they all sat at the dining room table, Elaine, who'd introduced herself to Beth as Bahira, said she'd never been happier with her choice of life paths. She had come there expressly to tell both of them that. She wanted them to hear it directly from her.

"Forgive me, but what makes you think either of us gives a shit?" Beth asked.

"Take it easy," Nate said.

Bahira was unperturbed. She stared calmly at Beth.

"You're very pretty. I can see why he went for you," Bahira said.

"Thanks. Where are the papers?"

Bahira removed a pen and a thick envelope from the large purse at her feet. She put them on the table.

"Nate, I have a favor to ask. I'm going away for a while. My mother hasn't been all that well. She still speaks fondly of you. I hope you can stay in touch, maybe call her now and then," she said.

"You haven't talked to your mother for years. She didn't even come to our wedding," Nate said.

"We've reconciled."

Now, isn't that handy, thought Beth. She wanted a drink. Nate had had four beers at last count, and she wasn't about to offer him another. She went into the kitchen and mixed herself a scotch and soda. The scotch was hers, because Freddie had none in the house. She drank some. She took out a pot and filled it with water. Maybe if Bahira thought dinner was underway, she'd get off her ass and leave. Pudgy appeared. He'd been sleeping on Lawrence's bed. At the sound of a strange voice, he took himself into the living room and barked at Bahira until Nate lifted him into his lap. Beth listened from just inside the kitchen doorway while she finished her drink.

"Seriously? Iraq?" Nate asked.

"Yes."

"Jesus! Why?"

"To work for an aid organization. Also to learn Arabic."

Good! The farther, the better, thought Beth.

"Maybe al-Qaeda will recruit you," Nate said.

"That's not funny."

"You'd be a prime target. Pissed off American woman. Wouldn't take much for them to talk you into showing up with a suicide bomb."

"Stop it, Nate."

Beth put her empty glass in the sink and went into the dining room.

"What were you doing in there?" Nate asked her.

"Drinking."

Beth sat down. She brought her hand to cheek. It felt smooth and warm. She could tell her neck was flushed. Being fair made that a sure fate every time she drank.

"You know, Muslims treat women like dogs," Beth said.

"Beth," Nate said.

"Their big theory is that a woman's body inflames a man's desire, so she needs to hide herself away, keep herself under wraps, lest he commit some sin."

"That's a very simplistic view," Bahira said.

"Really? Do enlighten me, then."

Bahira smoothed down the papers in front of her. She recapped the plastic pen in her hand. Her eyes were downcast, as if studying the surface of the table.

"The abaya gives us freedom," Bahira said.

"How do you figure that?" Beth asked.

"We aren't judged by how we look. No one of us is more beautiful, or sexier, or slimmer, than another. We're all the same."

"Is that why you converted? So you could walk around in some sort of uniform and get lost in the crowd?"

"No. Because I wanted to discover who I really am, and the abaya is only a small part of that. Small, but necessary."

"So, you promote modesty of dress, but really what you're saying is that women are first and foremost sexual objects, so you need to cover up—"

Like a nun. Exactly like a nun! Jesus, Mark. Why didn't you tell me that's what they're all about? Maybe they want piety, the pure connection to God, okay, I get that, but they also want to hide—

"—because men always want to undress us . . . they want us to be . . ."

Naked. And sexual. Anytime. Anywhere.

"Available," Bahira said.

Like in a strip club.

Beth rubbed her forehead. She was woozy. And hungry, too. She'd had half a grapefruit for breakfast, and a scrambled egg for lunch. She'd gained weight since moving back home, though Nate said she looked fine. Better than fine, actually.

Bahira signed the papers. Then she put them in front of Nate, and showed him where to sign. She handed him the pen.

"I assume you want to bring them to the lawyer yourself?" she asked him.

"Yeah."

"All right, then."

Nate stared at the documents in his hand.

"Can you guys give me a minute alone with these? I want to read them, make sure it's all clear."

Beth got up and went onto the back porch. She welcomed the cool air on her skin. After a moment Bahira appeared.

"Do you mind?" Bahira asked. Beth shrugged.

They sat side by side, observing the brown prairie stretching before them. A flock of birds lifted from the ground, calling loudly, diving and rising, and then disappeared. A lone cottonwood tree stood proudly in the distance. Beth thought if she concentrated hard enough on the view, she'd forget that Bahira was there, and even the faint spicy scent she gave off would disappear.

"You're curious about Islam, I can tell," Bahira said.

"Because I think it's stupid?"

"Because you think about it at all."

Beth wanted another drink. Bahira was between her and the kitchen. Wouldn't it be the craziest thing to offer her one? Muslims didn't drink, though, did they?

"You know, I wanted to be a scientist," Bahira said.

"Yeah?"

"Wasn't sure what kind. Maybe a chemist, or a biologist. But school and I didn't get along. To be specific, college and I didn't get along. I dropped out."

"Uh-huh."

"And when I first came to love Islam, I thought about what I used to want, which was to know the world, to really *know* it, and I realized it was impossible. That we can never really know the world, not all the way down."

"You're saying there will always be unknowns."

"I'm saying the more you know, the more you realize the extent of what you'll never know."

Beth wondered how much more time Nate needed by himself.

"That's not very optimistic," Beth said.

"On the contrary. It's the basis of faith."

"I thought the basis of faith was the admittance of a possibility."

Bahira turned her head in Beth's direction.

"Explain," she said.

"Once you accept that there a lot of things you never see or experience, you allow the possibility of something bigger than yourself." Beth had formulated that idea after listening to Father Mark's desperate ramblings on that very porch.

"And when allowing becomes seeking, you find faith," Bahira said.

"Something like that."

Pudgy came to the screen door and whined. Beth stood up, reached across Bahira, opened the door, and let him out. He stared at Bahira, but didn't bark. Then he went slowly and stiffly down the steps to the yard. He ambled over to an old truck tire Freddie used as a planter, and lifted his leg.

"So, you believe in God," Bahira said.

Nate was at the door. The women went inside, leaving Pudgy to wander around the yard, sniffing the earth. Nate had a fresh beer in his hand. He gestured to the papers on the dining room table.

"All done," he said.

Bahira reviewed the papers one last time, refolded them, and put them in his hand.

"Well, good luck, then," she said.

Nate nodded. Beth wondered if they'd embrace. They didn't. Nate walked her to the front door. Beth stayed put. When Bahira had gone, Nate asked what she wanted to do for dinner. They could go out and celebrate. Beth said they should stay in and order pizza instead.

Thirty-Nine

Beth's conversation with Bahira had unsettled her. Then, not twenty-four hours later, Father Mark called from Florida to say he was on his way home and needed to see her.

He didn't want to come to the house. He wanted Beth to meet him in a bar by the airport during his three-hour layover. Why not a bar *in* the airport? Because there weren't any outside the security cordon. She'd have to have a plane ticket in hand to get that far in. But if he left the airport to meet her, he'd just have to go through the security screen a second time. Wouldn't he mind? He said it was fine. But they'd question him, wouldn't they? They'd want to know what he'd been doing with his time during those few hours. Because who wanders away from the airport when he's got a plane to catch? His long silence said he found her concern confusing. Then he explained that he'd say he was called away by someone in need.

The right thing would be to tell him thanks but no thanks, and stay home. She couldn't help being curious, though. Maybe he was going to fall at her feet and beg her to come back with him. She sort of hoped he would. An emotional plea like that would be a huge ego boost. Since leaving Las Vegas she'd had to be satisfied with the occasional glances she got from men in public. Nate told her all the time how beautiful she was, but it wasn't the same. All her life she'd hungered for male admiration. She was bright enough to know that this stemmed from her father's constant disapproval of her when she was young. Yet it was more than that. It was a sort of power she had over the men who looked at her. Were she to

236

approach one, and make her interest clear, he wouldn't refuse. She knew it was wrong. She left Las Vegas to change not only her life but also her attitude. She was trying not to see men as hopeless morons enslaved by lust.

"It's more a question of how you see yourself, isn't it?" Nate asked her.

"Guess so."

"So, you won't meet him?"

"No."

She went, though. Nate was at work. On the drive, she told herself it was okay that she'd intended to meet Father Mark all along. If Nate found out, she would promote the idea of closure. *Have to shut one door before I can open another one, right?* Nate might say she was weak-willed and deceitful. He'd be right on both counts.

Father Mark, on the other hand, took her showing up as evidence of both her strength and her willingness to face the truth about their relationship.

"What truth is that?" she asked. The bar had a view of a runway. Seeing planes rise into the air made her feel both queasy and restless.

"That we will always be responsible for each other."

He wasn't wearing his collar. His hair had grown. So had his beard. He looked more like a college student than a man of the cloth. His drink had changed, too. He used to like martinis. Now he drank beer in a frosted mug. The only luggage he had was a worn backpack he'd thrown on the floor. A decent wristwatch that had been his father's had been replaced with a cheap digital one.

"You're dreaming," Beth said. She was on her second whiskey and soda.

"I don't mean we have any sort of a future together. Even if you wanted one, it's impossible."

"Because I split?"

"Because in loving you I discovered who I am."

"And who's that?"

"A weak man, a flawed one, too, but most definitely a man of God."

"Oh."

"You sound disappointed," Father Mark said.

"No, not at all. No skin off my ass if you're still devout. No surprise, either. I figure something a lot more important than me would have to come along to make you give all that up."

"There isn't anything more important than you, Beth. You were what tested my faith, and what made me find it again."

"Three cheers for me." She wished she hadn't come. She wanted to board one of the airplanes out there and disappear into the sky.

"And I hope that you think I was the one who nudged you into a new life, too," Father Mark said.

Beth shrugged. She wanted another drink.

"You were sick of things when I came along. You just didn't know it then. But you know it now. And you know you'll never go back to how it all used to be."

"Unless I get really hard up for dough."

"Not even then. I can see you've changed."

Another plane rushed down the tarmac. She thought of the people inside who might hate flying and did it anyway. Facing down a fear was tough. Learning you'd always be afraid of it was even tougher.

"I don't think I look so different," Beth said. She was aware of the belligerence in her tone.

"Not on the outside, maybe. But on the inside."

"Uh-huh."

"You forget, I'm trained to see inside people."

"Like Superman, with your X-ray eyes."

"Something like that."

Father Mark grinned, and drank his beer. She missed him all of a sudden in a way that made her heart pound. *What the hell*, she thought. *What the fucking hell?*

She wanted to know about Florida. He said it had been difficult to be in a new place. At first he intended to travel, but once there, he found a motel that rented by the week, and more or less settled in. He volunteered at a homeless shelter, then at a mission. He didn't tell anyone he was a priest on leave. He never wore his collar.

He'd gone to visit his wife some weeks before. She seemed to like the flowers he brought. When she smiled at them, something of the old Lydia appeared. He was surprised by how sad it made him—but strong, too. In fact, the last several months seem to have been one long trial to assess his worth as a human being.

"Heavy," Beth said. She knew exactly what he meant, though.

"Yes. It was."

"And now?"

"Back to Vegas, back to the church."

"Back to the arrogant snots who manage things out there."

"Arrogant snots are always among us."

Beth pondered her empty glass. She decided against a third.

Father Mark said it was time to go. Beth didn't want to leave, even though only moments before she'd been restless and ill at ease. She envied him his calm. Knowing what to do with yourself didn't come easily. She was proof of that, wasn't she?

"I'm getting married," she said.

"Congratulations."

Father Mark watched her, waiting for her to continue with the obvious details. In the old days she'd have conjured up a long bridal train, flower girls, and the whole works, or if she'd wanted to get a dig in, she'd have them running back to Las Vegas to a little chapel that rented by the hour. Now she said nothing, silenced by the enormity of her lie.

"Thanks," she said.

"Send me pictures of the wedding, won't you?"

"Sure."

"And give Lawrence my best."

"Okay."

Now it was her turn to wait. Why didn't he ask about her fiancé? Wasn't he interested? Or had he removed himself so far from her life that he didn't feel it was any of his business? She felt herself falling into the gulf that had opened up between them. She remembered him in bed, holding her. She remembered him thrusting inside her. He was the best lover she'd ever had, way better than Nate, though Nate tried. *Oh, God*, she thought. Her face grew warm. Father Mark looked at her calmly.

"Say hello to your mother for me," Father Mark said.

"I will."

"She's quite a woman, in her way."

"She's in Minnesota with my aunt."

"I see."

"She had a stroke. My aunt, I mean. And my mother went to be with her."

"Doing her Christian duty."

"Well, I don't know if I'd call it that."

Father Mark stood up. He put money on the table for their drinks. Beth had no choice but to stand up, too. They walked together out of the bar. The noise of traffic along the highway was loud. He gave her a discreet hug, the kind a friend gives a friend, with space between them. She pulled him hard. His arms went around her, and his face was on her neck. She wanted him to kiss her. He didn't, but he didn't he pull away, either. When he did, she realized that every time she made love with Nate, it was Father Mark she wanted and always would.

Forty

To keep her mind off Mark, Beth cleaned the house again. Freddie was due home the following day, and she didn't want to get any critical remarks about how she'd let things go. Her nervous energy even led her to give Pudgy a bath, which he accepted, but not without the requisite struggle and thrashing of limbs. She dried him as well as she could with an old towel. When she found him a bit later, standing miserably in the kitchen with his still-damp fur in peaks, she used her hair dryer on him, set on low, which furthered his malaise.

During Freddie's absence, Nate stayed over every night. He loved it, and wanted to get a place of their own. The problem was that a security deposit on a rental house was beyond the pathetic balance in Nate's checking account. Beth had money. She said so often enough. Her expenses since moving back to South Dakota had been few. Freddie was generous that way. He didn't want to ask her for help, but he had to if they were going to go on living together. She wrote him a check for two thousand dollars on the spot. That would be more than enough. Didn't she want to look at places with him? No, not today. Today she was up to her ears in housework.

She went to pick up Lawrence at school, as she did every afternoon. He was late leaving the building. She asked him why. He said his friend Ernie was crying.

"Why was Ernie crying?" Beth asked. She had trained herself to take an interest in what Lawrence said, to follow up and continue the conversation until Lawrence's attention jumped to something else.

"His grandmother died."

"I see."

"I told him it was okay to be sad."

"He must have been very good friends with his grandmother."

"Not really."

"Then why is he sad?"

"Because his mother's sad."

"Oh, right."

Beth was six, just about Lawrence's age, when Lorraine died. She never knew her. What she heard was scant. Wry remarks from her father about a drunken Bible-thumper. She didn't remember how the news had been received. A telephone call, most likely. But not on the day itself, or even a few days later. Some time had passed between the death and her mother hearing of it.

In her short life, Beth had often seen her mother angry. She had seen her turn cold and sullen, silent for hours on end. She saw the hard looks she gave her father. She saw warmth, too, and love. Her mother was also always busy with something, as if sitting too long might challenge her ability to get up again. There was a sense of lurking hopelessness, something held firmly in check.

That day, Beth saw her mother weep, and her father reduced first to utter helplessness, then to anger.

How the hell can give you a damn, after the way she treated you? he demanded. Beth watched them pace the kitchen from the corner of the couch she occupied, forgotten.

The weeping grew more frantic. Beth's father threatened to knock some sense into her mother if she didn't stop. Her mother told him to go ahead and try, to see where it got him. Her voice was ragged and halting, her face twisted and shiny with tears.

If you think she cared about you, you're wrong!

Beth began to hate her father then, not for the first time. He was sometimes mean to her, but often he just treated her as if she didn't exist. He spoke of her in the third person when she was in the same room. *Isn't she going to school tomorrow?* he asked when she'd been home sick. Or, *please tell her not to bother me when I'm trying to read.* Beth's mother, sitting right there on the sofa next to her could have said, *Tell her yourself* but didn't. Her mother, Beth noticed, seemed to want to say a lot of things and held back out of respect, or fear. Beth's father was a commanding figure, especially when he was in uniform.

His anger made him seem weak, desperate. Underneath the harsh words was despair. Beth understood that her father was scared of her mother's sorrow, afraid of what it would mean to all of them. Then her mother was no longer hysterical, just grim. She went into her bedroom and closed the door. Beth's father told her to go outside and play. Beth didn't move. He sat at the kitchen table with a bottle of beer and ignored her. The house was silent. Beth thought that her mother must have fallen asleep. She wondered who would make her dinner.

Beth walked quietly to her parents' bedroom. She slowly turned the knob and gently pushed the door open. Her mother wasn't on the bed, but on her knees, in the center of the room, her hands clasped tightly in front of her. Her eyes were closed and her lips moved. Her mother was praying. It was the only time she ever saw her do it. Some of Beth's friends went to church. Later, Beth asked why they didn't go, too. Beth's father, in a rare good mood, laughingly said that her mother was allergic to it.

"They're not putting her in the ground. They're going to burn her up," Lawrence said.

"That's called cremation. All that's left are ashes."

"Is that why they say, 'Dust to dust, ashes to ashes'?"

"Where did you hear that?"

"Grandma."

Beth thought that unlikely, despite her now remembering the praying incident. Yet that strain in her had always been there. Moments of quiet reflection with her eyes closed. There was no Bible in the house—at least Beth had never seen one. Yet her mother deferred to something beyond herself, something she never spoke of.

The anniversary of her father's death was less than a week away, and that, too, intruded. Beth's presence at the funeral parlor had been reluctant. Freddie said nothing about her being drunk. Lawrence had stayed behind in Las Vegas with friends. Death was no atmosphere for a child, but in truth that wasn't why Beth didn't bring him. She simply couldn't handle her own feelings and him, too. There was no love lost between her and her father, but she mourned him nonetheless. Just as Freddie had mourned her own mother. A connection was a connection, and when it broke, you felt it pretty hard.

Nate was on the front steps waiting for her. The day was cold; his jacket was zipped up. He rubbed his hands together for warmth. He pulled out a piece of paper, and waved it in the air.

"Lease agreement," he said.

"That was fast."

"What is it?" Lawrence asked.

"We're moving," Beth said.

"Where?"

"Not far. Just a few blocks, in fact. You'll be a little closer to school," Nate said.

"What about Grandma?" Lawrence asked. His nose had started to run in the cold.

"She'll stay here. This is her home," Beth said.

"I don't want to leave Grandma."

"Well, we couldn't stay with her forever." Beth realized that her tone wasn't particularly kind. She'd never been very good at reassuring him.

"But she'll be all by herself!"

They went inside. Lawrence whined for a few moments more, then turned his attention to the cookies he wanted to eat. Beth got them for him. She told him not to get crumbs all over the carpet, or he'd have to run the vacuum cleaner himself. He ate with one hand cupped under his chin to catch anything that fell. Beth said he could go and watch television if he wanted to.

When they were alone Beth asked Nate when they could move in.

"As soon as we like. Tomorrow, even. It's got a decent kitchen, and the bathroom's been upgraded. It's empty, though, so we should round up some furniture."

"Did you already give notice at your apartment?"

"I will as soon as you have a chance to look the place over and give it your seal of approval."

Beth flopped down on the couch. Suddenly the whole prospect felt exhausting. And confining. She still hadn't found a job. Nate could probably cover the rent on what he made, but she insisted on covering herself and Lawrence both. It wouldn't be too much longer before she ran through her savings. There was a strip club on the other side of town. It had been there for years, even when she was in high school. The easiest thing in the world would be to walk in there and say she'd worked in Vegas. She could stop worrying about money then.

"What?" Nate asked. As usual, he'd sat down opposite her and studied her face.

"How would you feel if I went back to pole dancing?"

"Like shit."

"I see."

"Don't get like that. You know I'm not a prude. But you need to do better."

"Thanks, Dad."

"Oh, for Christ's sake, Beth!"

She closed her eyes for a moment. Maybe when she opened them he'd be looking at something else. He wasn't.

"You think pole dancing equates with immaturity?" she asked.

"I think it sells you short. And I think it'll be hard for Lawrence to make sense of."

Beth hadn't thought about Lawrence. He was older now, more curious about life. Sooner or later, how she earned her money would cross his radar.

"Besides, didn't you tell me you couldn't stand it anymore?" Nate asked.

"I guess it doesn't seem as awful, now that I've been away from it for a while."

"Trust me, it wouldn't take long for you to hate it again."

His hands were dirty. So were his slacks. The company he drove a truck for distributed beer. All those dusty cases, going into the backs of bars all over Sioux Falls made Beth yearn for a beer right then. She needed to be outside, with air on her face. She told Lawrence she'd be in the backyard, and to yell at the door if he needed her. Then she told Nate to come with her. He put his jacket back on. She grabbed an old sweater hanging on one of the pegs in the hall. It had been there since she moved back, and she never thought about it. Now she realized it was her father's. Freddie had done a pretty good job of clearing out his stuff, and she'd done it mostly alone, because Beth had stayed in Vegas the whole time. Holly came out to help, and didn't stay long, apparently because Freddie said she didn't want to be meddled with just then. Beth didn't understand why the sweater had been spared her mother's purge, and had a ghoulish thought that sometimes, when she was particularly lonely, Freddie might put it on for comfort.

If she can handle it, I can, too!

"Where are we going?" Nate asked.

"Out there."

They were walking over the stretch of barren land that backed onto the house, through the prairie dog holes, which Beth cautioned Nate to avoid stepping in. Beth crossed her arms against the cold. The sweater's extra-long sleeves reminded her of a straight jacket.

"This guy I work with had a drug problem—major. Heroin, the whole thing," Nate said.

"And he got a job driving a truck?"

"He has to give a urine sample every week. Anyway, he says he gets tempted from time to time. You know, the stress of life gets to be a pain. And he says the best way to battle addiction is to realize that your life's not about the drug anymore."

"I'm not addicted to pole dancing. I'm just used to it."

"But it's not what your life's about now."

They paused. The wind was swift and fresh. Dead leaves from a far-off tree raced along the ground. Snow would fall within the week, Beth was sure. This would be her first winter in South Dakota in over ten years.

Nate and Beth turned back toward the house. Nate walked forward. Beth didn't. He turned around.

"Why are you crying?" he asked.

She shook her head.

"What is it?" He had his arms around her.

"I was just thinking that if my dad had lived another year, he'd have witnessed my miraculous transformation from slut to proper citizen."

"Would that have changed how he treated you?"

"No. He just had it in for me, no matter what."

"I bet it was more complicated than that."

Nate said he read somewhere once that a lot of cops were reformed crooks, at least emotionally. That's why they were drawn to law enforcement in the first place. Bad people doing bad things were appealing, not only because they were a challenge, but also because catching them was a way of sublimating their own urges.

"You're saying my dad wanted to be a criminal?" Beth asked. She used one ridiculously long sleeve to wipe her nose.

"No, but he was drawn to the world they live in. He'd have to be, don't you see?"

She shrugged.

"And you went right into that world. Or, up to very edge of it, at least."

"That's why he hated me."

"He was jealous. You flaunted authority. There must have been a lot of times when he wanted to do the same thing."

They continued walking. Beth was cold now. Nate was right. It wasn't just admiration she'd been after—she'd wanted to piss off her father. With his urn in the ground, she no longer had an audience. She could accept that. The question was, could she handle it from now on?

When she looked at the house again, Lawrence was on the back porch waving at them with Pudgy at his side.

Forty-One

On Freddie's last night in Minneapolis, when the snowfall stopped and the world froze, she and Holly sat in the kitchen below a cheerful ring of light. Freddie was comfortable there, in Holly's grand house. Holly wasn't. She was restless and dissatisfied.

"I've done nothing but drift," she told Freddie. "I put up a wall. I've lived as if none of it ever happened. We look at the pictures every year and I think, 'Okay, there they are again,' and then I forget that they ever existed."

"Isn't that what you wanted, though? To be free of the past?"

"We're never free."

Holly's brow was knitted; her mouth was turned down. She was a little girl again, in the shadows of the tent, back in a corner on a chair or cot, turning the whole world over in her mind.

"You're talking about Mother," Freddie said.

"She did a lot of lousy things, you know? But the worst was keeping us from faith."

"All she did was throw faith at us, morning, noon, and night!"

"Which turned us away."

Holly looked at her rings. On her right hand was a large aquamarine she'd gotten one summer in Norway. On her left was the diamond Jack bought her for their twentieth anniversary. It was over two carats. Freddie's diamond was a speck of light in comparison.

"If she wanted us to live in the Spirit, she should have let us find our own way, just as she did," Holly said.

"Maybe. But keep in mind, she was too wrapped up in it all to think clearly a lot of the time."

Freddie got up and put their wineglasses in the sink. She thought about washing them by hand and didn't want to. She had a long day tomorrow. She was a poor traveler, and flying always unsettled her.

Freddie sat down again. Holly looked grim. She lit a cigarette with a gold lighter—not a gift from Jack, something she bought for herself.

"Look, instead of looking back, why not look forward instead?" Freddie asked.

"You mean life as a divorced woman."

Holly had had enough. Maybe it was her health crisis that made everything clear—she didn't know. She just wanted out. But not quite yet.

"What are you waiting for, if your mind's made up?" Freddie asked.

"To talk to someone."

"A lawyer?"

"No, not a lawyer."

"Well, if you need a sounding board, I'm sitting right here."

Holly said nothing. Then, "I met someone through a friend."

"You mean a therapist?"

"No."

"Who, then? What's the big mystery?"

"It's a pastor."

Freddie saw something in the corner of her eye. The snowfall had resumed. She rose once more, retrieved the wineglasses, and opened another bottle. She had lined up several on the counter the day before. Jack had an extensive wine collection, Freddie had discovered, which he didn't typically share. He was sharing it now, like it or not.

"Don't look like that," Holly said.

"I don't look like anything. If you have a pastor, you have a pastor."

"I don't 'have' him. He's the husband of someone in my book club. He counsels people."

"Baptist, I suppose?"

"Yes."

"Must feel out of place here, in the frozen north."

"No doubt."

Holly said this man's grandfather had been the same sort of revival tent preacher that Joseph Swinn was. He was fascinated by Holly's accounts of her childhood. He suggested that she consider writing a book.

"I told him that would be too much work," Holly said.

Freddie drank her wine. She didn't know how much she'd had that evening. She'd lost track, but didn't feel one bit woozy. On the contrary, she felt keen and sharp-witted.

"And you want advice about getting divorced?" Freddie said.

"Just a chance to talk it through."

"He'll tell you not to."

"Maybe. I expect what he'll actually tell me to do is pray."

"Quite likely."

"And I would, but I don't remember how."

"To pray?"

Holly nodded. Freddie didn't know what to say.

"It's not just folding your hands and bowing your head, you know. It's a state of mind. Like going into some special place where you can hear yourself think," Holly said.

Preaching to the choir, eh, Ken?

Holly drank her wine, too. Her face was flushed and her eyes were bright. She looked calm, almost peaceful. She let her cigarette burn in the ashtray without smoking it.

"And you need his help to find that place," Freddie said. Her voice was level. She was good at controlling her inflections.

"More or less."

Holly leaned back and looked out the window. The snow was steady and light, swirling in the bitter cold. Her neck seemed loose, and her head lolled a bit. Freddie said they should probably get to bed.

Holly put out her cigarette. She was looking forward to sleep, because sometimes God came to her in her dreams, she said. Freddie went to her own room, double-checked how she'd packed her suitcase, and then slept, without visitors or dreams of any kind.

Epilogue
2012

Freddie's house is warm against the winter wind that seemed fiercer than usual this year. Pudgy grudgingly accepts being put into a lively striped sweater Freddie decided the weather made necessary. It doesn't fit properly, a bit too tight in the neck so that the folds around his head are shoved forward, giving him a tough, commanding air that is at odds with the gentle, retiring soul he truly is. They make their rounds several times a day, heads down, pace steady, always grateful for the walk's end and for returning to the peaceful brightness of their home.

Freddie won't put up a Christmas tree this year. She never liked them. The idea of chopping one down just so it could die in her living room always made her sad. Ken loved his tree, though, and put great care into decorating it. Last year, which she spent alone despite repeated offers of company from both Beth and Holly, she bought a tree as a tribute to his memory; but this year she will suit herself and be happy with her own traditions.

Beth still has no job and has made peace with a slow economy and living off Nate's income. Sometimes she volunteers at Lawrence's school. The other mothers have accepted her. One of the teachers is old enough to remember her as a student in the first and second grades, before her distrust and hatred of her father turned her away from wanting to learn and excel.

Holly will leave Jack after the first of the year, a decision she made on her own, without consulting the pastor she spoke of to Freddie. She refers to that episode as a "weak moment," and confesses that her stroke rattled her more than she saw at first. She wants Freddie to know that she's had no more visits from Lorraine. Freddie is glad to hear it. Holly also intends to quit smoking—again. Freddie is glad to hear that, too.

When Holly moves out, she will return to Sioux Falls and buy a nice house there. She considers making an offer on their old place, gutting it, and starting over. Freddie says that's probably not a great idea. In the spring, when the weather is gentle again, Holly wants to drive out to Coshocton and see the site of the old camp, which her research, borne of sudden and intense curiosity, says was torn down years before. She wants Freddie to go with her. Freddie doesn't know yet if she will.

Freddie discusses all of this with Ken, who doesn't respond as fast as he used to. She supposes that's to be expected. His spirit is moving on from hers now, finding all the other spirits of the dead. She vows to remember everything she can of him, and when her mind fails, which it must if she lives long enough, she will take on faith the man he was and wasn't.

She spends time now and then with her photographs, looking more closely at them than before. Anna is so petite and dark, Olaf tall and wide. Between them stands Lorraine, not looking at the camera, but to the side, as if listening to music only she can hear. Their boardinghouse grows dingy over the years, as if the money ran out, or their interest waned for some other reason. Maybe Lorraine running off drained them so much they lacked the energy to carry on as they once did.

How strange to think that the story of her family is written by women who fled. Anna left the country of her birth. Lorraine left Anna and Olaf. Beth left Freddie and Ken. Beth came back, though—too late to reconcile with Ken, but Freddie is pleased nevertheless.

I never escaped anything, Freddie thinks calmly. *I bore the brunt.*

She sits by her fire, Pudgy at her feet, and drops down into a quiet, safe place where she hasn't been for a while. It's time to return, and become familiar again with seeking out comfort and truth. It's time to ask and hope for answers, to be made whole simply by asking.

I've been away. Sorry about that. You know how things have been.

Pudgy twitches in his sleep. His front paws run over the field after a prairie dog, and the rest of him follows.

So, here's what I want to know.

Her mind wanders for a bit. Holly's new house. Beth's life with Nate. Her own future, built on sturdy bricks from the past.

Her heartbeat is strong, steady, not tired yet.

She concentrates.

Are You there? Are You listening?

Just tell me. I'm right here.

THE END

Acknowledgments

A portion of this novel appeared as a stand-alone story entitled "An Act of Concealment" in the Winter/Spring 2013 issue of *Crab Orchard Review*, and was a finalist in their annual Jack Dyer Fiction Prize.

About the Author

© John Christiansen

Anne Leigh Parrish's debut story collection, *All The Roads That Lead From Home* (Press 53, 2011) won a silver medal in the 2012 Independent Publisher Book Awards. Her second collection, *Our Love Could Light The World*, (She Writes Press, 2013) is a Kirkus Reviews recommended Indie title, and a finalist in both the International Book Awards and the Best Book Awards. She is the fiction editor for the online literary magazine *Eclectica*. She lives in Seattle.

SELECTED TITLES FROM SHE WRITES PRESS

She Writes Press is an independent publishing company
founded to serve women writers everywhere.
Visit us at www.shewritespress.com.

Our Love Could Light the World by Anne Leigh Parrish
$15.95, 978-1-938314-44-5
Twelve stories depicting a dysfunctional and chaotic—yet lovable—
family that has to band together in order to survive.

The Belief in Angels by J. Dylan Yates
$16.95, 978-1-938314-64-3
From the Majdonek death camp to a volatile hippie household on the
East Coast, this narrative of tragedy, survival, and hope spans more than
fifty years, from the 1920s to the 1970s.

The Geometry of Love by Jessica Levine
$16.95, 978-1-938314-62-9
Torn between her need for stability and her desire for independence, an
aspiring poets grapples with questions of artistic inspiration, erotic love,
and infidelity.

Duck Pond Epiphany by Tracey Barnes Priestley
$16.95, 978-1-938314-24-7
When a mother of four delivers her last child to college, she has to decide
what to do next—and her life takes a surprising turn.

Faint Promise of Rain by Anjali Mitter Duva
$16.95, 978-1-938314-97-1
Adhira, a young girl born to a family of Hindu temple dancers,
is raised to be dutiful—but ultimately, as the world around her
changes, it is her own bold choice that will determine the fate of
her family and of their tradition.

Bittersweet Manor by Tory McCagg
$16.95, 978-1-938314-56-8
A chronicle of three generations of love, manipulation, entitlement, and
disappointed expectations in an upper-middle class New England family.